SHADOWS AWAKEN

GEORGINA MAKALANI

ISBN: 978-0-6450346-3-9

Also by Georgina Makalani

The Last Dragon Skin Chronicles:
The Empty Crown
The Lost Endeavour
Shadows Awaken

The Magics of Rei-Een:
The Hidden Princess
Hidden Promises
The Hidden Phoenix

The Raven Crown Series:
Raven's Dawn
The Caged Raven
Raven's Edge

The Legend of Iski Flare (Novella series):
The Legend Begins
Red Wolves
The Riddle of Daralis
The Last Child
The Tree Maiden
Reflections
The Beast
Circus of Wonders

Other Stories:
The Mark of Oldra
The Heart of Oldra

Short Stories:
Stuffed Frogs and Spinning Teacups
Searcher
The Silence (in Glimpses)
Short Stories:
Stuffed Frogs and Spinning Teacups
Searcher
The Silence (in Glimpses

1

Drayton Sterling lay back along the narrow bench, which served as both seat and bed, and studied the shadows moving like smoke between the curved surfaces of the stones above him. Ana had left them to watch over him, but how they might protect him, he couldn't guess. Nor what they might do to him if he were to go against her.

He had, after all, allowed himself to be locked up. When the king had disappeared, he hadn't put up a fight. It hadn't been worth the effort. He would have gone to the cells no matter what he said or did, and he wasn't prepared to take down good men to prove the regent right.

Barlow had walked him to the cells and locked him away, although he had promised to try his best to get him out. How the man planned it, Dray wasn't sure. If he really wanted out of the cell, he could have accepted Ana's help and allowed her to spirit him away as she had the king. He continued to stare at the rough stone ceiling, imagining what might be going on in the throne room somewhere above him and what else Ana might do to help the king.

The sword master had hesitated in identifying the king, allowing doubt to be seen by those in the room when the king had changed. The boy had become someone else, and for just a moment Dray had thought he had been fooled himself. But he knew the boy. He had known him the moment he'd seen him and had hardly left his side. The only change Ana had made was to dress him as he should have been dressed.

It occurred to Dray, as the shadows moved across the rough surface, that the regent had never wanted the boy to be King. He had done everything he could to keep him hidden away and ignorant of the world, despite appearing to do all he could to make him the king he was destined to be.

Perhaps Barlow could talk to the tutors, discover what the king had been learning and what they had been teaching. The only one who had seemed to pay him the time and effort worthy of a king was the sword master, Forest. Dray could only hope that he remained safe, along with his daughter. The fiery little girl came to mind, although she was not as young as she appeared, given that she would have been born when the queen died. Although, there was something very odd about her, and yet familiar at the same time.

She had been determined to save Edwin, only Ende had managed to hold her back from the attention of the room. She was stronger than she appeared, and Dray wondered if she could have been stopped had anyone other than the dragon tried to hold her. He had noticed the burnt fabric on the back of the dragon's shirt as they had escorted him from the room.

Once he was alone in the cell, Ana had appeared before him, walking through the bars as though they were made of smoke. He had hurt her by refusing to go with her, but he was sure it was the only way he could save the king. He watched the shadows continue their slow journey between the stones, and in an instant they disappeared. Dray sat up slowly, taking in the man standing in the dim light by the bars.

"Have you thought about it?" the regent asked.

"About what?" Dray leaned back into the cold, rough stones and wondered if the shadows hid behind his back from this man. What might they do if the regent actually posed a threat? Dray looked past him for a sign of any other soldiers or the mage, but it appeared he had come alone. The regent had lost his main man, after all, when Ana had allowed her shadows to take him. If they were hers. Part of him feared they were using her rather than supporting her.

"Whether you continue to insist the imposter is the king."

"Where is the king?" Dray asked. He moved his focus from the man, who stood to his left, to the front of his cell where he remembered Ana standing not so long ago.

"Lost. Run away."

"How long can you keep that story going? Those girls, the tribute. They know what they saw."

"Do they? They also saw a witch appear in the middle of their camp. She might have done anything to ensure the young man appeared to be who she wanted them to think he was."

"What about his friend? Would you have given her to the mage? What might he do with a bright young woman like that?"

"I'm sure he would have found a use. He is always searching out some girl or other. And I believe he needs a new maid."

"I had heard she was somewhat altered," Dray murmured.

The regent shivered and moved his hand to his right forearm, rubbing over it.

"Did you vex her?" Dray asked, thinking of the maid, but the man dropped his hand and glared at him.

"Where is the witch?" the man asked, stepping around to stand before him. Dray thought he might step through the bars as Ana had.

He shook his head, wondering if now was the time for the shadows to show themselves and if that would help him or make the situation worse. A shadow of a man caught his eye, and Dray tried to subtly shake his head, thinking the shadows had returned. It wasn't subtle enough. The man before him growled, and Dray looked at him again.

"I could have you hanged before she could stop me," he said, his voice low and dangerous, and Dray believed him.

"You would need clear charges," said the man in the shadows, standing where the regent had been.

Dray sighed and nodded at the realisation it was Barlow.

"Who would know?" the regent asked.

"Given the uncertainty around the king, I would think his regent would be more focused on finding him."

"The boy has abandoned his crown."

"I'm sure that story helps you sleep at night," Dray murmured, wondering if he was seeing the shadows move around him or if his mind was going. After all that had happened, he put his trust in Ana first. When she had winked out of the room as though she hadn't existed, with the king in her arms, Dray wondered why he had ever followed her. Yet he knew the king must come first, that he had to be saved, and it was the only way.

He blew out a slow breath.

"Feeling betrayed by the little witch?" the regent asked. Dray looked into his grinning face, half hoping the shadows could take him away.

"She knows what she does."

"Does she? Do you have any idea where she took the imposter?"

Dray shook his head. He hadn't asked, and it wasn't something she had been willing to tell him. Not that he would tell this man if he did know.

"What if you crossed her?" the regent asked, leaning forward, his face close to the bars. "What might she do?"

"Something like she did to the major," Dray said, resting his head back.

The regent only glared and then walked from the cells, his hand on his arm again. Dray wondered when he might have injured it, and whether it had anything to do with Ana.

"I don't think he will change his mind," Barlow said. Dray glanced at the man, having forgotten he was there.

"It no longer matters," Dray said, lying back down on the bench.

"Here," Barlow said, and Dray caught the thin blanket as he tossed it between the bars. "It isn't much, but until I work out a way to get you back amongst the men, this is the best I can do."

Dray flicked the blanket out over his legs and stared back at the ceiling. Something shifted in the shadows and then, as Barlow left with the small lantern, whatever it might have been disappeared. He would be forever looking for what wasn't there, Dray thought, closing his eyes and hoping the large dark monster that had found them in the forest wasn't creeping through the shadows anywhere nearby.

The regent stood in the middle of the throne room and growled. The soldier wasn't going to give him anything of use to find the boy or the witch. He had demanded that the mage find a way to track the boy down and destroy him before the witch found another way to push him before the people. But he too had been somewhat distracted and wanted to wait. He wasn't sure what for.

Too many believed the boy was the king, despite the regent's best efforts at trying to show him to be something else. Travelling with the tribute had done nothing to help that story. Thom rubbed at his arm and then pulled at his sleeve. It ached all the time, yet there didn't appear to be any injury. He wondered if it was some trick the witch had played, to make him think he was hurt when he wasn't. He sighed and pulled down the sleeve, wincing as the material moved across his skin.

The room was still a mess from the evening before. Tables had been moved and chairs overturned. A tapestry had been burned, and no one seemed to know how that had happened. Food and wine had been spilt across tables and floor. He wondered when it was going to be put right. This wasn't the dining hall, after all. It was where the people came to see him.

He sat heavily on the throne, then leaned forward quickly, half expecting Ana to jump from the shadows. She had always been watching. Again, he thought of the mage's certainty that she could help them, yet she had been just as the mage had feared when he had first seen her. If only she hadn't managed to convince the soldier to save her. He still had no idea how that had happened.

The soldier had appeared quite resigned in his little cell. Thom wondered if he was bitter that she hadn't saved him when she'd saved the boy. They were still to find the young blonde woman the mage had been so interested in. The regent sighed out his frustration. Amidst the mayhem, he had yet to assign the tribute. He stared at the mess before him and wondered if he should rethink who he was to give them to.

Thom vividly remembered the dark eyes of one of the women. Her olive skin, her soft dark hair. She had been disappointed, it seemed, when the boy had gone, and he wondered if she longed for something better than what she had. He sat forward, and a soldier appeared in the doorway.

"Fetch the tribute with the dark skin," he said, waving the man away again. Perhaps he needed some time to determine just what she did want and whether he could use it to his advantage. He still had ten tributes and, despite the debacle of the night before, he could hardly blame any of it on the Lord of Near Forest. In fact, it would be better at the moment to try and keep the peace. For the boy might have tried to make an ally of the man. The Lord of Near Forest was young, Thom remembered, having taken over when his father died. But he hadn't visited the provinces as Barric had, and as Edwin had claimed.

The blonde girl had called him Ed. Had she known who he was, or could Thom claim she was misled? For a young woman couldn't refer to the king by name, no matter who she was. A boy named Ed, trying to claim to be King. He might be able to use that.

The woman appeared before him, and his breath caught. She

curtsied deeply and then stood, head bowed. "You wished to see me, Your Highness." Her voice was light, her face beautiful, and when she raised her dark eyes to him, he stood and stepped forward to take her hand.

"Tell me where you come from," he whispered.

"The Near Forest," she said, her eyes downcast.

"I know they claim the tribute comes from the province, but it isn't always so," Thom said conspiratorially, leaning in towards her and breathing in her subtle citrus scent.

"In this case," she returned, a smile forming easily on her lips, "it is true."

"Oh," he said, leaning back.

"My brother is the lord," she said, raising her dark eyes to meet his.

"Did he send you away?" Thom asked, raising a hand to his heart.

"I chose to go. He wished to keep one for himself, and I saw the opportunity."

The regent tried to keep the anger from his face. Keeping a tribute destined for the capital was not something that would win favour. "Which one?" he asked, hoping the question didn't sound as short and bitter as he thought it did.

"Belle, the king's friend." She put a hand over her lips and blinked as though realising her error, but he knew it was staged. "He wasn't the king."

He shook his head. "And she has run."

"Why did you wish to see me?" she asked. Her look was expectant, but he was sure the girl guessed more than he hoped to tell her.

"I wonder at who I might gift you to," he said, stepping away and sitting down.

She followed, standing before the throne. "I thought you might have been interested yourself," she whispered, looking down, and he wondered if she was hoping rather than questioning.

"I am an old man," he said carefully.

"Hardly," she said, sitting at his feet and resting her hand on his knee.

He gaped at her openness. No woman before had thought to get this close. He rested his hand on hers. "What would you want? Or do you want for your brother?"

She scowled then, pulling from his hold and standing. She brushed at her skirt and patted at her hair, the movement accentuating the lowered front of her dress, and when he raised his eyes from her cleavage, she was smiling.

"I am not here for my brother," she said clearly.

"You are here for a brighter future," he said, beckoning her forward.

She nodded once, but was reluctant to step forward again. He motioned again, and she stepped closer.

"Would you be a loyal wife?" he asked.

She curtsied so low before him that she almost sat upon the floor. He stepped forward and offered her a hand. As she rose, she stepped in close to him, but he pushed her back a step when she reached for his arm.

"Your Highness," she whispered.

He rubbed his arm as he nodded.

"It will be announced soon," he said, waving a soldier forward. "Escort the lady to her room."

She bowed her head and followed the soldier from the room. He watched her go, willing her to turn back at the doorway and smile. When she didn't, he feared his arm had got in the way again.

2

Ana breathed in the salty air and was reminded of home. Despite all that had happened, she didn't miss the world she had left behind. And she doubted she would ever want to return. Her toes dug into the cool sand as the water lapped around her legs. It pulled at her skirts and dragged on her cloak. She sighed at the quiet comfort it provided.

The breeze pulled at her hair and blew across her skin. The wind had scared her not so long ago, but no more. Although the only real change was the lack of height to fall from. She moved her toes through the sand, grounding herself further.

There was nothing beyond her, the sea a slowly undulating green-blue beast that comforted her. A short distance along the coast was a small town built around a port. Although there had been boats when she had watched the people from the shadows as the sun rose over the water, there wasn't a single vessel visible from her place on the beach.

For a moment she wondered what was across the sea, what she might find if she sailed away. It could be an option for the king, suddenly confident in her presence. She had been reminded of how comfortable they were together in the mountains, the connection Ende had sensed, and yet she hadn't been as confident of it herself of late. They needed each other, but how she no longer knew.

She closed her eyes and focused on the world around her, the cool water and the gentle breeze. Behind her, the marshland filled the world between the sea and the capital. It was a strange landscape. Several people lived amongst the grasses, but few seemed to pass that way.

Despite his concerns when she had first taken him, Ed was not trying to go anywhere. He was too keen to stay, and it unsettled her a little. It was what she had promised him, after all—to help him, to give him what he wanted. And he wanted it now. All that indecision, yet he had looked at his uncle sitting on the throne and seemed to know it was his for the taking. If she had allowed him, he may have taken a sword to the man.

In the end, she hadn't given Ed the option. They needed a more determined plan to remove the regent. She hoped he would be the one to find it and prove himself a king. Not that she had returned to him since the evening before. He needed the time to be sure it was what he wanted. She provided fresh clothes, water and food, and remained hidden in the shadows to ensure he was safe.

Despite the woman in his arms, he had not said anything further. He only needed to know that Ana would support him, that she had the power to support him. The little dragon came to mind. Ana wondered if Salima would find him, search him out as she had been so determined to do. Her only focus was the brother she didn't know she had, and Ana wondered then at the single-mindedness of the girl. Was there something else, or did she just understand the danger to him?

She stepped deeper into the cool water, the fine silk of the dress still far too light.

'Miss?' a young man called from further down the beach, and she watched as he raced towards her.

He appeared puffed when he stopped by her, but she couldn't place his face. She wasn't sure if he was someone she should know or just someone passing by.

"There are things in the water," he said, pointing out at the waves.

"What things?"

"You might drown."

Ana looked down at her feet, the water barely reaching her knees. "I don't plan to swim."

He stood there for a time, watching her and then the water.

"What do you want?" she asked, allowing the shadows to fill her voice. He took a small step back. "Go home," she hissed.

He bowed his head and turned away, walking quickly down the beach and occasionally turning to see if she was still there. She sighed and turned back to the water. Something moved beneath the surface, something dark, but it didn't come near her. She took another step deeper into the cool water.

Two small children ran and squealed further down the beach, racing at waves and then running away as the water chased them back and lapped onto the shore. She wondered at the two girls she had seen in her room at the mage's workshop. She closed her eyes, remembering them; there was something very special about them, but she wasn't sure what it was. The shadows pulled on her.

Take them.

"I don't want them," Ana whispered over the waves. "Do I?"

I can feel the power within them.

"Like ours?" Ana asked. Could they also be linked to the shadows? But Belle was something very different, not that Ana had seen her shine since she had her pulled from the throne room. The mage had wanted Belle too, and Ana was sure he had seen for himself just what she was.

Ana watched the water rise and fall before her as it lapped against her thighs, her cloak heavy with liquid. She hadn't seen the light in Belle until the carriage, and Ende hadn't mentioned anything. Was there a reason she'd been called to the king's side?

She sighed, thinking of Ed again as he stood in the tall grass with the woman in his arms, her feet muddy, her arms holding him close. He had real wanting on his face, as though the crown was the only thing of importance. She wondered what would have happened to him if he had stayed in the capital all those months ago instead of running to the north to find his mother's friend.

She had wanted him to use her, to allow her to help him be the king he was meant to be, and now he would. Yet she wondered if it was for the same reason he wanted it now. She should visit with the mage. She might be able to learn what she couldn't before and see what these little girls were.

The maid stays close.

Ana cocked her head to the side. The creature the maid had become belonged to her, in the same way as the shadows were hers. Yet the hatred in the little maid joined with the darkness might not allow her to take what she wanted from the mage. Ana turned and pushed her way back to the shore, the cloak heavy about her shoulders and the dress clinging to her legs.

"I want to see Dray," she said.

Leave him be, the voice inside her hummed, although Ana knew full well that her magic longed for him as much as she did. She needed his approval, his reassurance, and his friendship.

"Show me," she breathed, closing her eyes to the world around her and allowing the cool wind to pull at her wet clothing.

Dray appeared in his cell. Ana watched from the shadows as he tried to exercise in the small space, half hidden by the wooden bench. He grunted through another push up and then collapsed, rolling over on the stone floor, his brow sweaty, his hair wet. His eyes appeared focused on her as he stared at her shadows on the ceiling. How hard was he trying to make this a viable option?

"It appears you are right," a man said, reaching through the bars and setting a cup on the bench.

"I usually am," Dray said, a smile pulling at his lips. Ana wanted to be there to help him to his feet. He huffed and then sat up, resting his arm across the bench and taking the cup, which he held up in salute to the man on the other side of the bars before he took a sip.

"The history tutor is surprisingly talkative, and not particularly bright."

"Did he say if they were directed to mislead the king?"

"No," the other man said, a little disappointed. "But it appears his understanding of history is not what it should be. Our king was also too eager to shirk his classes, which the tutors were only too happy to let him do."

Dray sighed and ran a hand through his hair, pushing it back from his face. Ana wished she were lower so she could see him front on rather than from above. She willed the shadows down the wall, but as her gaze drew level with his, he looked towards the wall and then glanced quickly at the other man. Barlow, Ana realised.

She sighed and pulled them back again.

I won't allow him to be taken.

"He already has been," Ana said softly, although he was using the time appropriately. She only hoped that Barlow wasn't discovered seeking information on his behalf. But there would be more soldiers amongst the ranks who would help him. He was a good man, even if he had run away with a maid.

3

The girls all lined up before the throne as Thom tried not to look around at the state of the room. It had finally been cleared, but it still felt stale and messy. He wanted desperately to check the shadows behind him, sure that the witch wasn't far away. The mage had assured him that he had his own beast in the shadows, but Thom doubted the man could control it as well as he thought he could.

Thom wasn't as trusting as he had been. The mage was supposed to be working for him, to ensure he was not only safe but remained on the throne and became the true heir. That hadn't gone very well. Other than the tribute, there were only soldiers in the room. He stood slowly and bit his tongue rather than touch the arm that seemed to ache all the more as he stepped forward.

He raised a hand towards the guard by the door, and a man was shown in. One of the nobles, vying for attention. In fact, it was the one who, not so long ago, had been keen to see if the witch knew more of the king. The man looked serious now, and he bowed low before the regent.

The tribute stood perfectly still, lined up before him. They were all perfect. The Lord of Near Forest had managed to provide the best of the kingdom, no matter where he might have gotten them from.

Thom had been willing to allow some of the men to choose

their own from the line, but as he looked them over now, he made eye contact with the beauty from the forest and she gave him a small smile. The man walked down the line as they all looked to the ground and selected a blonde girl at random, taking her hand and pulling her forward. She flushed, the colour highlighting her beauty, and the man drew in a sharp breath.

"Your wife," Thom said, directing the woman towards him.

"I thank you, Your Highness," he said, bowing again. He held the woman's hand too tightly in case the regent would change his mind and take her back again.

The regent waved him out, and another man entered. "If you could choose," he prompted the man, whose eyes moved to the dark woman in the middle of the line. The regent gave a small shake of his head. The man stepped forward and took the hands of the dark-haired woman beside her. The regent nodded.

"Go," he said, bored with the event already. His eyes met the forest woman's again.

He wasn't bored, he thought, his eyes refusing to move away from the dark beauty. He just wanted this over and her for himself. In truth, he had invited ten men of the capital forward this morning. Some of those he had invited were different from those he had initially considered. He had almost been tempted to offer one to the sword master, after all. But he had won his small battle with that man when he had struggled to identify the king.

Thom grinned and waved the next one forward. He had determined the order in which they were to attend. He had kept them separated, so they would not be any the wiser if he changed his mind. They could compare young wives later.

An older man stepped forward. His eyes travelled over the line of women remaining, and without a look at the regent he walked forward and looked them over one by one. He turned and travelled back down the line. As he passed the dark forest girl, she glanced up at him. Did she want what she had indicated? The man stopped by the girl who appeared to be the youngest of them all and ran a finger down her cheek. He leaned forward and whispered something that made the girl blush as he took her hands in his.

'A good choice,' the regent said.

'Thank you, Your Highness,' the man said with a bow, the girl clinging to his arm, and Thom waved them towards a door.

He looked over the waiting girls then, and back to the door.

The soldier appeared, a question in his glance.

"Not yet. I fear this young lady doesn't feel well," Thom said slowly, motioning forward the woman he wanted for himself. "Take her through to the west dining room and fetch her some cool water."

The soldier nodded and indicated the way. Without looking at Thom, she followed. As soon as she was out of sight, he waved towards the door and held up two fingers. Another soldier in the doorway bowed his head and sent in two young men.

They looked at each other and then the women before them. Whether by luck or not, they selected different women and then were gone. He cared little for the remainder of the choices and stood silently as the men he had chosen entered and then left with the girls of their choosing. He looked over the empty room as the soldier reappeared.

"There is a gentleman waiting," he said.

"Keep him waiting." Thom strode through the other door and towards the west dining room. He only hoped no one else would have thought to visit the small space.

As he entered, she stood quickly and curtsied. He stopped, closing the door behind him, then glanced around the room to see if anyone had stayed to ensure she was seen to.

"You have made your choice," she said, looking down.

"Are you not happy with it? I have another eager lord wishing to please me, if you would rather someone else."

She smiled up at him, but made no move. He tried not to sigh. She was more beautiful than the witch, and he wondered if he could dress her differently. Although, the pale golden gown suited her dark skin. Without hesitation, he gently ran his fingers over her bare shoulder. She was as soft as she appeared to be. She held him with a steady gaze, and he knew he wouldn't have to fight her to get what he wanted, wouldn't have to fear her… he wasn't sure what. He stepped back again.

"May I?" she asked, gesturing to his arm.

He nodded once and she helped him slip the coat from his shoulders, then stepped behind him and pulled it carefully down over his arms. She folded it and placed it over a chair at the large round table in the middle of the room. He made to roll up his sleeve, but she held up her hand, reaching instead for the ties by his throat. He felt a nervousness he hadn't felt before as she pulled his shirt from his breeches. He looked down at her concentrating as she guided one arm out and lifted the fabric over his head before very carefully removing it from his injured arm.

He flinched as she held her hand above it. "What did she do?" she whispered, leaning forward, her breath soft over his skin.

He shook his head.

She rested her hand over the skin and looked up at him as he grimaced. His skin prickled, but it wasn't the burning sensation he feared. Then she ran her other hand over his chest. "Not an old man," she breathed, pushing him gently back towards the table. She lifted her skirts enough to step over his leg and leaned into him, her hands on his chest.

He closed his arms around her, wincing as his injured arm brushed against her. She pulled away and turned back to the arm.

He winced as she took his wrist. "It doesn't look damaged," he said, unsure how to explain what he was, what it was, when he didn't know himself.

She bent over it and pressed warm lips to the skin, and he cried out. But instead of moving away, she moved her soft kisses along his arm. The skin appeared to bruise where she touched, and he pulled her tight against his chest with the other arm. Holding out his injured arm, he watched the forearm slowly turn a dark bluish purple.

"I only…" she stammered, tugging at his arm across her throat as he pulled her closer. "Please," she whimpered, and he released her. She dropped to the floor, her hand to her throat.

As he studied the arm, the strange colour disappeared. He flexed his fingers and stretched, then placed a hand over it and was surprised it felt as it had before. "What did you do?" he asked, looking down at her.

She shook her head. He squatted beside her and held out the arm. "Touch it," he commanded.

She raised damp, terrified eyes to his and then reached out to lay her fingers gently on the skin.

"More," he said, dropping to his knees.

She rubbed her hand across his forearm and, when he didn't move, grabbed him firmly. "How?" she asked, her eyes on him, her breasts heaving with every frightened breath.

"I don't know," he whispered, leaning over her. She leaned back, her skirts showing more of her leg than he anticipated, and he pushed his hand along her smooth olive skin. "Show me what else your lips can cure," he demanded, hooking a hand around the nape of her neck and pulling her to him. Her fingers bit into the skin she held as he dragged her closer.

The two girls stood side by side, their smocks covering their skinny frames and their strange golden eyes studying the mage across the book. He tapped it again with his finger. "Read it," he said.

They looked at each other first and then to the page. One twisted her head to the side, as though reading from another angle might help. The other screwed her eyes into a squint and leaned closer to the page.

He sighed and glanced around, hoping his little maid could

assist them, but she hadn't been seen since he had brought the girls to the capital. He worried that they might take the children when he needed them himself. He saw the power, but he wasn't sure yet just how he could use them. They hadn't found their link to the other side.

The glow of the girl being dragged away from the young king was burned into his memory, and he longed for her. She had something he had not seen, and he wanted it. Although he wondered what that would mean for the shadows. Had she always glowed in such a way, and did Ana know what she was? She had sent her shadows after the girl and stolen her away. Everyone else thought she had run, but he knew what it was the moment the lights had gone out.

She was bright, shining in the dark, and then the dark closed around her and dragged her far away. What was Ana up to? He would like the chance to sit and talk with her, learn what skill she had, for she was much stronger than he had anticipated. Much stronger than the darkness he had envisaged envelop the regent.

He looked towards the door then. He was surprised the regent hadn't reappeared after all that had happened. The man had searched out the mage when he'd been looking for the girls. That had taken far longer than he had anticipated, and the mage wondered if he wasn't as strong as he used to be.

"He is busy sharing tribute," a voice hissed from the shadows, and the mage smiled. He had done the right thing in giving her away. She remained close despite her loyalty to Ana. Looking now into the shadows for the beast he couldn't see, he wondered if she was only there on Ana's bequest, spying on him.

"Perhaps the man should have kept one for himself," he mused. It might take the regent's mind from Ana for a time. The mage would need to find a way to deal with her, but so far, they had only succeeded in angering her further.

"He did," the shadows hissed.

The mage looked away from the girls before him. Interesting.

He hadn't expected such a turn of events. But the regent was a man like any other, he supposed. He'd had feelings before, usually for someone untouchable, unattainable. Mariela and then Ana.

"Can you sense the king?" the mage asked, closing the book the girls were still struggling to make sense of.

They glanced at each other, and he wondered how well each of them would function alone. He would need to be careful if he wanted to use them to their full advantage. They turned back to him, sharing an apologetic look as they shook their heads in unison.

He tapped his finger on the cover of the book, waiting for the shadows to share any news, but there was only silence. He looked down at the cover and then at the image of the queen on the desk, the edges a little burnt. He lifted it to his nose. "Why is this not where I left it?" he asked.

"We haven't touched it," the girls said quickly. Again, thinking as a pair.

"You are not to touch him," the shadows hissed, and the image disappeared.

The mage growled, pushing up from the table, and the girls stepped back. He waved them away, and they ran through the open door to what had been Ana's room, shared by others before her. The outer door was locked, a guard standing on the other side. The mage wished he could send his little maid out to test them now. She was no longer his to direct.

"Are you to follow your queen over me?" he asked, staring into the shadows as the door closed behind the girls.

"Yes," she hissed, appearing as his maid for just a moment in the shadows, the face so familiar before it was gone.

"I gave you…" he roared into the darkness, but the cold hand on the back of his neck caught his voice in his throat. He gulped down his fear and hoped it was a game the creature played. Then something pulled at his short beard, a claw scratching at his chin. He was sure it drew blood, but he couldn't see any sign of the creature. He looked towards the wall where the girls had just run to and wondered if they would be what he needed them to be—or if they would be stolen away.

"What do you want from me?" he asked, aware he was doing as required now, not the girl he had given away.

"You want to save your regent," a voice hissed in his ear, the creature still unseen.

"I want what is best for this kingdom," he whispered.

Something sharp poked his side.

"You want what is best for you."

"What do you want?" the mage asked again.

"I want a way to destroy her."

The mage waited. She did Ana's bidding, would not go against her, and yet the hatred in the child within called to him. He smiled and nodded once. "Her soldier," he suggested.

"She has protected him."

"More shadows?"

"She has called to them, uses them. They will do her bidding. Unless she is gone, and then they will be free to do mine."

"You are sure they won't follow the other creature?" he asked, fearing the reaction to the words. The air became cooler.

"I was first," the shadows hissed.

He bowed his head as the pressure was released and the beast disappeared.

4

Ende stood silently in the dim light of the cells and watched the man sleeping on the narrow wooden bench. He seemed comfortable enough with one leg hanging down, an arm behind his head, his breaths soft and slow. Ende took another step, aware there was no one else nearby, and then stopped, surprised by a puddle by the bars. He squatted down and put his fingers to the cold water, then raised them to his lips. Salt water. He shook his head, wondering what tactics they were using to try and coerce this man.

"Are you going to explain the child?" Dray asked, his voice croaky.

Ende looked back into the cell and shook his head.

The man opened an eye and looked at him.

"What could I explain?" he asked, trying not to sigh.

"I saw the marks on your back," Dray said, sitting up and leaning forward slowly, as though the movement was difficult.

"Are they feeding you?"

Dray mumbled something unintelligible, which may have confirmed he was being fed, but he didn't look himself. Several days in a cell can do that to a man.

"I thought she might have taken you away," Ende said.

"She visits," Dray said, indicating the puddle. "She keeps watch." He waved his hand around him. Something dark moved in the shadows.

That could explain his low spirits. "Does she not want you?"

"I am better situated here," Dray said, running both hands through his hair, his eyes down.

"Yes," Ende said slowly. "I can see how you can get so much more done from your cell to save the king."

The soldier leapt to his feet with surprising speed, and Ende stepped back from the cell. Dray grabbed the bars and pushed his face forward. "Ideas then?" he growled. "How are you going to save the king? Or are you even here for him?"

Ende watched carefully. Ana had determined quite quickly what the child was, but then she was far stronger than he had anticipated. Stronger than any of them had anticipated, he thought at the idea of the soldier being consumed by the shadows. What might she do to him if she thought he wasn't here for the king?

The soldier sighed and sat back, the shadows moving slowly behind him, and Ende watched the wall. It appeared she was keeping a close watch on the soldier. He wondered what she might do for this man if he were in danger. "What does she want?"

"To put the king on the throne. I think."

"She has always said as much," Ende said slowly. "Does she have a plan?"

"She hasn't told me if she has."

"Has she returned home?"

Dray looked up then, and Ende pointed to the puddle on the floor. She was somewhere near the sea. That could be anywhere around the continent, as they were surrounded by water. Ende wasn't very sure of the little mage, but he would rather have her in his sights.

"She is keeping the king safe, and that is all I need know." Dray sat back and closed his eyes again.

"We could get you out of here," Ende offered, wondering just who he could talk to.

"Barlow says the same—to give the regent a few days to calm

down. Be fussed over by those he has shared the tribute with. Another ten loyal men might be more willing to kill a king for him. If they can find him standing before them."

"Rumour is that he only gave nine."

Dray squinted up at him. "He kept one for himself?"

Ende nodded.

"Was she a lord's sister?"

"Perhaps," Ende said.

"I think the brother believes he will get more from such a match. But the regent wouldn't take one without good reason. There was something about her," Dray mused, closing his eyes again.

"What kind of something?" Ende asked, stepping closer to the bars.

Dray shook his head, his focus on the ceiling above. "Someone else is coming," he whispered.

"How do you know?" Ende asked, sniffing at the air.

"I have friends," Dray said, pointing to the ceiling. After a few moments, a guard appeared at the bars, looked them over and then left again. "Are you going to tell me about the girl?"

Ende shook his head. It was too hard. Salima was struggling herself with what she had done and what she held inside her. He needed to calm her enough to be able to start some discussion and lessons. She was too worked up about Ed, too emotional, and she had nearly burnt her father's rooms to ashes as it was.

"I'll do all I can to help," he said to the man inside the cell.

Dray nodded silently, back in his reclined pose with an arm behind his head, one leg bent and the other hanging over the edge of the narrow bench.

Ana had been tempted to send her shadows to watch over the little dragon and her father, but she had seen the girl in the throne room and feared what she might do. Ana might be using them, but she didn't want to lose them. They might become far more than what they currently were. Instead, she trusted Ende to watch the girl and hopefully help her find what she was while keeping it hidden from others.

She could only imagine what the regent would do to her if he discovered a dragon in his midst. Let alone two, although she doubted he knew what Ende was.

The man across the small table looked at her expectantly, and she tried not to sigh. This was why she had taken him, after all. He was the king, and she was to put him on his throne. He had taken so long to decide that was what he truly was, and now he held himself differently. She hoped his father would have been proud. His mother was not someone she could guess at now.

"Where have you been?" Ed asked.

"Out, away, watching the world," Ana said, bowing her head. Her magic pulled at her chest every time she did so. But this was her king.

"Will you tell me?" he asked, his voice firm. Although part of her was proud in that moment, the rest of her resented him.

"If I had found something of importance, I would have told you."

"Did you see Dray?" Belle asked, sitting in a chair by the little fire. She didn't look away from the flames. She had rarely looked at Ana since she had arrived back at the cottage.

Ana tried not to stare, thinking that Belle might be starting to glow a little. "No," she lied.

"What if he needs help?" Belle asked, swiveling around, but she looked to Ed and not Ana.

"I have help nearby," Ana said.

"Ende," the girl said, looking back to the flames.

"Him too," Ana whispered. She turned back to the expectant face of the boy across from her. "I don't know."

"We can use your magic," Ed said hurriedly. "Like my uncle

uses the mage."

Ana stared at him, unmoving, and the confident smile faltered. She nodded once and the grin returned.

"All she can do is disappear," Belle said, then screamed as a shadow moved and twisted from the wall. It wasn't solid, but it wanted to be, and Ana wondered for just a moment what her light would look like in the dark.

She turned back to Ed, his face serious. Then he leaned back from the table as the shadows pressed in around her. She nodded slowly as they hissed in her ear and whispered over her skin.

"What is it?" Ed's voice was low, as though he was too scared to know the answer.

"My servant bows down to another."

Ed turned a wary look towards Belle.

"I thought all the shadows followed you, or at least obeyed you," Belle whispered, looking around in fear of what Ana could bring forth.

"I did not create this."

But you are the queen.

Ana nodded once, then looked at the two worried faces before her and pulled herself from the damp marsh cottage.

She pressed her back into the wall of the castle and breathed out slowly.

You are the queen, we are the queen.

She nodded, but it wouldn't help Ed. Her only reason for being was to help Ed, to get him to the throne and return his crown. It was what she had dreamt before she had met him, what she knew in her heart when the mage had allowed her to see the fuzzy image of a boy handing it away. It was the reason he still wanted her dead. For he had seen what she would become and the threat she would be to the regent.

She stood straighter, looking out across the marshes where she had hidden the king so close. She was stronger with them. When they had held her, even Ende had seen something else. And in the forest, when she had scared the darkness away, darkness that wanted to devour the king and Dray. She looked down at shaking hands.

That was me.

"That was us," she whispered. "I didn't have the strength to push it back until they stood with me. I couldn't do it without them. I can only help Ed with Ed and Dray."

You don't need them. You needed the idea of them. The boy you had sacrificed so much for. For the idea of his crown.

"Dray," she breathed.

You don't need me to tell you what you already know.

Ana blew out a long breath and leaned back against the wall.

You know what you are. You just needed them to show you.

She nodded slowly and flexed her fingers, then pulled the hood of her cloak up over her head and straightened her shoulders. "Let's test that," she whispered. She closed her eyes and imagined the creature with the maid at its heart. The darkness that would follow her and yet followed another. It wouldn't touch the king, for she had forbidden it. But it would try to find another way to defeat her.

Are you sure?

Ana nodded once. "Come!" she commanded.

The creature appeared before her. Anger flashed across its dark skin, and then it bowed low before her. "My queen," it hissed. They hissed. The internal battle twisted their features, and she smiled.

"You would defy me," she said, her voice low as she sensed someone on the wall above walking closer.

"Never," they hissed, bowing lower, their forked tongue flicking over scaly lips.

"Prove yourself," she said.

"Anything, Majesty."

"The girls," she said, and the beast turned dark dangerous eyes towards her. "What would you do for the girls?"

A smile split their face, sharp teeth glinting in the sunlight. "They are special, Majesty."

She nodded. "Watch them, and when I say it is time, they are yours."

The creature held out a dark long-fingered hand. The sharp claws caught the light in much the same way as teeth, but Ana rested her hand in it. The creature leaned forward, flicked their tongue over her pale skin and purred.

"I see you trust me, Majesty," the beast said.

"Ensure you honour that trust," Ana whispered, leaning forward. "Or I shall tear you apart."

The creature bowed again and then was gone. The man above continued walking along the wall. Ana leaned back into it, her heart racing.

A risk, the voice inside her whispered.

"One worth taking," Ana responded. And she hoped she was right. She had more power than she realised, and she didn't need the boy and the soldier standing by. But if she had more power in another realm, she would use it to keep them safe, whether they realised they needed her or not.

The creature appeared before her again, with a bow and a grin. "Someone comes whom you should see," it hissed, and then it was gone.

Ana followed the thread of shadows to the throne room and hid in the darkness behind the throne as the doors flew open. She almost stepped forward into the light as Phillip staggered forward. A tall blond man with olive skin followed behind him, his face cruel. Something moved beside the throne, and Ana moved to another hiding spot deep in the shadows of the room.

The young woman, a woman Ana had seen at the inn with the tribute, stepped forward. The young man glared and then shoved Phillip to his knees with a boot to the back of his leg.

"I understand…" he said, without any greeting for the regent or the woman Ana thought bore a resemblance to the man, "that the little boy who stowed away with my tribute was not the king as he claimed. He lied and he stole, and he killed several of my men. I am here for payment."

"And this is?" the regent asked, pushing himself up lazily from the throne and taking a step forward. The girl reached out and took his hand, and Ana wondered if she had been kept willingly.

"A farmer," the man snapped.

The regent turned back to the woman. "A farmer pushes his way in here and demands what?"

The woman grinned as the regent turned his attention back on the man.

"I am not the farmer," the man spluttered. "I am the Lord of Near Forest."

"And you forget who you address and where you are," the regent said calmly.

"The King's Regent of the Kingdom of Ilia," the woman announced. "The whole kingdom, brother, not just a little bit of it."

He glared at her and then bowed to the regent. "Forgive me, Your Highness," he mumbled. "I am still angry at the betrayal. For the young man stole my sister."

The regent looked then at the beauty beside him. She smiled at him and gave a little shake of her head. Ana wondered how much he had given her.

"Well," the regent said. "My wife says she was not stolen. Let's forget that."

Was he happy? He stepped forward, and the girl wrapped her hand around his arm. Ana waited for him to flinch, but he didn't. She might have to see what she could do about that.

The lord pushed Phillip in the back with his foot, and he tumbled forward. His hands tied before him prevented him from stopping himself. "This man killed my men!" the lord bellowed, and the regent raised an eyebrow.

"I was defending my daughter," Phillip wheezed.

What could Ana do? The darkness beside her longed for

something, and she looked into the shadows. "You can play with him," she whispered, "but don't harm him."

The woman's eyes grew wide, and she ducked behind the regent as her brother turned slowly to take in the black creature looming behind him. They blinked slowly, grinned and flicked the long tongue through the air. Ana could taste the fear.

The mage appeared not far behind. Ana sighed as he pointed at the creature and it cowered from him. "Where have you been?" he growled.

It hissed and then disappeared. Ana was somewhat disappointed, as the regent had looked more than a little uncomfortable himself.

"Has the witch returned?" the regent asked, and she was tempted to walk out into the room just to scare him. But her eyes focused on the beautiful woman beside him who had been all smiles. She might be able to use her.

The mage shook his head. "Who is this?" he asked, pointing to the man on the floor.

"No, you don't," Ana whispered. "Take him to his daughter."

The shadows moved across the floor, curled around Phillip and then disappeared with him. It was surprisingly easy to move people to where she wanted. Again, she thought of Dray.

He will not appreciate it.

No, she thought, not yet. And she too disappeared to the sounds of the woman's screams and the lord claiming that the regent was stealing from him.

5

Salima growled, and more flames pushed forward. Her father ran a hand over his face, and for a moment she worried she might have burnt him. Ende, on the other hand, just nodded.

"Make it stop," she grumbled, more flames spewing forth.

"Only you can control it. Only you can find it."

"That is hardly helpful," she snapped, then slammed her mouth shut as the words were followed by hot flames. She was still surprised that although she could feel the heat, it didn't burn her. It burnt the furniture easily enough. They had moved to the practice halls as there was more space, yet she looked nervously at the grass mats. There was no chance anyone would find them. No one had come since the boy had been slaughtered and then disappeared.

"Ice," she whispered as she tried her best to hold the flames inside, but failed.

Ende shook his head and Papa chewed his lip. It had been suggested before that the cold might help hold her flames inside, but her father was too scared the same thing that had happened to Ana would happen to her. They might be discovered and she might actually die, although Ende thought that unlikely. Nothing could cool her that much.

"I don't understand," she whispered, the flames reduced.

"Your mother," Papa whispered, glancing at Ende. But he couldn't continue, and she wondered what he hadn't shared about her. Was that why she had died so young?

"You need a chance to stretch your wings," Ende said. "If you get a better feel for what you are, you will be better able to control it. I would like to…"

"No," Papa snapped.

Ende stood back and held out a hand. She needed him. She needed the heat in him to help her own. She stepped forward then, standing close to him.

"Salima?" Papa whispered.

"What are you?" she asked. The rush of flame washed over him, and yet she wasn't surprised when he blinked at her unharmed, with a wide smile and his eyes appearing solid black.

"I, little dragon, am an old dragon."

The relief that flooded through her was overwhelming. That was how Ana knew what she was. She had met Ende and knew the fire inside him. "Do I have wings?" she asked.

"Let's find out," he suggested, leaning in close. The warmth flowed from him, pulling at her. "Will you come with me?"

She reached out to take his hands before Papa could say anything. "Where will we go?" The flames washed over him, and he was unharmed although his clothes were burnt away.

"Somewhere you can stretch your wings and not burn anyone."

She nodded slowly, looking to her father. She doubted she could be this close to him and not kill him.

"Bring her back to me," he whispered.

Ende smiled, but she noted that he didn't give any reassurances, and she wondered then if she could return. Before she could doubt the decision, Ende pulled her from the building. She was all too aware of his naked chest, yet people only glanced at them as they ran across the courtyard and towards the main gate of the castle. Instead of heading out, he led her up the steep steps to the wall, and then they were running along it. She was surprised she could keep up, but he got faster and faster, and then they were overlooking the marshland rather than the city. He stopped suddenly, dragged her to his chest and wrapped his arms around her.

"Hold tight," he murmured. She could feel him grow taller behind her as she squeezed her eyes closed. His arms, still tight, became thicker and stronger, and then they were falling through the air. As she opened her eyes, she heard the whomp of movement above her. But she couldn't look. Someone shouted behind them, but they were moving too fast to be stopped. The world dropped away beneath her as they flew across the sea of golden grass, wetness glinting amongst it as though it grew in water. The sea sparkled in the distance, but he turned away from it. The capital was a grey blur in the distance. Green fields stretched out before them as they climbed higher and higher, the world less clear beneath them.

And then she was falling. It wasn't that she had slipped; his hold had been too tight. He had let her go, and she screamed as the ground rushed up to meet her.

Salima allowed the fire burning through her to consume her, and then she was gliding rather than falling. Although somewhat shakily. She felt different, as she had when she had returned the bars in the ice cell, as though she *was* the fire. One giant ball of fire. The world around her looked different too. Orange and red, as though she saw through the flames. She rolled her shoulders, felt the strength in them and pushed higher into the sky with strong wings.

She faltered, pulled higher and then dropped. She had control and yet didn't. In the distance, she aimed for a craggy cliff that overlooked the water. The more focused she was on the rock, the smoother her wings beat. She sighed out with relief when she landed, feeling the cool earth beneath her large claws, and then she was kneeling on the hard rock. She sat back and shivered, watching the giant dragon soar over the water.

She had flown. She had actually flown like a bird. She tried to see over her shoulder at the wings that were no longer there. And then took in her nakedness. She squealed and squeezed her eyes closed, pulling the warmth around her and then clinging to the dress that appeared. She breathed out slowly and turned to the man who walked towards her across the rocky outcrop.

She grinned from the exhilaration. Her heart still beat so fast in her chest, and she wanted to cry all at the same time.

"Tell me of my mother," she demanded as he drew closer.

"Tell me of Ed," he returned, and she was confused for a moment. What did he want with Ed?

"You know who Ed is," she said, standing in the wind, wondering how they would return to the castle. "Are you able to find him?"

"Who is Ed to you?" he asked, his voice soft and coaxing.

She sighed and looked out over the water. "I don't know," she admitted. "I care for him, as though he is far more important than anyone else. But I don't feel like you think I do about him," she added hastily.

"How do you think I know of how you feel?"

She smiled despite her fears. "Why?"

"You are very focused on him. You are driven to find and protect him. I want to know why that is."

She shrugged then, looking back to the water and away from the expectant face of the man who watched her too closely. The dragon who watched her too closely. And he knew what she was.

"You knew my mother," she said softly, and he nodded once. "She is the reason I am like this," she said, indicating her body. But she wasn't angry, exactly. How had Papa thought he could keep her safe when she could have killed him?

"In a sense, but she is not to blame."

"Blame?" Salima asked. She looked from his too-serious features across the water and then turned back towards a castle and capital she couldn't see. "She wasn't a dragon," she whispered, feeling the flames on her tongue. But they didn't spew forth as they had before.

He shook his head without looking at her.

There were so many questions, and in many ways, she already knew the answers. "Why did he take me?"

"Because he was asked to."

"Did he know?"

Ende shook his head.

"Did you know?" she barely whispered, scared of his response although she wasn't sure why.

He looked down before he shook his head. "I thought you had died with her." His voice caught, and she felt his pain flow through her as though it were her own.

"You loved her," she said, feeling the connection between the two.

He turned dark, sad eyes towards her. She could feel that love still.

"Who was she?"

He shook his head and turned back to the water.

"Who was she?" Salima demanded. "She was my mother—I deserve to know."

"No," he said firmly, stepping towards her, and she took a step back. "Knowing will make no difference except to put you in danger."

"You can't just tell me part of the story and then not the rest. This is my history you are keeping."

"Tell me of Ed," he pressed again, taking another step closer.

"He is my friend. He is… I don't know," she snapped. The flame burned hot inside her, longing to be pushed out. "I just need to be with him." Her hands dropped by her side, and the fire was suddenly cooled. "Ana felt him in me."

"What?" Ende asked, reaching for her, and she allowed him to take hold of her arm.

"She felt the connection. The blood." She looked up at him.

"None of it made any sense. She told me…"

"What did she tell you?"

"Who I am," she stammered. "You know who Ed is. You know what he is to me because you know what and who I am." She turned then and ran towards the end of the rocky outcrop, her feet sure, the fire burning hotter inside her.

"Salima! Where are you going?" he cried after her, and she knew he wasn't far behind.

"To find my brother." She leapt into the air and felt the fire wash over her. The strong wings lifted her into the air, and she flew out over the water before turning towards the capital.

6

The regent tried not to sigh as he looked out over the dining hall. People talked in hushed tones, and there weren't quite as many as he had hoped for. Excited about the tribute and the new brides, many had come to show off their favour with the regent. One or two weren't present, and of the others he could only guess. The Lord of Near Forest sat beside him looking happy enough, but Thom doubted that was due to anything he had said. He really thought the man's sister had helped raise him up. Although how much higher than a province lord this young man could climb was beyond him.

"Old royalty," his father had called it. The royal families of the old kingdoms. Yet he had also said something about other people who didn't have a place in the new kingdom. They had a place, but not recognised. Thom wondered if they would ever stand up against the capital. He hoped not.

He glanced again at the young man. He certainly saw himself as a king. And the talk amongst the soldiers was that he had hoped to marry the sister to the king and thus put his family back on the throne. Thankfully, there were not many remaining who believed Edwin was who he claimed to be, and the witch hadn't helped him.

She was also the reason not many were present for such a celebration, and the reason the staff had been too afraid to clean the throne room after the debacle with the king. She was frightening people. His new wife's hand closed around his forearm, and he smiled at her. No matter what the witch thought she could do, it appeared it wasn't as bad as he had first thought. She was a girl with some little power. The mage had his shadow creature, after all, which still seemed to follow his instructions. Thom turned from the woman beside him to the brother on the other side, his eyes searching the wall behind him.

The man flinched and turned to look as well, then turned his angry glare back on the regent. He had the room well lit. Servants had placed torches along the walls, and there was no space for shadows. She couldn't creep up on him if she couldn't hide. Although she seemed to be able to appear from nowhere well enough. She might very well appear in the middle of the room—and steal away anything or anyone she chose. Thom took the hand of the woman beside him.

"My dear?" she asked, her voice soft.

He shook his head. It had been surprisingly easy to become attached to the young woman. And so far, she seemed to present as everything he wanted, although there were moments when he wondered if that was due to her brother and what he might want. But she had hardly spoken to the lord, nor looked at him.

Someone stood from a table, scaring a maid who dropped a tray. In the following silence, the Lord of Near Forest cleared his throat. "About my payment?"

"I understand…" the regent said, looking to his wife rather than her brother once the noise started again, "that you stole most of the tribute from the rest of the kingdom as you didn't have enough beauties of your own to offer. Your men were killed during this process, by a man whose daughter was stolen from the grasslands. I think you should consider yourself lucky that I haven't sought compensation for your lies." He turned to the young man, who glowered at the woman at his side rather than the regent. "Will you insist on following through with your demands? Are you not loyal to Ilia?"

The man's scowl deepened.

The regent turned back to the woman beside him, who offered him a warm smile. "Does he wish to take his own part of the kingdom back?"

She seemed confused for a moment and then looked at her brother. She shook her head.

"Are you certain?"

She shook her head again, but she didn't look at him.

"I could make you an example to the other lords," he murmured, but his eyes were on his young wife. As much as he wanted to love her and as beautiful as she was, there was something he did not trust. He would need to find a way to ensure she was loyal to him first. And his position.

"So, the boy disappeared," the lord said, as though he weren't being threatened with a cell. "Could this witch return him?"

"He isn't the king, so what does it matter?"

"Where is the king?" the man asked, leaning in close, his voice low.

"That is a question many have asked. He is a boy, not ready to rule. He has run from his responsibilities, and if he has managed to survive, I doubt we will see him again."

"Will you always be regent?" Dahli asked, her voice as low as her brother's. Did she doubt him? Or was she asking for herself?

"When do you return to the forest?" Thom asked the lord without acknowledging his wife's question. He might need to talk to the mage.

"I think I should stay and see my sister settled."

"I am settled, quite comfortably," she said, giving the regent another smile.

"I could arrange a tour," he said half-heartedly. He meant the words for the lord, but as the young woman's face lit up, he wondered that he hadn't offered her the same. They were new to the castle and the capital. There were markets a woman might be interested in, and although she had fine dresses, it wouldn't hurt to take her around and show her off.

He nodded slowly, taking her hand in his. "Tomorrow," he promised. Then he waved a soldier forward. "Take the lord down and show him the accommodations below," he said to the man as he leaned in towards him. "Bring him back again, but I would like him to see why he is here."

The soldier bowed, and the lord sat his cup back on the table with a thump, spilling the wine.

Ed tried not to sigh as he watched Belle talk with her father. The small cottage appeared to be getting smaller by the day. He was relieved to see the man alive, although somewhat battered and bruised. Phillip hadn't made it back to the forest with Eilke as Ed had thought, and he was disappointed with himself that he hadn't tried harder to find the man. But when Belle had found him missing, Ed had spent most of the night comforting her. Not once had either of them suggested looking for him around the place they'd been staying, and he wondered if she was as disappointed with herself as he was.

Dray also hadn't made any such suggestions, but then he hadn't been himself. Not since before Ana had arrived to scare off the shadow beast. Although she seemed to have made friends with the shadows now. Dray had been distracted, and Ed wondered what he knew that he hadn't shared. He hadn't spoken to her then, and he hadn't seen her since she was taken. But they were connected. He wondered if they had something that told the experienced soldier she wasn't what she had been.

Each time Ana appeared, she scared Ed more and more. Yet her focus was always to make him King. To help him be the king he was. He was certain this was what he was meant to be. What he had always been. With Ana's help, he could be exactly what he needed to be. She could help him defeat his uncle and he would be sitting on the throne before he knew it, his father's crown on his head.

Yet she didn't appear to be moving very quickly. And he had seen very little of her. Ed had no idea if she was working on something or just hiding away from him. Belle hadn't been as friendly as he had hoped she would be to Ana either, when she was there. They had been friends. They had been holding hands when Ana was pulled from the mountains. But much had happened since then, and again he thought of Dray and his reservation with her.

If only Ed could reach the soldier and ask what he might know. Or if he could reach Ende and send him to ask. He hadn't seen anyone since Ana had pulled him from the throne room, and he had no idea just how far from the castle they were.

"Have you settled in?" Ana asked Phillip, appearing in the middle of the room, and Ed wondered for a moment if he had conjured her by thinking of her.

The old man jumped and then nodded.

"I am sorry," she said, lowering her head to him, although Ed thought she grimaced as she moved. "I had little option."

"I'm grateful." Phillip reached out to take her hands, but she pulled them back.

"Are you hurt?" Ed asked.

She looked at him and shook her head, a familiar smile on her lips.

"You don't look comfortable."

"I don't quite feel the world in the same way," she whispered as she sat slowly at the small table. "Perhaps we need somewhere a little bigger," she mused, looking around the space.

Belle sat a hot cup before her, and she nodded thanks as she lifted it to her lips. Something flashed greener within her eyes. As Ed turned to take her in completely, she lowered them to the table.

"How is the captain?" Phillip asked, but she remained looking down. "I thought he would be here," he continued when Belle shook her head.

"He thought he was of better service in a cell," Ana said. There was something dark in her voice, and again Ed thought there was something more around her.

"I'm sure he is using his contacts from there to find out what he can," Phillip suggested. She looked up at him and gave a small smile. She nodded once, but there was something unsettling about her. Ed wondered if Dray had seen that, either in the forest or since.

"Did you see Dray?" he asked, and she turned her brilliant gaze on him, cocking her head a little to the side. "Before?"

"Before what?" she asked.

"Before the forest, since the forest," he breathed. If she could transport herself anywhere in an instant, she could have been popping in and out of their camp all along. Although if that were the case, why hadn't she shown herself to him?

"He does not want to leave the cell. At least not with my help," she said, unblinking.

"That doesn't answer my question," he said, sounding firmer than he intended. If she was to help him, he had to know he could trust her.

"And what will you do if you can't?" she asked, her voice scaring him more than he'd realised it could.

"Can't what?" Belle asked for him, as his mouth went dry.

"Do you want me to be King?" he asked instead.

"You are the king," she said, bowing her head to him. Again, he thought he saw the faintest grimace as she looked down. And then she was gone.

"I can't get used to that," Phillip said.

"What did she mean?" Belle asked. She stood, but didn't come any closer as she looked at the seat Ana had vacated.

Ed shook his head.

"Ed!"

"I'm not sure," he said carefully.

"Was she talking about Dray?" Belle asked, her hands finding her hips. He looked back to the empty chair.

"I was thinking about whether I could trust her," he whispered.

"Does she know you doubt?" Belle asked.

"She knows you doubt, and yet we are still here," he returned.

Belle dragged in a ragged breath. Phillip reached out and took her hand.

"Who exactly is she helping?" Belle asked.

"The king," Phillip answered.

Ed nodded, but he had more doubts now about Ana and her help than he had thought possible. She was the only one who believed in him. The only one who knew above all else that he was the king. She had stolen him away to protect him. He only hoped Salima was all right. And that Ana's contact with her over the time they were trying to reach her wasn't something else he should worry about.

He looked around the small room. The fire warmed them. Nothing surrounded them. Belle stood staring at him while her father sat beside her, holding her hand. And Ed sat at a small wooden bench staring at a chair that had contained a witch not so long ago.

He didn't want to think of her that way, but the people did, and she was using their fear to her advantage. To his advantage. He certainly hoped she was helping him, as he didn't think he would be able to work against her.

7

"There is talk of a dragon in the castle," Barlow stammered.

Dray continued to stare up at the shadows that crawled over the ceiling above him. Had Ende shown himself, or was there another?

"Captain Sterling," the man asserted.

Dray sat slowly, dragging his eyes from the shadows. He wondered if she watched him all the time, and whether she would protect him if needed. Although what he needed protection from, he wasn't sure.

"How big was it?" he asked.

The man actually laughed out loud and leaned against the wall opposite the cell. "You knew the witch, and now I learn you know a dragon."

"If it is the same one."

"How many dragons are there?"

Dray dragged his hands through his hair. He had asked that question of Ende himself, he thought. Or had he? He had the idea that the man was the only dragon out there. "Don't try to hunt it," he said, rising to his feet to find himself more unsteady than he'd expected. He clung to a bar. How many days had he been lying on that wooden bench?

"I'll get something more substantial sent down," Barlow said, leaning in closer to him. "And it was seen leaving the castle, not arriving. I don't think anyone is senseless enough to go hunting after it."

Dray nodded, but he wasn't sure what he could say. He had no idea what Ende might be up to. And as the king had gone, he might not have anything to hang around for. But he had come to the capital before that. He had abandoned them in the forest in search of something else. "What was he here for?"

"The dragon?"

Dray nodded.

"You do know it. How can anyone have hidden a dragon in the castle?"

Dray shook his head. They had hidden a witch well enough, although he hoped that wasn't who Ana was. He wasn't so sure now. He longed to see her, and yet she scared him more than he would like to admit when he did see her. She knew he wanted her to stay away, and yet he knew she came. Sometimes when he couldn't complain, such as when he was sleeping, he would wake to some sign that she had been there.

"I think I'm ready to get out," he whispered through the bars, and the man on the other side nodded once. "I don't want to risk you."

"The regent is occupied, and if there are any questions we can claim your witch stole you away."

"She is hardly mine," Dray murmured. "And where would you hide me?"

"Plain sight," Barlow said with a wink. "But we might wait until after dark."

"You mean it isn't dark now?"

The man laughed again as he disappeared. Dray sighed. He wasn't sure this was a good idea, but Ana had been right. He wouldn't last much longer here, no matter how determined he was to do the right thing. This wasn't helping the king, and it wasn't doing anything to stop the regent. Not that Dray was really sure he could.

"You're helping him, aren't you?" he asked the shadows. "You still want him to be King?"

"Of course," she whispered, her hands on his. He looked up into her green eyes, glowing in the dim light of the dungeons. "What would you have me do?" she asked. Her voice was soft, and yet there was something about it that wasn't her own. He clung tighter to the bars, his head spinning, her hands over his, the same warmth he remembered. And then she was beside him, holding him up, helping him back to the bench. "You need to eat more," she whispered, her fingers in his hair, her other hand tight around his bicep as though she still held him up.

"Barlow is sorting it."

"You should have let me help you."

He shook his head, pulling her hand from his hair. She sighed and rested her head against his shoulder.

"Do you need help?" he asked, too scared to move in case she disappeared. Yet it unsettled him more than he could explain having her so close.

"Phillip is with us," she said.

"Phillip?" he asked, and she nodded once. "I thought he went back to the forest."

"The lord had him captive."

Dray shook his head slowly and then jumped to his feet, holding the bars to keep him steady. "I thought…"

"You were wrong," she said, her voice soft and comforting, yet with something accusatory in it. "You don't seem to be as focused as you were."

He studied her then. The woman he thought he had known so well as a girl not very long ago now appeared something very different. And he couldn't place how it had occurred. He should have held on to her tighter in the mountains, and this wouldn't have happened.

"You couldn't have stopped any of this," she said, standing and smoothing her dress. "It is not your destiny."

"What is my destiny, Ana?"

She smiled up at him, and he remembered the girl he wanted to be there. "What I deem it to be. Let me save you."

"Barlow will help me."

"Why will you not accept my help?"

"Because it is not the way it is to be."

"Now you think you know better. I see far more than you ever will, and you will come to appreciate that gift."

"Not like this," he said, closing his eyes and leaning back against the cool bars. Something about them grounded him and helped to clear his head. "Not like this." When he opened his eyes, she was gone, and he slid slowly down the bars to sit on the floor. It was easier when she stayed away. But he knew she wouldn't.

Barlow came for him some time later. It didn't appear any darker than it already had, yet when they arrived somewhere on the other side of the castle gates, it was not only dark but quiet, as though the world slept around them.

"Any sign of the dragon?" Dray asked quietly.

The other man shook his head and motioned him forward.

"I thought plain sight?" he said.

"For now that means far from where people might see you. And maybe not as one of the King's Men."

"That is all I know," Dray said, following Barlow along quiet narrow streets and between small buildings.

"You are about to learn something new."

Dray tried not to sigh as he followed the man further and further away from the castle and any way he might have had of finding a way around this—although at this stage he really had no idea what that might be.

The small building they ended up in could have been anything other than a home, for it didn't have any indication of people, and the spaces were empty. The shadows seemed to overwhelm him for a moment, and he was sure that if Ana wanted to find him, she would have no trouble. She might have even had him followed. A board squeaked above him, and Barlow drew a sword as Dray reached for one that wasn't there.

He allowed the other man to lead the way up the narrow steps to another room. A single lantern in the middle of the space revealed several soldiers in full armour and swords standing around, fidgeting.

"You did send us ahead," one said, and Dray stepped into the light to get a better idea of the man.

Barlow put his sword away. "These are men I know we can trust. They were part of the contingent that was sent for the tribute."

"Your men, not mine," Dray said.

One of them held out a sword in a scabbard, the belt attached. "This is yours, I believe," he said.

Dray nodded and took the offered sword, pulling it out and looking over the blade. He was reminded of another bright sword. "No one tried to take the king's sword," he mused.

"Did you see how fast he drew it?" the same man asked. "Even you couldn't have bested that, Captain."

Dray raised his eyebrows and nodded once. The boy had some skill, although Dray hadn't really had the chance to see it yet. He had bloodied his sword on his way to the mountains, but Dray hadn't gotten many details on that, except that he had managed to kill several men. "Could we talk to Sword Master Forest?" he asked.

Barlow raised an eyebrow.

"He knew the king well, and other than whatever trick the mage played in that room, he knew that the boy king is very much the man we know."

"It might not be that easy. The regent has men watching all over the castle."

"Although that number is diminished, if only by one. What of Major Field's men—where do they stand?"

"Out of the way for now," Barlow said. "But other than those in this room, there are few I trust."

"There are my own men," Dray suggested.

"Those who thought you had run away with a girl in the mountains?" one of the soldiers said.

"Did you know of the king then?" another asked.

Dray shook his head. He had only thought of saving Ana, and he'd had no plan at all. Like now, she had been his only focus, although it was just as likely to get him killed now as it had been then.

Ed stood slowly at the sound of something he couldn't quite place as both Belle and her father remained focused on the fire before them. He tried not to sigh. They had been so determined to help, yet they weren't able to do anything now but sit and talk.

Ana hadn't said they couldn't leave the cottage, and they had walked a short distance on that first day. He was doing nothing of use, and he wasn't sure what Ana was up to when she wasn't with them. She had visited the castle. He knew that much, for she had found Phillip and returned him to them. Despite Ed's own guilt, the man didn't seem to hold any hard feelings.

The noise drew closer, and he opened the door.

There was nothing moving towards them across the golden grass, but there was something in the sky. A large smudge against the blue moved closer and another further behind it. Ed stood too long trying to determine what it was, his hand on the door. As it drew closer, he couldn't seem to focus on it clearly, before it dropped into the tall grass, and as he stepped forward, Salima came barrelling out of the grass at top speed. She threw her arms around him, nearly knocking him on his back as she pushed him back into the cottage.

She was warm from the exercise and clung far too tightly. Then, as he looked up, Ende walked from the field. Salima leaned back and grinned up at him.

"I told you," she said in a sing-song voice.

"What did you tell?" Belle asked somewhat nervously as Ende pushed the door closed behind him.

The cottage appeared even smaller than it had before. Ed thought he would rather wait outside given how he usually dealt with small spaces.

"That I could find you," she said, pressing her face back to Ed's chest.

"How?" he managed, taking in the dragon standing far too still by the door.

"I sniffed you out."

"You have to let me go," Ed said, pulling at her arms. "You are going to cut me in half."

"Sorry," she murmured, standing back, but the grin remained.

Ed looked between the two of them, and something dark flashed across her eyes as she looked up at the man beside her. Ed sat suddenly on the wooden bench that ran by the table. "How did you sniff me out?" he asked, although he wasn't sure he wanted the answer.

She chewed on her lip and glanced at Belle and Phillip before looking back to Ed. Then she shook her head.

"We will give you a moment," Belle said, taking her father by the arm and leading him outside.

As soon as the door was closed behind them, Salima blurted, "You're my brother."

"What?" he asked slowly.

The grin slipped a little, but she took a deep breath and continued, "Ana said she felt the magic and my link to you in my blood. I didn't know what she meant exactly, and she seemed to know far more than she shared. Then when I found her in the ice cells, she called me a dragon. And she has always called me Princess."

"You are a dragon?" Ed hoped his voice didn't tremble as much as he thought it did.

"Because of my mother," she said with a short nod.

Ed opened his mouth and then closed it. He knew his connection to Salima, but he was fairly certain his mother had not been a dragon. His eyes moved from her smiling face to Ende's serious one focused ahead of him as he remained stock-still by the door.

"Explain this," he said, standing slowly.

"My mother," she said, her voice shaky now, "was your mother."

Ed nodded once.

"You knew," she whined, and he smiled at her.

"It wasn't for me to tell you, and I thought that kept you safer from our uncle."

She pursed her lips and nodded slowly, as though showing her understanding, yet she had never appeared so young to Ed as she did then. "I've always tried to look out for you," he said.

"Except when you ran away and left me."

"That was to protect you," he insisted. "Tell me how Mother made you a dragon."

"Ah," she said, looking up at the man beside her again. "That is probably more to do with Ende."

"Ende?"

The man remained unmoving, and Ed wondered what he thought Salima was going to claim he was. He took a step forward, looking again between the two of them. Salima grinned and then looked seriously at the floor. Ende continued his stare ahead, and Ed realised then just how similar their eyes were. Although Ende looked nothing like he did when Ed had first met him.

"Did you look like this before?" Ed asked him.

"I can look how I like," he whispered.

Ed looked again at the little fiery-haired girl he knew to be his sister. There was nothing alike between them. "You sniffed me out," he said.

She nodded once.

"We are linked as siblings," he said slowly, "but I'm no dragon."

"I'm her father," Ende said, his voice level and careful. He focused his dark eyes on Ed, not as a challenge but to see what he might do.

Ed sat back on the bench. "I didn't know her as a woman," Ed said finally. "I can't say why she would have risked so much for you."

"I didn't intend for her to risk what she did," Ende said, the sadness creeping in.

"You loved her," Ed said, as though it couldn't have been a possibility.

Ende nodded once, and Salima threw her arms around him, burying her face in his side as he pulled her closer.

Ed blew out a slow breath and ran his fingers through his hair. "Ana knows."

Salima nodded.

"That is why you wanted to spend time with me," he said.

"I still do. I want to help you be the king you are meant to be, and then…"

Ed looked up, but her eyes were on the tall man she was wrapped around.

"Then I'm going with Ende."

The tall man looked down at her and pulled her closer still, although Ed couldn't read the look on his face. Whether it was worry or content.

Ed wasn't quite sure what he should think. He was pleased, in a way, that she finally had some connection to family. Despite all that Master Forest had done for her, he wasn't her father, and she had never had the chance to learn of her mother. Although, Ed thought as he looked at the tall man before him, he didn't really know her himself.

"How did Ana know this?"

"She was stronger than she realised when she was first in the capital, and she had a connection to you," Ende said. "She found that same connection in Salima."

"Would she tell who she is?"

"Of course, she wouldn't," Salima answered. "She might scare me, but she is my friend too."

"And it wouldn't help you for such a secret to come out," Ende added. "Whatever she is, Ana still focuses on you and your crown first."

"Is that what she is doing now?"

The man nodded, but he didn't appear as confident as Ed had hoped.

"Why are you staying so close?" Salima asked. "If it isn't safe…"

"Close?"

"You are within a couple days' walk to the capital. Within the marshlands between the castle and the coast."

Ed looked beyond the man to the door.

"You didn't know?"

He shook his head. "Ana can go where she wants."

Ende nodded and then moved further into the small cottage, looking around the room and into corners.

"What are you looking for?"

He shook his head and continued to move around the cavern.

"Ende!" Ed cried in frustration.

"She left shadows to watch over the captain. I thought she might have done the same here."

Ed looked around himself then, but it didn't look any different from how it had before. "She sees more than I thought she did," he murmured. "Where is Dray?"

"Locked away. Ana won't let anything happen to him, no matter what he wants."

"What do you mean?" Belle asked as the door creaked open. "Can we come in?"

Salima moved to allow them in and Ende, now on the far side of the cottage, sat down at the table.

"I think Ana offered to help him, but he thinks he is where he is meant to be."

"He always has the king's best interest in mind," Belle said.

Ed hoped that was true. The man had certainly supported him well enough, but something had not been quite right in those last few days before they made it to the capital. He was distracted, and Ed would have given anything to know why that was.

"Do you want us to take you back?" Salima asked.

"I think we need more of a plan in place," Ed said. "Only I have no idea where to start. If I reappear now, my uncle will just have me killed, claiming I'm someone or something else."

Salima nodded, yet she looked as unsettled as Ende usually did indoors.

"Do you want to return to your father?" he asked.

She opened her mouth and closed it before nodding and then shaking her head.

Ed stepped forward and wrapped his arms around her, and she returned the embrace a lot less violently than she had the first time.

"I just want to help you," she whispered.

"You can, but without putting yourself in danger."

"I'm much stronger than you realise." She grinned up at him.

"Still a way to go," Ende murmured from the table.

Ed felt her suck in a deep breath as the temperature rose somewhat in the room, and he wasn't sure for a moment if she might scorch them all. But she nodded and kept quiet.

"Who knew such change would create such restraint," Ed said, and she squeezed him just a little too tight.

"I can visit again?" she asked.

He nodded. "If it is safe to do so."

"When you have a plan, I can be your man on the inside."

Ed nodded again. If he had two dragons standing behind him, his uncle would certainly not have the chance to deny him. But he doubted it would be so easy.

8

Ana was struggling. She wanted to help, she wanted to be seen and she wanted Dray, yet she was standing in the shadows of the mage's workshop again. Her frustration pushed at the world around her. It wasn't what or where she wanted to be.

Most of the bottles on the shelves pulled at her and called to her. Some of them were suspiciously quiet. She still didn't have a plan. The regent was key, she knew that much, but it did little to quell the turmoil she felt building inside her. He held all the power at the moment, despite her best efforts to unsettle him. She also had the means, but it was not enough to simply destroy the man; she had to set it up for the people to accept Ed as the king he was.

The regent had been too well prepared when the king had appeared with the tribute, and he had too easily turned the people against him. They doubted Ed, and she needed a way to show the people just who he truly was.

The regent stood now in the dim light, trying not to look nervous as the mage worked through one of his books again. Ana tried not to sigh. The mage had skill, although not to the same level as she did, and she wondered just what he thought he gained from all those words.

The shadows kept to themselves, although she knew they were there, as they did her. Despite the little maid and her hatred, Ana was still her queen. She would do as she was directed, no matter how much the mage thought he was in control.

She wanted the creature to step forward just to unsettle the regent further, but he trusted in the mage and she wanted to know their plans.

"I still don't understand why you can't just send your creature after him. It was why you created it," the regent said with a groan.

"I called it, not created it," the mage murmured, not looking up. "Something else did that long ago. And I have explained this." He put down the pen and sighed. "Ana has a way to direct them."

"But if you called it…"

"It will not kill the king. It will do nothing that will bring him harm."

"But what of his friends? The soldier might tell us more, or the girl he stole from the tribute. You want her, don't you?"

"Don't tease me, Your Highness. I know what I want and why. There was something special in that girl. But she is also under Ana's protection."

"Ana!" the regent fumed, and she was tempted to step out into the room to see what they would do. "She was just a maid from a faraway part of the kingdom. If we hadn't sought her out, she would still be serving tea to an aunt who didn't want her."

"But we did. We are part of that child's destiny," the mage muttered, tapping his finger on the page. "I saw what she could be, and then what she was destined to be. In seeking her out, I made her. In trying to destroy her, I made her stronger. At each step we have been intertwined. Me thinking I can gain from her, or end her to stop her harming us. Ana has only grown with each interaction. She survived her parents' loss. She survived the Walk, and the frozen cells. She is exactly what I feared her to be."

"Then use your creature against her, or creatures. Find something. Because I can't destroy the boy until the girl is gone."

"You aren't listening." The mage looked back to his page. The regent stepped forward and leaned over him. The shadows moved behind him.

"You must find a way to destroy her. If she has something of the beyond in her, take it away—send it away."

The mage looked up at the mage then, but before he could speak the creature appeared at his side, the usually broad grin absent, the flicking tongue still. Ana felt more unsettled by the change in the creature than the regent appeared as he took a step back.

"You will not touch my queen," it hissed. Just one, Ana thought, as though there was nothing of the maid. They had always been two, but Ana couldn't sense it now. "Do you understand?"

The regent nodded wildly. The creature bowed its head and then the feeling of two returned, the maid pushing back into the being. The grin split the face as the forked tongue tasted the air.

"My Queen," they hissed, staring at her and bowing their head.

The regent turned slowly to where the creature's focus was directed, and Ana smiled and disappeared without showing herself.

The cell was empty. Dray had found a way out. She was disappointed that she hadn't been able to keep him closer.

He might be free, but they were all in danger. No matter what she tried to do, others wanted to hurt them, and mostly to get to her. The shadows at least would protect them and, despite the direction of others, would not harm them.

Her shadows moved over the walls, just where she had left them, as Ana realised she hadn't seen any sign of the girls in the workshop. Should she go back and look for them?

She stepped forward through the bars as though they didn't exist and put her hand to the rough stone wall. The shadows whispered towards her fingertips between the stones like fog through a valley. She felt the cool comfort of them as they travelled along her arm and settled on her skin.

Dray was watched over by more than Ana, but she wondered if Ende's visit to him had been because he cared or if he had been trying to determine what was happening with her.

He will not appreciate a visit.

"But I must see him."

Dray pulled at the jerkin and tried not to grumble. He seemed to be grumbling a lot, and he had asked Barlow to get him out. He understood the risk to the king and that the need for action was coming fast upon them. Dray had traded in his small band of maids, dragons and farmers for soldiers. They might be more likely to succeed, but if they were found out to be working against the regent, none of them would survive the day.

And everyone in the room looked like they belonged with the King's Men but him.

"You said plain sight."

"That doesn't mean as a soldier," Barlow returned. "No one will expect you out of your armour."

"Including me," Dray said, chewing on his lip as Barlow raised his eyebrow. "Fine. I trust you are better able to determine how to save the king. I've been too long out of the capital."

"Firstly, we need to prove that he is the king. Show the people. He looks so much like his father that it was clear to anyone looking at him at the presentation who he truly is."

Dray was reminded of how the general was so drawn to Ed sharing his mother's eyes. Anyone given the chance to look at the boy would know who he was.

"Secondly," Barlow continued, "we need to find him."

"First let's work on how we can show the people he is who he says. I think we should be able to find him easily enough when the time comes."

"You think the witch will give him back?" Barlow asked.

"She isn't a witch," Dray said, looking into the shadows of the room. She was here somewhere, not just with her shadows watching him, but in the room. He wasn't sure why, but he was certain of it.

"She certainly seems like one."

"Ana is using what she can to keep the king safe."

"Shame she didn't do the same for you."

Dray moved his focus back to the captain, whose sandy brown hair and stubbled chin made him look far younger than Dray. "I told her to leave me."

"You told her? And she listened? Perhaps she is *your* witch."

"She is not a witch!" Dray snapped, leaping to his feet as another man entered the small room. He wore the King's Men armour, and he stopped to scowl at Dray from the doorway.

"Why are you helping us?" the man asked.

"Helping you? You are helping me. And we are supposed to be helping the king."

The man remained where he was, and Dray looked at the shiny armour with more regret. He put his hand to his sword, but as comforting as it was, it wasn't enough.

"We have been trying to find the king since his disappearance," the man returned. He was someone Dray had recognised, but not someone he knew. He looked to Barlow as though he could explain to Dray why they didn't need him.

"Kemp," Barlow said, raising a hand as though to placate him. "Captain Sterling has been travelling with the king for some time in an attempt to keep him safe."

"No one seemed to pay him much attention before he left," Dray said, tightening his hand around the handle of his sword. "Other than the sword master, his tutors were of little use. His uncle showed him nothing of what he should be, and no one of the kingdom questioned why the boy from so long ago was still locked away like a child."

"Where were you when he was locked away?" Kemp asked.

"Doing as I was told," Dray murmured, "and I've learnt of my mistake. We know now what he is and what he should be. The uncle should step aside for the son, the heir, but we all know he won't do that."

Barlow nodded, and Dray was distracted for a moment thinking the shadow behind Kemp moved. But when he focused on the wall, he couldn't see anything.

"So, what is the plan?" Dray asked. "How do we force the regent's hand without risking the king?"

"We've been working on a few ideas, but after he appeared in the throne room for the tribute presentation, I think we can try to win over more of those who saw him. We need to convince them that the mage altered him, and that the regent doesn't want him returned."

"Most of those men would have been the regent's men, there for a gift of a wife. Would they go against him?"

"That is hard to say," Barlow admitted, "though someone missed out, as the regent kept one for himself."

"Is that enough?" Kemp asked.

"You did see them," Barlow said. "We all travelled with them; we know just how beautiful they are. If you were hoping for a beautiful young wife, would you not be disappointed when the regent kept her for himself?"

"Perhaps," Kemp admitted to Barlow. "We are too busy working to protect the crown to think of women." But he looked at Dray as he said it.

Dray nodded, but he didn't think that was true. He had been thinking far too often of a woman of late, and that had prevented him from protecting the king. He glanced again towards the shadows and noticed Barlow watching him closely. "How do we determine who was promised and missed out?"

"The presentation didn't go to plan, and the regent invited guests to the castle to hand out his gifts. We just need to find someone from the castle who watched over the guests and is willing to talk."

"Would it be that easy?" Dray asked. "Would you share information on the tribute given you watched over their journey? Would you tell of what happened in the throne room, of the major, or Ana?"

"It might depend who was doing the asking," Barlow said. "You have influence over the younger men. If you were to ask the right one, they would tell you well enough."

"They may not know the names of the men waiting."

"They may know more than you give them credit for," Barlow said. "How many meetings and the like have you been present at where you pretended not to hear what was going on, where you couldn't get involved?"

Dray watched Barlow closely, wondering just who would speak out.

"Only you got involved, didn't you Sterling?" Kemp said, his arms crossed over his shiny breastplate.

Dray looked the man square in the eye. They were supposed to be on the same side, but he doubted the man trusted him any more than the regent. "That was different," he murmured.

"Was it? How could it be different from any other time you were expected to stand by when someone was threatened, or killed, at the whim of the mage or the regent for the supposed benefit of the kingdom yet you knew it was only to benefit them?"

Dray continued to stare. He couldn't explain Ana to this man. He wouldn't understand. Dray knew then that this soldier wouldn't have done as he had, if he had been in the same situation, despite his working against the regent now to save the king. "Are you really here for the king?" he asked.

The man didn't respond, and Dray noticed the shadows moving again. He knew she was there, yet he still had not seen her. What might she do if she thought he was in danger?

Kemp turned quickly to look over his shoulder. "Did you bring your witch?" he asked.

"Enough," Barlow snapped. "We are on the same side here."

"I hope so," Dray said, but his focus remained on the wall behind Kemp. He hoped she was on his side too, but she scared him more than he thought possible. He closed his eyes and drew in a deep breath, trying to remember her sleeping features from when she had curled against him in the narrow cot. He didn't know what Ana was now, but she certainly wasn't the little maid he had pulled from the air onto the Walk.

"We will investigate those promised a tribute, and you ready your witch for the return of the king," Kemp spat as he marched back out of the small room. Barlow gave him a reassuring nod, but as he listened to the other soldier stomp down the stairs and bang the door loudly behind him, Dray wondered if he wouldn't have been better off in his cell. The king was likely safer being watched over by Ana than these men.

9

The regent paced his room, trying not to groan aloud. Nothing was going his way. Nothing had gone his way since that girl had been discovered. He had been so keen to send the mage after her, so sure she was a strength they could use, and he couldn't have been more wrong. She had been nothing but trouble, and now she would be the undoing of him if he couldn't find a way to get rid of her.

The creature the mage had raised to destroy her was working for her, and he had no way to stop her. Thom shivered at the idea of the major disappearing in such a way. The scream still echoed in his ears, and he wondered if he would ever be able to forget it. Had she called the shadows that had surrounded her in the field that day? Were they working with her?

He looked around again. "Where are my torches?" he called.

A man appeared in the doorway, glancing about nervously. "Your Highness?"

"I wanted more light in here," he snapped. Like in the other rooms where people gathered, he didn't want her to have the chance to hide.

"Your wife asked for more subtle lighting," the man said, looking about for the woman to back him up.

The regent looked about himself then. Had she gone against his wishes, or did she not fully understand the need? She hadn't been present when the major was taken, but she had seen what Ana was capable of in the throne room at the presentation.

"Dahli," he called, but there was no response. He hoped she hadn't disappeared with her brother. She hadn't seemed very pleased to see the lord, but Thom was realising he wasn't as good at reading people as he'd hoped. He ran a hand over his forearm, reaffirming that the strange lingering pain had disappeared. Whether Dahli had done that, he wasn't sure. He had heard rumours of the tree people having powers of their own. He didn't think that Dahli had such powers, but again his doubts outweighed his certainty.

When she didn't appear, he waved the man away and headed into the room she had disappeared into earlier. He wanted the chance to spend some time with her, but she was young. She appeared to be attentive every time he sat down, but he was certain it was not genuine attention.

He stood in the doorway and sighed, looking over the bed and the quiet figure curled beneath the blankets. The brother hadn't come close, he thought, watching the slow, regular rise and fall of her shoulder with her breath. They had talked little at dinner. She hadn't appeared to want him here, and he hadn't called upon them to ask any particular favour. Other than to demand that the boy return the woman he had stolen.

Thom hadn't paid too much attention to the girl. Like the others, she had been very beautiful, but there was something about her that had grabbed the mage's attention, although he wasn't saying what that was. Thom headed back out to the main room and his balcony. He wouldn't be able to sleep, and he was disappointed he wasn't getting from his wife what he needed.

He leaned across the railing and looked out at the lights of the city below. A hand ran over his forearm, and he tried not to turn from the view as his young wife pressed her body into his side.

"I thought you were going to join me," she breathed in his ear, and a tingle travelled across his skin. He was reminded of a woman long ago who had created the same response in him, and he tried not to remember the look on her face when he had last seen her. "How is your arm?" she whispered as her hand ran over it, and he thought a slight burning sensation returned.

He smacked at her hand, but she grabbed at him and he turned to her intense gaze. Her beautiful dark eyes stared up at him, a smile he hadn't seen before lighting up her face although she looked darker, as though surrounded by shadows. She wore very little. He was taken in by the shape of her body and the outline of her features beneath the thin material. He turned quickly and pulled her close, her young body firm. As he leaned forward, she turned her face to accept his lips against her cheek.

"I can't wait any longer," he whispered hoarsely as his lips worked across her chin and down her throat. For a moment he thought she shivered, and he pulled back. "Are you cold?"

She nodded, running her hand across his cheek and down his neck to rest on his heart. "Let's go to bed," she whispered, chewing on her lip. He nodded as he released his hold on her, and she moved quickly across the room and back through the door.

By the time he reached the door, she was already back beneath the covers, just as he had spied her before. He stood at the side of the bed and put his hand on her shoulder. She groaned as though sleeping. He looked up and around the room, then pulled the covers back from her. She was as he had seen her moments ago, yet different.

"My love," she whispered sleepily. "What is the matter?"

"Get out," he growled.

Her sleepy eyes grew wide, and she warily climbed from the bed to stand before him. Her outfit was a little less transparent than when she had stood by the balcony. Her curves a little softer. He suddenly pulled her against him, and she squealed with surprise. As he wrapped his arms around her, his arm started to ache.

"What have you done?" he whispered in her ear, holding her too close.

"Thom?" she asked, but he could hear the fear in her voice.

"What has happened?"

She felt different against him, and he released his hold and raced back to the door that led down the steps to the courtyard. He pulled the door open to find a guard and the servant waiting for instructions. They both looked at him with surprise, and he closed the door again.

"The witch," he murmured.

"What?" the woman asked, shivering as she stood in the doorway.

"The witch was here," he said more clearly.

"You saw her?"

"I saw you," he said, looking around the room again, "although it wasn't you."

"You aren't making sense," she said, stepping out to meet him, but he pushed past her and into the room to see if she was still sleeping. The bed was empty, the covers pulled back.

"She was here," he said. He wasn't safe anywhere. He looked over the woman before him. The light in the room was dim, but the shadows didn't close in around her as he thought they had at the balcony.

"You don't trust me," she said, clearly disappointed.

"Now is your chance to prove yourself," he said.

She looked around nervously, then locked her eyes with his and nodded once. She motioned him forward but stayed within sight. When he reached her, she took his hand and pulled him into the room, pushing the door shut. She directed him to the bed, then took the candle from beside the bed and lit the others around the room, making it brighter and reducing the shadows.

Ana stood in the cool night air beside the hut. The smell of grass and mud was comforting, and she smiled into the dark. It might have been a little trick, and she hadn't been sure she could pull it off. Yet the regent had truly thought her his wife. She wondered if he would work it out and what he might do, but it had been enough.

Her aim had been to unsettle him, which she had done, and to put her back in the forefront of his mind. The niggling pain she created would do that. As she wasn't quite sure what she had done the last time, she didn't know if it would remain in the arm or travel throughout his body. Either way, he would be somewhat more nervous of the dark.

If that nervousness caused him to reduce the shadows, she would have to work out a way around that. She wondered if the Lord of Near Forest had managed to get any payment in return for what he was so sure had been taken from him. Belle was safe. Maybe promises had been made for the next tribute.

Ana sighed and looked up at the stars above. She had only ever wanted a simple life, but she was far from that now. Dray was working with the soldiers to find a way to the regent, and she was protecting the king. She could wear the regent down, but she still didn't have any clear idea of how she could get him to step down. Maybe the soldiers were right and they just had to show the people who Ed was. Hadn't she thought the same at one point?

It will not be enough for him to step down. He will always be a threat to the crown.

Ana nodded. They would have to destroy him, but they would have to get the crown first. "And the girls?" Ana whispered into the night.

Interesting, we could use them.

"I think the mage has that idea."

The shadows want them.

There was something about them that drew Ana's attention as well. Perhaps the mage saw them as a replacement, thinking they could be what she would not. "They don't have our strength," Ana whispered.

No, they don't.

"I will think on it." Ana walked through the wall of the hut, appearing in the shadows on the other side. It was late, and Phillip was sleeping in the narrow cot. Another had been set up perpendicular to it, across the end wall. Ed and Belle shared it, curled together in the small space.

Ana sucked in a breath. She had expected something between the two, yet it felt jarring to see it. The small room was too warm for the small fire, and she glanced around before stepping out of the shadows to sit at the table. Ende and the little dragon had been here. Ana could taste their heat on the air. Salima was still very focused on Ed, and Ana wondered if she had discovered a way to find him. Perhaps now that more of her dragon was emerging, she had sniffed him out.

Ana wanted to find them, but she was tired. Using the shadows to disguise herself as someone else had taken more than she thought it could. She lay down across the table, resting her head on her arms. She rarely slept now, and not nearly as well as she had that night wrapped in Dray's arms in a similar narrow cot as Ed and Belle.

But he knew what she was now, and she didn't think he would allow such a moment to occur between them again. He had watched the shadows with real fear in his eyes while speaking to the men, as though he knew she was there and worried what she might do. She would protect him. In her own way. He was so determined to protect himself, and yet if he had been able to, he wouldn't have ended up in a cell.

10

Forest no longer felt comfortable in his own space, and he didn't feel like himself. Ende sat in the worn chair beside him, focused on the fire. He had always known Salima wasn't his, that he was raising her for someone else, and yet she had become his. She knew nothing of her mother or father, and although she had formed a connection with Ed quite quickly, she hadn't known he was family.

But her being the child of the dragon was something very different. It didn't change how Forest felt about her—she was still his daughter—but it changed whether he could continue as her father. Ende would take her away.

It had been Salima who said she wanted to go with him, to understand more of what she was. She had felt the connection to the man, and once the dragon became clearer, not just the heat in her hands but the fire and then the wings… He sighed.

When he had checked on her not so long ago, she was curled in her bed sleeping peacefully, and yet he felt as though he had lost her. She had called him Papa and hugged him close when they had returned, the relief that she had found a way to stop the fire short lived as she blurted out who she was and what she was going to do.

"She wants to help Ed first," he murmured.

Ende looked around from the flames then, his expression sympathetic. Or was it pity? Forest no longer knew. "I will keep her safe," the dragon rumbled.

"Tell me how this happened," Forest said, leaning back in his chair, trying to look relaxed.

"The stress of seeing the boy in such danger triggered the change. Although I'm surprised it didn't happen sooner. She is more dragon than girl."

Forest looked down at his hands. He wanted to know what this would mean for her, but it wasn't the question he had asked. "Teressa," he said.

"Ah." Ende sighed, looking back to the flames. "That is much harder to explain."

"Did it start because you were causing trouble? You were always playing tricks and pushing boundaries."

The man shook his head, his gaze locked on something far away.

"You loved her?" Forest asked, as though it wasn't possible. She had been an amazing woman, but she had been the queen.

"I didn't mean to fall for her," Ende said softly. "I am loath to say it was one of those things that just happened. But it did. If I could have taken her far away, I would have. When I learned she was with child…"

Forest looked at the man staring into the flames as a lone tear rolled away.

"Did you know what that would mean?"

"I assumed she and Barric had conceived. I loved her so intensely that I couldn't bear the idea of him touching her. I told her I was leaving, that I couldn't watch her being loved by him."

Forest waited, glancing quickly at Salima's door, hoping she still slept.

"She begged me not to go, assured me the child was mine. I wanted to take her away then, take her far away from everyone. But she wouldn't come, and I knew it wouldn't end well. Dragons and men." He turned from the flames, his gaze intense. "I might look like a man, but I'm not."

Forest nodded, understanding that what at first had been joy was now what he knew would kill her.

"When news came of her death and no mention of a child, I knew they were both lost. There was nothing to return for, nothing to live for."

"And then there was Ana," Forest said.

"Such strength," Ende said, a small smile brightening his sad face, his eyes still damp. "I was reminded of Essa, but there was something else. And within a short time of finding her, I felt the boy, felt Essa in the boy moving towards me. I had to see him. I knew he had come to find me, although I wasn't sure why, and the connection between the two was so strong."

"What of Sterling?"

Ende shook his head and turned back to the flames. "A stronger connection. And although I thought that was because she had called to him, demanded to be saved, I wonder now if there wasn't something else to it."

"What sort of something?"

He shook his head. "I don't know. But he might be the only one to reach her in the darkness."

"You think she is dangerous," Forest said, sitting forward.

"One of them is," Ende murmured.

He had said something similar before, and Forest wasn't sure he understood just what he meant. It had something to do with the connection to her magic, he thought as he glanced around the room, searching the shadows. Although she had allowed him to stop her moving through the shadows, or whatever it was, she did. Holding her seemed to be a way to keep her grounded.

Ende's attention was turned back to the fire, and the conversation had stilled. Although Forest felt he understood the dragon better, he still didn't understand how Ter-essa had allowed herself to become involved with him. But as he thought about the little witch and the feel of her soft dress and too-thin frame when he had tried to hold her back, he wondered if he too could feel something for a woman he shouldn't even consider.

"She is not what you want her to be," Ende whispered.

Forest gulped down the thoughts that were forming and glanced back to the dragon, who hadn't even looked up. "How do you do that?" he asked.

Ende shrugged.

"She isn't the girl who first arrived. It is almost as though she has changed to fit the expectations of what she is."

The dragon nodded, but he didn't turn to look at Forest.

"I don't trust her; I have never trusted her. What is she?"

Ende turned, but said nothing.

"I was reminded of her mother, but there is very little of her mother in her. She scares me."

"And yet you remained close."

"I thought if I knew where she was, she couldn't cause any trouble. Couldn't hurt anyone." Yet she had seemed just as lost herself. Unsure of who and what she was, scared of what she might do. Even when she had hidden in the storeroom, he had wanted her as far away from Salima as possible. And yet she had looked so frail, as though she needed him. "What skill does she have over men?" he asked.

When he focused on the silent dragon, Forest found him grinning. "The same as any other woman. But her focus is the king, and her only interest is the soldier."

"Are you sure? I would have thought she would have taken him first."

"The king and then the soldier. She went for him, returned for him to the cells, but he wouldn't go. She ensured he was protected and visited him even when he told her not to."

Forest looked down at his hands. She hadn't come back to him. Not that he wanted her to. He wasn't sure what he could do or say if she did appear. It was probably for the best. "What are we going to do for Ed?" he asked.

The dragon shook his head.

"Do you think she wants to help him regain the crown, or just keep him safe?"

"I think the crown is very important in whatever it is she is planning."

Ed shifted his legs as he woke, Belle's warmth pressed against him, and he opened his eyes to her blond hair. He breathed in the scent of her and tightened his arms around her. Phillip snorted in his sleep. Reminded that they weren't alone, Ed looked around and noticed Ana sleeping across the table. He pulled carefully away from Belle and lifted himself up to watch the woman at the table. The pale light of morning pushed through the window, and she appeared both relaxed and uncomfortable.

It had been so long since he had really seen her, and since he had seen her sleep. She appeared to lie too still. He carefully crawled over the woman beside him, who murmured in her sleep and threaded her arms around him as he tried to move over her.

He would have longed to see her bright blue eyes smiling up at him then, but he needed to check on Ana. He continued moving as Belle moved into the space he had been, and then he was sitting on the edge of the cot. The room was quiet. He stood slowly, pulled the covers over Belle and padded towards the table.

One arm was bent beneath her head the other stretched out across the table. Even standing close, he couldn't determine if she was sleeping or not. She didn't appear to move at all. He gently ran a finger along her temple, capturing the hair that had fallen across her face and brushing it back. Her nose twitched, and he thought she smiled before she sighed. She appeared to be sleeping soundly. He wondered what she dreamt of that would put such a smile on her face.

He sat down on the bench beside her and watched the smile slip away as she returned to the serious, still woman she had appeared as when he woke.

In the quiet room, he sat and watched her remain motionless. He wondered if he had seen the movement and smile or if she was in fact lost. He reached out and took the wrist of her outstretched arm, pressing his fingers against her cool skin as gently as he could. He could feel the slight pulse beneath the skin and sighed with relief, then looked back to find her watching him.

He let her go. She pulled her arm out of reach and sat slowly.

"Sorry," he whispered, aware that the others were still sleeping. "I was worried."

She said nothing, only stared at him.

"I didn't expect to see you," he said, although he wondered at his own words.

Ana only looked past him to the beds at the other end of the small cottage.

"Do you have an idea of how I can face my uncle and win?" he asked.

Ana looked back at him, and he wondered what she was thinking. She would know what he was thinking, as she seemed to be able to work that out with a glance. But she was scaring him again.

She raised her eyebrows and then crossed her arms. He was tempted to fill the silence as he had been, but he bit down on his tongue to wait.

"Ende was here," she said after some time. "And the little one."

Ed nodded. He thought she knew what Salima was, but he wondered if she had realised why that was and what it meant for her.

Ana nodded once.

"You have to stop doing that," Ed whispered hoarsely.

"Then you need to talk to me."

"I'm sorry." He sighed. "There is just so much for me to wrap my head around."

"I know what she is and who. I know her father is not yours. I also understand why your mother did as she did."

"Really?" he asked, honestly surprised by the thought. "I thought she loved my father."

"I'm sure she did," Ana said, looking towards the door.

"Are you going again?"

She looked back, but said nothing.

"Where do you go?"

"To find a way to help you."

"Can Dray help?"

"He works on his own plans. They aim to help you all they can."

"They?" Ed asked, and he thought she looked sad again. "Do you wish he were here?"

"He is where he needs to be," she said, pushing up from the table. Ed closed his hand around her wrist, wanting to keep her close, hoping she wouldn't just disappear again. "He has found some soldiers willing to help you."

"Can he trust them?"

"I think so," she said softly, pulling at his hold, but he wouldn't let her go. "The sword master thought such a move would hold me in one place." She leaned forward, studying his face as though trying to read him. "It is not what I am." Despite his hold on her wrist, she was gone, and his hand fell away. She had felt safe enough to return to them and sleep, although he wondered what she had been doing that she was so lost to it.

Did the constant moving through the shadows, if that was what she did, drain her so much? And had she been to see Dray before them?

"Ed?" Belle said, standing behind him. He jumped, then turned as she took a step back.

"Ana was here," he said quietly, looking over at the sleeping man. Phillip seemed to sleep far more than he had before, and Ed worried about his time with the lord of the forest.

"What did she want? Does she have a plan?"

"Not one she was willing to share, if she does. She said Dray was working on something. She was sleeping; she looks tired."

"She always looks tired," Belle whispered, stepping up to him, and he held her warmth close. "She is on the move all the time, and yet we don't know what she does. Are you certain she is trying to help you?"

Ed nodded and allowed his arms to drop away. "We need more wood on the fire," he murmured, padding out onto the small covered porch. He took his time to collect an armful of wood, then returned to find Belle sitting where Ana had been at the table.

"I understand that you won't hear a word against her. But we don't know what she is doing."

"I'm sure she helps, or why would she stay? She didn't have to save me. She didn't have to hide us away from my uncle." He dropped the wood into a small pile by the fire, wincing as the noise filled the space, before putting two of them over the dying coals. He wondered what they might do if it ran out. There didn't seem to be any trees nearby, and he wasn't sure if he could ask Ana for supplies. As he looked up from the flames, he saw a basket on the table he hadn't noticed before.

Belle turned to look and then dragged it closer. "I suppose she isn't leaving us to starve."

They sat in silence for a time, looking over the food. When he looked up, Belle was staring at him. She flushed.

"Do you feel guilty about doubting her?" he asked.

She shook her head. "I was thinking of something else."

"What sort of something?" he asked as her face flushed a deeper red. "Belle?"

She sucked in a breath. "Where is Dray?"

"You were thinking of Dray?" he asked too loudly, and as she put her finger to her lips, Phillip groaned and rolled over in his narrow bed.

"Don't you worry where he is?"

"Yes," he said quickly. "But not in a way that makes me blush."

Her face coloured again, and she looked down at the table. Ed stood too quickly and moved to the doorway. He really needed to focus on what he was doing and how he was going to remove his uncle. Dray was working with soldiers, Ana was out searching… even Ende and Salima had gone. Maybe if they were all together again, they could come up with something sensible. Although he wasn't quite sure what it would be like to sit on the throne. Would Ana remain to offer her advice, or would she disappear?

Belle's slender arms threaded around his waist, and she leaned into his back. He put his hands on hers and was reminded of the feel of her body against his when he had woken. He wasn't quite sure how it had come about that they were sharing a bed, but once her father had arrived, it had just happened.

"I was thinking of you," she whispered.

"What about me?" he asked, trying to picture himself sitting on the throne in a room he had barely visited since his father had died.

"How I like sharing your bed."

"You aren't disappointed that you didn't find some old man for a husband?" He meant it as a joke, but her hold released and he turned to find her looking down, her face flushed again. Her arms hung at her sides, and her blond curls were almost as wayward as Salima's. On impulse, he stepped closer, closing the small gap between them. Although he wanted to wrap his arms around her and hold her against him, he ran his hands across her jawline and tilted her face up to his.

Her eyes sparkled with unshed tears, and he wondered if he would only upset this woman. He leaned down and pressed his lips to hers before he had a chance to say anything else that might upset her. She was so soft, and her hands clung to the front of his shirt.

11

"Did you talk to Master Forest?" Dray asked as the captain entered the small space. He was starting to think that he had traded one cell for another. He couldn't go out. He was still trapped far away from Ana, and he had no real idea what was going on.

"He is hard to get to," Barlow said.

"Why?" Dray asked, climbing to his feet from the dusty floor.

"The practice halls are still closed."

"Surely he could train somewhere else."

"He doesn't appear that keen. He spends his time in his rooms with his daughter."

"Maybe she isn't well?"

"Keeping out of the way, more like. We have discovered the man we thought was to be offered the last tribute, but he isn't being very clear on why he was at the castle at the time and what he might have missed out on."

Dray tried not to sigh. "Who is this man?"

"Some noble or other, Charles Man-something. Kemp knows."

"Mandering?" Dray asked.

"Possibly. Do you know him?"

"His family is influential."

"And maybe the reason why he isn't saying anything, even though he missed out."

"Let me talk to him."

"And what would you say?"

Dray glared. He was tired of doing nothing. He had started out with no plan, trying to save a girl from the mage. He still had no plan, but they weren't running anymore. Well, in some ways they were trying to do so much more, and they couldn't do it in hiding any longer. "You said plain sight," he murmured.

"Fine," Barlow conceded. "No one will recognise you, although I suggest…" He raised a hand to his own face, and Dray wasn't sure if he should shave again or neaten up what was developing into a beard. Barlow shook his head. "Do you want someone to escort you?"

Dray shook his head. He would be better on his own. Soldiers tended to draw attention, and he didn't need that at the moment. Barlow indicated the door, and with this hand on his sword, Dray headed eagerly for the stairs. He skipped down and into the street, then hovered by the edge of the building.

It had been too long since he had been out, and he felt somewhat exposed without his armour. He rearranged the jerkin, tried not to look like a lost boy and headed along the street. He was almost disappointed when no one paid him any attention. He passed stalls and small shops selling all sorts of wares, including cloth, bread and gems. He saw a small silver dagger at one stall that made him think of Ana, but aside from not having any coins, he didn't know when he could give it to her or even if she would appreciate such a gift. She really wasn't the girl he had met so long ago.

A cart filled the narrow road before him, and he moved out of the way to let it through, wondering at what it carried. Had it been so long since he had walked away from the castle? So much seemed to have happened. He had been separated from Ana for much of it, and yet she was at the forefront of every thought.

Standing to the side of the road as the wagon passed, he looked into the crowd hugging the stalls opposite and was sure that Ana was among their number. He looked away and then back, thinking it was all in his mind. But she was there, standing in the crowd, the thick cloak pulled up over her head and her bright eyes shining from within. He stepped forward, and she watched him come. When he held out an arm, she slipped her hand into the crook of his elbow without hesitation and allowed him to lead her along the street in the sunshine.

He wondered how long she would continue with him in such a way, for she seemed to hug the shadows all the time.

"Where are you going?" she asked, raising her voice to be heard over the crowds they moved through.

"To meet a man about a bride."

She looked up at him, her eyes sparkling and lips smiling. "Is this to do with the girl from the trees?"

He nodded and then pulled her to the side of the road as several soldiers rode past. They didn't even glance his way.

"Dahli," he said.

He looked down on her, and she glanced back at him, the soft smile turning to a smirk. "I think the regent might doubt his choice of bride."

"Why?" he asked, pulling her to a stop.

She shook her head. She didn't appear as comical as she had in his cloak. She looked scary, as though she had a secret he didn't want to learn. When had it come to this?

He waited, but she said nothing. When he started walking again, she kept pace easily enough, her hand still tight on his arm. She paused by a stall with soup, but when he looked at her she dragged him away. She had been too thin last time he had seen her, and he wondered if she ate or rested.

"I hope you have a plan," she said.

He nodded, but he didn't. It wouldn't be enough to ensure the kingdom knew Ed was the king. He knew that. "What do you propose?"

"I have some ideas, although I'm not sure you would approve."

He glanced down at her, but she was looking in the direction they were walking. "Do I want to ask?"

"I just want Ed to be what he is meant to be."

"We all want that. He is safe, isn't he?"

She glared up at him. "Why wouldn't he be?" she asked in a soft, dangerous whisper, and he was tempted to remove himself from her arm.

"I know you would keep him safe; I just needed to ask. So many ask me."

She only continued to glare, then focused on the road before her. It took him a moment to think about where they were, but he was just walking, too focused on Ana again rather than where he needed to go and who he needed to speak to.

He redirected her along a narrow street that led to a wider one, with houses larger than the little ones they had passed.

"Growing up, I assumed everyone of importance lived in the castle," Ana said quietly. Dray was taken back to the walk through the mountains with her. He rested his hand on hers. "No one lives in houses like this in Sheer Rock."

"Long histories of gold and connection have allowed for bigger homes."

"How will you get in to talk to him?"

Dray opened his mouth and then closed it. He hadn't really thought about that. The man was unlikely to allow a stranger into his home to talk about a gift he hadn't received from the regent. They would assume he was working against them, and it was likely he would wind up in a cell by the end of the day. Again.

When he glanced at Ana, she was grinning. Closing her hand so tight around his arm that he thought he felt claws, she shut her eyes and the world went dark around them. He sucked in a breath as the darkness disappeared and they were standing in a small room. Narrow windows looked out across the city towards the dominating castle of the capital, and a man sat at a round table eating. The food stopped partway to his mouth, and then he was standing with a small blade held out.

"We want to talk to you of the king," Ana said, releasing her hold on Dray. He wondered if she might leave him there, although he didn't really want to move with her through the shadows again.

"Didn't he run away?" the man asked cruelly.

Ana was beside him in a heartbeat. Dray wasn't even sure if she had moved across the room or disappeared and reappeared. Her hand rested on Mandering's hand that held the knife. He squealed and released it, jumping back.

"Have a seat, sir," she hummed, and the hairs on Dray's neck stood at attention. "We only have some questions. You were in the throne room on the night that was to be the presentation."

He nodded, even though she hadn't phrased it as a question.

"You saw him."

He opened and then closed his mouth. Ana leaned closer.

"I saw something," he stammered. "A young man, not a boy—a man, who looked very much like King Barric. Very much," he added softly.

"Did you believe him to be King Edwin?" Ana asked, her voice coaxing, and the earlier uneasiness Dray had felt lifted somewhat.

Mandering nodded slowly. "But then he looked so different. His clothes, his face, his hair."

"The mage," Ana growled. Dray was tempted to take a step back as the man at the table leaned back.

"Ana," Dray said softly.

She glanced at him and then back to Mandering. "I changed his clothes. He is a king, after all, and he hasn't been given the opportunity to dress as one, be one, learn what it means."

Mandering sighed and nodded. "What do you want?" he asked.

"Just for you to tell others who you believed the man to be."

"If I start telling others that the boy king has returned and his uncle has him locked away, what would that mean for me?"

"The regent was trying to win your favour."

"He might already have it. Who is to say the boy would rule any better?"

"I am," she said, leaning in closer to him. Dray was sure the man paled.

"No one will believe me. They will think me bitter because I didn't get a bride."

"Were you expecting one?"

The man shook his head. "I hoped, but he promised those ten girls to many more than he could give them to. He did the same with the last tribute. He had promised Harold so faithfully last time, and he had to wait seven years. If I go against him now, I might miss out next time."

"Unless you meet a nice lady on your own," Ana said.

He glanced up at her even more nervously than before. "What are you proposing, witch?"

Ana straightened and Dray stepped forward, taking her arm and pulling her back despite the feeling that he was in as much danger as the pompous man at the table.

"I am proposing that you back your king, so you don't lose your head when he sits on the throne."

Mandering blinked up at her, but he made no movement to indicate he would do as she asked.

"Who else at the presentation believed him to be the king?" Dray asked.

"Most," he murmured, his eyes still on Ana. "Until he changed and the doubt outweighed what they had seen."

"Maybe rumour will be enough," Dray said, his hand around Ana's too-thin wrist. "Thank you for your time, sir." He bowed his head and tugged Ana towards the door.

"It is not enough," she whispered. "But I will leave it with you."

Dray opened his mouth to protest, fearing she would leave him there, and suddenly they were again on the street outside the house.

Ana was frustrated. She hadn't gotten what she'd wanted from Mandering, and she wondered what Dray thought he would do. The hideous man was too keen to keep the favour of the regent. The people didn't believe that Ed could be king. It wasn't that they didn't believe he was who he said—they just didn't think he would win. She needed a way for him to prove himself to them. Being seen was not going to be enough.

She had tried to focus on Dray. It had been a relief to be with him again, near him, her hand on his arm. But there were too many people, and she hadn't been around such crowds for a long time. Walking with him amongst the stalls and shops, she had almost been excited. It was what she had dreamt of so long ago. Visiting the capital, where there were so many different things to buy.

But the shadows had called to her from the crowd, and for a moment it had seemed too easy to allow them to come. They could almost have lived as she had, hidden within the people of the capital. But it wasn't what they wanted. It wouldn't be enough. And for a moment, walking in the sunshine with Dray, it was what she had wanted too. For them to come.

They had walked in silence back through the streets towards where Dray was staying. She could sense that he wanted to ask so much, and yet he didn't. She wanted to return such interest, but she knew his thoughts. None of which were going to get the king any closer to his throne or crown. They knew who he was. That was what frustrated her most. The people of the kingdom and the capital knew very well that the man who had appeared before them in the throne room was their king, that he was meant to be where the regent was, and yet they wouldn't back him.

She had slipped away from him before he had the chance to ask her what was on her mind, and she had watched him return to his dusty room from the shadows.

Fear, she thought, looking into the shadows of the practice halls. Still no one came here. What that meant for the sword master with nowhere to teach his trade, she didn't know. But then, the kingdom didn't seem to be missing the lessons.

Forest had returned the king's daughter to find she wasn't what he had thought after all, and it was likely he would lose her himself. If he didn't have a king to support, what might he do? Where might he go?

What could she do to have the people see Ed was the king they needed? At least Ed had been willing to use her. He was scared of her, but he would use her, and that was all she needed.

Ana took a breath and leaned against the wall. She was so tired. She stepped forward as the boy who had died in this very room formed in the shadows. She closed her eyes, feeling the strength of them. Almost as strong as the maid in her creature.

"Majesty," they hissed.

"Who sent you here?" she asked.

"I sought you out."

She waited, longing to lean against the wall again. It hadn't been so long ago that she had slept in the cottage in the marshes. She hadn't felt this drained since she had first escaped the ice cell.

"I will watch over you," they hissed, stepping forward, concern on their reptilian face.

"I don't need you to," Ana said quickly, but she wondered if she did. She wanted somewhere comfortable, safe. She didn't feel safe anywhere at the moment. For a brief instant, she thought of Dray and his little room in the barracks and sleeping so soundly in his arms.

Allow them.

Ana sighed. "What is the mage planning?" she asked instead.

"He would destroy the king."

Ana sucked in an angry groan. "I have said he is not to be touched."

"He is trying to find another way."

"The girls," Ana murmured.

The creature bent its awkward frame down and knelt before her. "Majesty."

"I have promised the girls to another," she said quickly. "Although perhaps we could use them ourselves. Do you know what they can do?"

The creature remained unmoving.

Ana blew out a long breath and leaned back against the wall. Had moving Dray through the shadows been what had drained her? She had dropped food off at the cottage, but she didn't think she had eaten herself. Although food didn't seem to taste the same. It didn't satisfy her as it had, so she hadn't really bothered of late.

The creature looked up at her with large, round black eyes. The long, forked tongue tasted the air of the room. "Allow me, Majesty."

She nodded once, mostly from curiosity as to what it proposed. If she were better able to focus, she could work on a way for Ed to be the man she needed him to be to win his crown back.

The creature reached out long-fingered clawed hands and gently took her own. She stared into the large dark eyes as the room disappeared around them. Shadows closed in around her, but they didn't dissipate as they usually did when she moved through them.

"Where?" she murmured, but she knew where they were.

Welcome home.

As the shadow creature before her released her hands, a black apple appeared in one. It felt as firm as any apple she had held before, and she took a bite. It wasn't sweet, but it was the best thing she had tasted in a long time. As she moved further into the room, it was dark but comfortable. A small table held a range of food before her, although it didn't look like anything she could recognise. When she stepped up to the table, a bed came into focus across the space. It was broad and inviting. She looked from the table to the bed and back again, unsure what she wanted more.

It was almost as the visions in the castle in the mountains had been. She couldn't see the walls; only the table and bed were clear.

"You have had others watch over what is important to you," the creature hissed. "It is time for us to watch over you."

Ana bowed her head and took another bite of the apple.

Although she was still tired, she felt more nourished than she had for some time, and she wondered at the food on the table. It was familiar and yet not. Something tugged at a memory from her dreams of a distant past.

Ana shook the idea away and climbed into the bed. It was the most inviting place she had ever been. It was as though she had come home. As she lay down, the soft bedding moved around her, snuggling her in its embrace. She was reminded of her childhood, her father and his gentle words as he tucked her in of a night.

She wondered then who he had been trying to reassure, the child or himself. Thinking that perhaps the woman he loved would come back to him. As Ana drifted to sleep, she wondered whether her life would have been different had her mother not left them. Although, believing her dead was better than knowing she had left them by choice.

The woman she had seen in her visions of the past returned to her dreams, yet she wasn't in the small cottage with her father. She was lost in the shadows.

12

Ed stood out amongst the tall golden grass, his feet sinking further into the boggy ground and the water rising slowly up his trousers. Why she had left them there, he wasn't sure. It didn't really seem like the best place to mount an attack, but then Ana hadn't given any indication that was what she intended to do. The more he thought about it, the more frustrated he became. He had no idea what she intended. She had been so sure she had to save him, but was that from his uncle or something else?

Ana seemed to be the one in control of the dark shadows that frightened the kingdom. Despite the mage having sent the first creature to end him, it was Ana who directed them. She had promised to give him whatever he wanted. He wanted to be king. He had been so unsure of himself, but finally he knew who he was and what he wanted, and it wasn't getting him anywhere. And he rarely saw her. She had slept at the table not so long ago, but he hadn't seen her since. He didn't know if she was working in his favour or not.

Although he constantly told himself she must be working to assist him, there was something very different about the girl he had met in the mountains. That first night he had felt so threatened, and then she had sat beside him at the table, taken his hand and listened to his stories. She had been a friend, someone he'd felt instantly comfortable with, someone he'd needed to be near.

Not now. Now she frightened him. Now she knew his every thought. He wasn't sure what to do with that. And he worried it would put those with him in more danger. He glanced back at the small cottage, almost lost from view in the grass. Belle had been sleeping soundly when he had left, her father the same. Ed worried for the old man. Phillip was not himself either, but far more had happened to him with the lord of the forest than he had realised, and more than he was willing to tell. Ed could see the guilt on Belle's face when she looked at her father, and he felt the same.

They were too far from those who might help them. The dragon, the soldier. Even Master Forest had been a better friend to him all these years than anyone else within the castle, and had kept his sister safe. Yet Forest too had hesitated when the regent had asked if he knew Ed. Without Ana to ensure that didn't happen again, he wasn't going to be able to just walk into the castle.

He hoped Ana could use her monsters to get rid of his uncle. Maybe it would simply come down to a fight. Unsure if he was headed towards the castle or away, Ed walked deeper into the marsh. Salima had said they were close, and yet he had no idea where they were. Again, he was reminded of how little he knew of the kingdom. By the time his father was his age, he had probably visited every part of Ilia. Had been seen by the people as the man he was. He had become king at a young age. Although not as young as Ed had been when his father had died, and not as young as he was now.

Despite all that had been done and all the ground he had covered, Ed still felt like a boy. A boy who shouldn't be king. He turned and realised he couldn't see the cottage. Not that he had come too far, but far enough to get lost. He studied the ground and quickly found his footprints, then retraced his steps back.

Belle stood in the doorway of the cottage looking out over the grass. She smiled as he approached, but she didn't seem to have been searching for him. He wondered at her feelings.

"You weren't worried I had gone?" he asked, his words a little sharper than intended.

"You wouldn't leave me behind," she said, her voice calm, her smile bright and her arms outstretched.

When he didn't step into them, she cocked her head a little to the side but didn't let them drop. "Changed your mind?" she asked.

He stepped forward, and she closed the gap between them. "Why do you have such faith in me?"

She ran a hand over his sparse beard, and he wondered how ragged he must look. But she still smiled. "How could I not? I know you, and you are a good man."

"Are you sure?" He leaned into her, wanting her lips against his.

"You don't want to wait here any longer," she said, as though she too could read his mind.

"I don't know what Ana might do, but I can't hide. I'm King and I need to show myself to the people. I can't allow my uncle to continue as regent."

"Could Salima help us?"

"Maybe." He sighed. "I don't want to use her just because…" He stopped. He hadn't explained to Belle just what his sister was. He wasn't sure how easy it would be to explain, and she didn't know of Ende. Perhaps it wasn't really his story to tell. Would she believe him?

"She said she would be your inside man."

He nodded. "Maybe we head for the capital. I think it would be easier to do this from inside."

"Now?"

"Should we wait for Ana?"

She shook her head. Not that she had said, but he got the idea Belle was just as uncertain of Ana and the changes in her as he was. The dark cloak had played on his mind too, and he wondered at the connection between her and Dray. She had left him, yet she seemed to cling to the idea of him.

"Let's see what we can do," he said, heading into the cottage. Phillip sat by the fire, a small loaf of bread in his hands although he wasn't eating it. They couldn't drag him through the marshes. Perhaps he could send Salima with supplies if they were to leave him behind. If they left without telling Ana, Ed wasn't sure she would take the interest in Phillip to keep him alive.

"Do we have anything else we could take with us?" he asked, looking around the small cottage.

"Have you asked the girl?" Phillip replied, still staring into the fire. "She would do anything for you."

"What girl?" Belle snapped.

Phillip turned, and Ed followed his gaze to find Ana sitting silently at the table, her back to the wall. It was as though she was lost to the shadows of the room, and yet he could see her very clearly.

"What is the plan, Your Majesty?" she asked. Her voice made him shiver.

"To get back to the capital."

"How do you propose to do that?"

"Walk," he said firmly. "It isn't that far."

She remained unmoving as she stared at him. There was something different about her. It was as though every time he saw her, she was less and less the woman he knew—or the girl, he thought, remembering her as she had been in the mountains, holding his hand.

"Why do you think I am so different?" she asked, but there was nothing in her voice to give away whether she was upset or angry at his thoughts.

"How long until you do something to help him be King?" Belle asked, allowing her anger to be heard.

"So that you can be his queen?" Ana asked, her voice just as undecipherable as before.

What doesn't she know? Ed thought.

Ana moved her attention to him slowly, and he bit down on his lip.

"Is that what you want?" she asked him.

He nodded once, too afraid to speak. He didn't need to speak, for she knew it all. She pushed up from the table, but didn't disappear as he expected her to.

"You could take us," Ed suggested. "You would be the safest way into the castle."

She raised her eyebrows as though unbelieving of his words.

"You could take us to the others. Dray would be able to help."

Something shifted in her look then. The hard, unreadable face softened a little as she partly opened her mouth and then closed it.

"Ana?" Ed said softly, stepping closer. "Has something happened to Dray? Will he not help?"

"He will always help you," she said softly.

"Does he not want to see you?" Belle asked, also moving closer. As she came level with Ed, she took his hand. Ana's gaze shifted to it, and the hardness returned. Was she jealous?

A growl emanated from the corner in which she stood, and Ed wasn't sure if it was her or one of her creatures. At the idea of it, one of them appeared beside her, the large dark eyes focused on Ed. Its long, narrow tongue flicked out as though tasting the air. But despite the fear coursing through Ed and Belle's shaking hand in his as she moved behind him, the creature bowed slowly, awkwardly.

"Majesty," it hissed. "What would you have us do?"

Ed stared, unsure how to answer the beast and unsure his voice would work if he tried to address it. They were certainly her creatures. They did her bidding. And it wouldn't matter what he said or how it addressed him.

"I…" he stammered eventually as the creature slowly blinked its large eyes.

"Take them to…" Ana sighed, leaning back against the wall, and the creature turned as though worried for her.

"Allow us to care for you," the creature hissed, although Ed could feel the compassion and worry in the strange being.

"I don't need your worry," Ana said, standing taller. The

strength returned. "The soldier," she said, her voice hushed as though it hurt her to talk of him. Ed wondered what had happened between them that she had abandoned Dray so easily.

Her face hardened, and Ed gulped down the rising fear. Despite the size of the cottage and the creature within it, he was certainly more afraid of Ana than what the creature might do to him.

"All of them?" it asked.

Ana looked to Phillip, who stood by the fire but didn't appear to show the same amount of fear that Ed was sure he did.

"I will stay," Phillip said. "I am of no use in this."

Ana nodded once, then snapped her fingers, and Ed looked down at the clean travelling clothes that were so similar to the ones he had worn when he'd left the capital the first time. Belle was dressed simply. She wore a fine dress, but she could have been any lady in the capital. Not anyone of wealth, but they might be able to blend in if required. Although Ed wasn't sure that was what he wanted.

"He will know what to do." Ana bowed her head and disappeared. Belle let out a small squeak as the creature stepped closer. Ed hoped it did her bidding after all as the world went dark around him. The only sensation was Belle's hands clinging tightly to his arm.

13

"It is not going to be as easy as we hoped," Dray said as Kemp stared at him. Then Kemp's eyes grew wide, he drew his sword and, as confusion crossed his face, he dropped to a knee.

Dray stared at the man and then turned to look behind him as the shadows withdrew. The king stood in the room, Belle clinging tightly to his arm, her eyes closed just as tightly. His mouth opened and closed several times, and then it was as though he took Dray in.

"You aren't wearing your armour," he stammered.

Dray laughed, unsure what else he could do. "What has she done?" he asked through the laughter.

Belle peeked around the room. She looked more scared than the king, and the laughter died in Dray's throat. "She sent her creature," she whispered.

"I…" Kemp said, and Dray turned back as the man stared at the king, still on his knee.

"You saw it?" Dray asked.

The man nodded. Dray turned back to the king as though he could explain what was going on with Ana. "Did she send you here?"

"I thought it was time to return. I thought I could do more from here…" The king's voice petered out as he looked around the dark, dusty space. Several turned-over crates served as seats, but there wasn't even a bed. Dray had been sleeping on the floor, and the others rarely stayed the night.

"She isn't herself," Belle said, and Dray found himself nodding with her.

"Does she have a plan?" Dray asked.

"Not one she is sharing," the king said. As Dray opened his mouth to ask more, the king continued, "We rarely see her. She isn't talking about what can be done, and I wonder if she is as invested as she was before."

"What are you suggesting?" Dray asked, trying to keep his voice level. This was the king, after all, and although he wanted desperately to believe in her, he too doubted Ana. She wasn't herself. Or she had become someone very different.

The king sighed. Kemp indicated a crate for him to sit, although his face burned red at the idea. The king nodded and took the offered crate as Kemp moved another, which he brushed off before indicating Belle could sit. She had clung to him when they had arrived, and as she sat down slowly beside the king, he reached for her hand. Dray looked between the two of them and wondered what had changed.

"The witch?" Kemp prompted as they looked at each other in the silence.

"What happened between you?" the king asked.

Dray shook his head.

"She trusted you. If she no longer does, it may be a problem for us all," Belle said softly.

"If she didn't trust me, you wouldn't be here." Dray looked them over. He couldn't explain the changes in Ana to himself, let alone these two.

"Have you seen Ende?" the king asked.

"Not since I was released from the dungeons."

"He visited you there?" Belle asked.

"Have you seen him?" Dray asked, and the king nodded.

"What is your plan, Your Majesty?" Kemp asked.

The king looked towards him and then back to Dray before giving a short shake of his head.

"We are trying to find others willing to stand before the regent and the people and swear to your identity," the soldier continued.

"Will that be enough?" Belle asked. "The mage might change him at any time."

"And Ana might not be able to help."

"The people fear the witch," Kemp murmured.

"Stop calling her that," Dray growled.

"They are not alone," the king said.

Dray studied the man sitting before him. He looked neat and tidy, probably just how he had looked when he had lived in the capital attending classes and reading in his room. Ana had done that. She was the only way he could be here, and yet he feared her.

"She is not the woman she was," the king said, his gaze direct, as though he too could read Dray.

"I thought she needed us," Dray said.

"It appears she is strong enough without us."

"She needed you in the forest," Belle said.

"I think she needed us to find herself. Now that she has found whatever power she had within, she does not."

"Might she need us to be what she was?" the king asked.

Dray blew out a soft breath. "I don't think she will ever be what she was." He hoped he didn't sound as sad as he felt. He missed her, despite having seen her only recently.

"So how do we get Ed in front of more people so they are willing to stand up and agree he is the king?"

Kemp made a strange squeak at the use of the king's name, and Dray smiled. He had heard Belle use it before, but there was something far more comfortable in it now.

"And are we to stay here? I could really use a decent bed."

The king squeezed her hand and gave her a small smile, but Dray feared it would be some time before any of them were comfortable.

"I don't think getting you into the castle is the best option, for it puts you directly in the path of the regent. We need to be able to stand before him with more evidence, more support. People willing to challenge him. As it stands, even if the people are willing to stand behind you and call you King, they won't go against him."

Salima looked at the two men standing before her and wondered which would be more likely to give her what she wanted, which was to see Ed. She had a better understanding of the pull towards him, now that she knew he was her brother. So much made sense now that she knew. She also knew that he was well aware of who she was, and that he hadn't shared that information.

He had tried to feign surprise when she had told him, but she had seen in his eyes that he knew. He just hadn't known who her father was. Although, looking at them, she wasn't quite sure herself. She felt a connection to Ende. She had right at the beginning, but it wasn't like what she felt for Ed, and she wondered why that was. But if anyone was to ask her who her father was, the sword master was her father. Even if he had thought he was raising the king's child, he was her father.

"Let me go," she tried again.

Ende sighed and looked to Papa, who shook his head slowly.

"I'll be fine."

"Will you?" Papa asked.

She was a dragon, after all, but could she just turn into the dragon if she was threatened? And what would it mean for her father and herself in the long run if people discovered what she was? Ende didn't protect himself by turning into a dragon. Although he might say he had protected himself by turning into a man.

She looked at him seriously for a moment, and he shifted under her direct stare. "Are you dragon or man?"

"Dragon," he said without hesitation.

"Then what am I?"

"Maybe more human than dragon. It is hard to say. Maybe you are more dragon than human. I can look like a human, but I'm not one. Your mother was very human and…"

This wasn't helping. Salima had no idea who she was. She was at least relieved that she had learnt control of the dragon within her, if that was how it worked. She wasn't spewing fire with every word. She wasn't a threat to her father. "I need to see him."

He shook his head again. "It is not safe."

"But I can…" What could she do to protect herself?

"What if you could hold a sword, or blade?" Papa suggested, his voice trailing away with the idea of what she might be capable of. He didn't seem very sure of anything.

"That is actually a good idea," she said. "Can I?"

He nodded. "If you are as strong as it appears, then you should be able to wield a sword as well as any of my students." He looked to Ende as though looking for reassurance he might be right, and Salima felt the initial excitement falter.

The tall man—dragon—beside her father carried a sword himself, but so did most men of the capital. She had yet to see him draw it, or use it.

He looked back at her as though reading her thoughts and drew the sword. It looked heavy. As he held it out to her, she reached with a hand and then paused. Chewing on her lip, she took the sword with both hands and found it wasn't as heavy as she had anticipated. She had been carrying equipment for her father long enough; perhaps it had nothing to do with her dragon blood.

"Why have I taken so long to understand I am a dragon?"

"Do you understand it?" Ende asked.

She wasn't sure what she could say to that.

"It may have something to do with your mother. You have been or appeared to be human for so long, it was only the threat to Ed that caused your fire to ignite."

"Either way," she murmured, "this isn't getting me any closer to Ed."

"Can you lift that?" her father asked, his arms crossed over his chest. "I'm not letting you race out there. What good would it do if you were killed? How do you expect to be able to help Ed that way?"

She had taken the sword from Ende easily enough, and she stood holding it out. Taking a step back, she moved it slowly in front of her.

Ende tilted his head to the side, and her father gave her a look she thought he only reserved for his students. She dropped one hand and, with her right, held the sword out at shoulder height. Her father actually smiled, and Ende raised an eyebrow.

"Maybe we could do some practice," she suggested.

"What did you have in mind?" Papa asked.

"The practice halls, an opponent."

"An opponent?" he asked.

She swung the sword slowly around, still holding it at shoulder height towards her father. As he was taller than her, it pointed more towards his heart. The smile changed to a grin.

"How long can you hold it?" he asked, stepping away from the sword and circling around her.

"It seems easy enough so far."

"Give the sword back, and I'll find you something to wear that would make it easier to move. Then you can meet us in the halls," Papa said as he looked her over.

"Really?" she asked, almost dropping the sword in her excitement. She just needed to show them that she wasn't a little girl anymore and that she could look after herself, and then they would let her find Ed and help him. How hard could it be? She moved the sword in a slow slashing motion before her and then handed it back to Ende.

She rolled her shoulder, and her father looked at her seriously. "Are you aching? Sore?"

"No," she said. She could feel the weight of the sword in her hands as though she still carried it, but she wasn't sore from holding it. And she was surprised she had managed to hold it for so long.

Papa glanced at Ende, who gave a small nod. She sighed with relief.

Her father left the room, and she sat in a chair while Ende continued to look her over. "So, it wasn't too heavy?"

"No, although it might be different using it against someone or trying to hit something."

He nodded and sat slowly in the chair beside her. "Why do you want to help Ed? What do you think you can do?"

"I don't know," she admitted. "I just know that I have to be with him."

"You don't feel the same for me," he said. She could hear something in his voice, although she wasn't sure if he was sad or if it was something else.

"I feel connected to you," she said. "I care," she added, surprising herself with the idea. "But there is a pull with Ed, like I can't be away from him. It was so hard with him gone, and then he was back, and although I know he is close…" She stopped, tilting her own head to the side as though hearing something. She sniffed at the air.

"What is it?" Ende asked, sitting forward in his chair and reaching for her.

"Ed," she whispered. She had no idea that she could sense him so clearly now. "He is back in the capital."

"You're certain?" Ende said.

"I don't know how, but yes." She looked at him, all seriousness beside her. "Did you feel this way about my mother?"

"In some way, yes. It is hard to explain. I needed to be with her, but I didn't sense when she died, and I didn't realise that you had survived."

"Did you feel the same for me when you discovered I had

lived?"

He nodded slowly. "I had to see you. I have to be with you."

She reached out then and took his hand. The warmth was comforting, as though she knew him. She could feel the dragon trying to stay a man. She could feel the love and certainty of who she was flowing with the heat through the grip she had on his hand. The door banged shut, and she looked up at Papa standing by the door, a bag in his arms. She could feel the hurt and pain roll from him too, and the fire within her flared. She released her hold on the dragon and stood.

"This is not as easy as I want it to be. I am not what I thought I was, and I need to relearn how to live," she said softly, taking the bag from his arms and stepping into the space against his body. It was safe, but not nearly warm enough.

He pulled her tight against his chest and dragged in a ragged breath. "I know that," he whispered. "And it is as much my fault as Ende's."

She pulled back to look up at him. "It is no one person's fault," she said softly. "It is just the way it is."

He pulled her close again, and she allowed him to hold her.

"I've found some training clothes, old ones from various students that have been left behind in the practice halls."

"Ew," she said before she could stop herself at the image of sweaty young men leaving their clothes behind.

"They've been laundered," he said with a laugh. "Now get changed, and let's see what you can do with a sword."

14

The child raced between the shelves. She seemed clear on what she was searching for, but so far, she hadn't been able to find anything the mage had sent her for. Her sister on the other hand was somewhat better, although neither were as good as Ana.

Her fair hair reappeared before the mage, and he tried not to sigh. He might be able to train her as a maid, but he doubted she had enough skill even for that. He missed the girl, although she appeared often enough as the beast he had given her to. He missed her face, and missed the tasks she did so well for him. This child would never replace that.

She grinned up at him as she sat the small glass jar on the desk before him, and he wondered what had drawn him to them. Although the maid's creature was keen enough to have them. He took a second look and then nodded. Not that he thought she had managed to find it through skill. More likely luck. He tried to ignore her sister moving through the shelves behind her. Trying to be silent, but the world cried out around them. She'd had help to complete the task. At least one of them had an idea of what they were doing.

"Did it call you?" he asked, lifting the jar up to his face to stare into it. The contents, which had screamed in fear earlier, were now silent, and yet he could sense the uneasiness. Ana had not been able to sense them initially, but once her magic woke she had become something very different. He needed to find a way to unlock the power within these girls.

The creature appeared as though called. The girl looked up at it, her eyes wide, as though she could sense something within it. Power ebbed from it. The mage thought anyone with even a little magic would sense it easily, and yet it had hidden well enough in the shadows of the throne room.

The idea of the throne room made him think of the regent, who had become even more demanding, if such a thing were possible. The mage had placated him for a short while by changing the king and fooling the people. It wouldn't last long, particularly if Ana was nearby, which she always was.

"Is there nothing we can do with her?" he asked.

The creature leaned forward, its gangly form more frightening when it tried to do what humans did. It flicked its black tongue over the girl's face, and she flinched.

"She may be what you hope," the creature hissed. "She may not."

"Can you sense the magic within?" he asked.

The sister's face appeared from the depths of the room. He could sense it in her, and despite her saying they felt the same, he was sure they did not.

"It might be there."

He sighed. This wasn't what he wanted. He had allowed Ana to find herself; he only wished he knew what had triggered the full strength of the magic within her.

"Tell me of Ana," he demanded of the creature. It turned its black eyes on him, its face level with his. The cold tongue was both wet and dry as it touched his skin. He did all he could not to shudder.

"You will not touch her."

He put his hands up in defence. "I only wish to know how she unlocked the magic."

"As her mother did. It is only known to her. I am not aware of what she did, what she felt when the magic came to her."

"Could she have been trying to perform some magic?" the sister in the shelves asked, and for the first time the mage thought it might be worth knowing her name.

He beckoned her forward, and she stepped up beside her sister. "Magic?" he asked.

"I am sure she had some, or that you sensed some," she said hurriedly, "or you would not have called her here to learn. Perhaps she was trying something specific to trigger the magic."

"Reaching for the king," the other sister said, her eyes closed.

He looked between them. Something very different and yet the same ebbed from them. "Tell me your names," he said.

They looked at each other and then at him. "Sarah and Ruth," they said at the same time.

"Which is which?" he asked, looking between the two.

"Guess," they chimed.

The creature beside him growled.

"Sarah," the girl who appeared to know more said. She was the first one he had been drawn to. As he looked at her sister, he wondered if she could share her gifts when they were close.

"Sarah," he said slowly, "how do you know she was searching for the king?"

"I felt it in the room. I could sense her on the painting." She pointed to his desk, and he wondered at the painting he thought he had tucked away, which still sat out on his desk. Was there something he had missed in the ink image of the queen?

"Have you seen my queen?" the creature asked, and the mage wondered at the question. For the maid had seemed so adamant to destroy Ana, even though she was connected to the creature. Had they come to some arrangement? He looked back to the girl, realising that he had been staring at the creature and had missed her response.

"Where?" it hissed.

She lifted a finger and pointed beyond the shelves.

"She came back to the room?" the mage asked.

They nodded in unison.

"When?"

"Several times," Ruth answered. "She appeared, saw us and left. The last time she came, I thought it was to look at us and see what we might be."

"What do you think you might be?" he asked the girl.

She looked to her sister rather than answer.

"Did she reach him?"

The creature nodded slowly.

"She was trying, but she didn't have the skill," the mage insisted.

"She found a way," Sarah said.

And that had unlocked the power she needed. Given her the power to create the wind in the room and the hold she had on the regent. She was all he had wanted her to be, but he knew the danger of that. She would be his undoing, unless he could find a way to stop her or distract her.

He looked up again into the intense gaze of the creature. "You are mine," he said, and it nodded slowly. "But you would do her bidding first."

"She is my queen," it hissed, then disappeared.

The mage looked back to the two expectant faces of the girls before him. "What do you want most in the world?" he asked.

"To be what you need us to be," Sarah said.

"Then the workshop is yours to find a way."

They bowed their heads, and before he could offer any further advice, Sarah was disappearing through the shelves. Ruth took a moment to look after her before following. He needed the two together. They were much stronger together, but what use Ruth might be on her own he couldn't guess.

Ana stood in the shadows watching the world move through the courtyard of the castle. She had moved around through much of the capital during the day, watching people, watching crowds, watching for familiar faces. She was desperate to see Dray, but he needed to help Ed, and she would only distract him from his task.

Or it might be that he would distract her. She watched, but she rarely interacted. Ed was sure they all needed to be together again, and she wasn't sure if that was a good idea or a way for them to move forward.

The kingdom had heard of the possible return of the king, that he had left the capital and returned with a young woman. But there was little else. No one seemed concerned that his uncle still ruled, and few spoke of the regent's claim that he was an imposter.

Ana moved through to the bathhouse of the barracks. It appeared that men gossiped more than women when they had the chance, and many soldiers thought the privacy of the baths was a safe place to do that. Although she found much of the conversation still guarded, even there, with the fear any of their fellow soldiers might report them to the regent.

At another point in her life, she might have been a little excited about the sight of so many naked men, but it was the conversation she was interested in, not the physiques.

"He certainly looked like the king," someone said, his voice hushed.

"Like his father," another added.

"The regent is sure he was an imposter. Surely he would know." Silence followed.

"How often did the regent spend time with the king?" someone asked.

Mumbling agreement followed.

"What if he asked the mage to step in and change him, rather than undo what the witch had done? What if they were trying to keep the king away—or worse, kill him—so that the regent could stay on the throne?"

Ana wondered if they would act on such a notion.

"Captain Sterling," someone whispered, and Ana tried not to step out from the wall. Was he here? "He was with the king. He wouldn't follow an imposter."

"True," someone else said.

Another soldier joined the growing number in the room, and the conversation stalled again.

"Didn't Sterling run from his position?"

A man raced forward, splashing awkwardly through the water to swing a punch at the man who spoke, although the other soldier dodged the clumsy move easily. "You know the captain would never do that," the man huffed.

"The regent said he ran away after a girl."

"A girl?" someone asked. "The captain?"

Laughter followed.

"Anyone who thought such a thing clearly did not know the captain. There has never been a more dedicated soldier. Wouldn't matter who she might be, or how pretty—he would never leave his post."

"Where is he now then?"

"The regent locked him up."

"I heard he disappeared."

"Maybe he is searching for the king."

They settled into quiet again, and Ana was about to leave when one man asked, "What of the witch?"

She paused, wondering what they thought she would do. Did she really care what these men thought? She had only come here to see if they were loyal to their king or the regent.

"She took the king," someone offered.

"If that was the king," someone else said and was met by jeers and splashing.

"She told the captain to keep him safe. Maybe she took him to keep him from the regent."

"So, where is he now? And where is she?"

"I thought the captain liked the witch."

"Maybe they share," someone snickered.

"Did you see how scared he looked?" another asked. "The captain knows better."

"You were the idiot who suggested he ran after a girl."

"I was caught up in the news. I've known Captain Sterling a long time. Very dedicated man, he would be drawn in by a witch even less than a pretty girl."

"Who said she was pretty?" someone across the room asked.

"I heard she was beautiful. The girl, that is. That witch might be scary, but I wouldn't mind pulling her close of a night." Someone else chuckled, and Ana blinked from the room before she gave the man something else to dream of.

The lights in the practice hall were a surprise, and she hugged the wall at the sound of blades meeting.

"Perhaps we should start with something smaller," the sword master suggested.

"Are you being soft, Papa? If I was any other student, you wouldn't make allowances."

"This is your first lesson," he returned.

"And I don't want to slice you open in front of your father," Ende added quietly.

Salima blocked another blow with skill, and Ana doubted there was any risk of injury.

She wondered at the girl with the sword, as she did the dragon she was fighting. She had never seen Ende with a sword, nor had she seen him wield one. This version of Ende was unfamiliar to her.

Would he stand beside the king and fight if required? Would he have done such a thing before? For his queen, perhaps. But if Salima were in real trouble, he would likely fly her far away rather than put her in danger.

It would all be for Ed. All the girl did was for him. The sword she swung was huge, on par with something Dray would carry, and Ana wondered at the strength of the little dragon. Had she always had this, or was it something she had only just discovered?

"You know what you are," Ana said, stepping forward. "That is how you found Ed."

Salima turned, the sword still outstretched, as Ana stepped into the practice area. Ende put his hand on hers, forcing her to lower the sword.

"Ed is here, isn't he?" the girl asked, although Ana knew Salima felt him in the city.

She nodded once.

"Why are you here?" Ende asked.

"I am searching for allies. For those who have recognised the king and are willing to stand up with him."

"I'm sure there are many," Salima said confidently.

"Oh, there are," Ana said. "Yet they won't stand against the regent."

"What are you thinking?" Ende asked gently

"That I don't know how to fix this," she said quietly. "Why are you learning to use a sword?"

"My father worries that I can't protect myself."

"You could always turn into the dragon and eat them."

Salima grinned, but she shook her head. "That is not how a princess would behave."

Ana smiled, despite herself.

"You must keep quiet," the sword master murmured.

"No one has been in here since the boy died."

"People are not the only ones who may overhear you," Ana said softly. "The information once shared could be your undoing."

"My undoing?" Salima asked, her voice a little shaky.

"Your death. Your capture. A way to get at Ed."

Salima looked to the dragon then, fear evident on her face, and Ende glared at Ana. She could feel the heat increase in the space.

"Not all the shadows follow me," she said.

"I thought you were their queen," the sword master said, his voice unusually cruel. Then he took a step back as a shadow creature appeared beside her. Not the maid, the boy. It looked around the space, squinting into the light of the torches.

"The windows have not been cleaned yet?" Ana noted.

"Too hard to reach," the sword master murmured.

The girl opened her mouth and then closed it, and Ana wondered if she thought about flying up and cleaning them for him. How big a dragon was she?

The creature beside her hissed as though trying to consider what to say.

"We can meet elsewhere," Ana offered.

It looked around the room, tasting the air with a long tongue.

"Robert?" the sword master asked, and it stepped forward and then drew back level with Ana.

"No more," they hissed. "The king is safe with the soldier. He has allies."

"Thank you," Ana whispered.

"Majesty," they hissed. Although she could sense there was going to be more, perhaps an insistence that she rest, they said no more. The creature winked from the room, Ana was tempted to follow. She was more rested than she had been in some time, and she knew where she could go for more. But she needed to see what the regent was up to, who else might support the king, and if Dray had a plan before she left them.

15

Thom looked at the beautiful woman beside him, still somewhat disbelieving that she was his wife and that she cared for him as much as she did. Or at least that she gave the impression of caring. Her brother had remained in the capital, and that wasn't what he had imagined for his new family. The man seemed too sure that his sister and the regent would act for his benefit.

"Has he been caught yet?" the Lord of Near Forest demanded as he stood before the throne. He hadn't even pretended to bow or show his respect.

Thom kept his eyes on the woman. Dahli. She had sat at his feet not so long ago, but he'd had a chair brought in so she could sit beside him. He wanted to show her that he cared and would look after her. He hoped it was only a matter of time until she bore him a son.

He turned to the man standing impatiently before him. "What are you talking of?" he asked, although he knew full well, for the man hadn't stopped talking of it since he had arrived.

"The imposter!"

"I think the whole kingdom would know if we had managed to find him," the regent said, trying his best not to sigh. He wished he had Ana's power to ask the shadows to take him away. At the thought of her, he glanced around. More torches had been lit around the room, despite the midday sun shining through the large window, to ensure there were no shadows for her to hide in.

"What are you doing about it?"

"Brother," Dahli chastised before Thom could say something. "Remember who you are talking to."

The man huffed. "He stole from me." He sounded more subdued, but Thom stood slowly from the throne and stepped forward.

"You provided tribute. Ten women, as required. If you are to continue with this, I shall have no option but to investigate where the women came from. It is very clear they were not all from the forest."

"My sister was…" He stopped as Thom took another step forward.

"Enough." Thom said it quietly, but there was sufficient strength behind the word that the man stepped backwards. "She is *my* wife. Your debt is paid. Perhaps you should pay again in seven years to prove your loyalty."

The man scowled. "That is not how the tribute works."

"You are telling me now how to run the kingdom. The tribute is to show the fealty of the lords of each province. Proof that they will remain loyal to the kingdom of Ilia, that they will not try to take the throne or break up the kingdom. Are you challenging that? Are you saying the forest will not show fealty?"

He shook his head, opened his mouth and then closed it again.

"You will do as you are told," the regent said, with the same dangerous note in his softly spoken words. "You have no children. Who will take over as Lord when you are gone?"

The man's mouth open and closed like a fish out of water before he turned on his heel and stomped out.

"There are others without children," Dahli said. He turned back to her, wondering if she was protecting her brother, but she looked concerned. She stood and stepped forward, resting her hands on his arm. "There is a rumour that the Lord of Edge Mountains is gone. The Lord of Sheer Rock also did not marry."

He looked at her seriously. "The lines have come to an end?"

She nodded slowly. "Unless my brother finds a wife and produces an heir, he too will be the last."

"A child of yours…" Thom started.

"Would inherit your seat in the kingdom," she said, glancing over her shoulder.

He smiled at the idea and pulled her close. She melted into him as he stared over her head at the throne. There were other provinces he hadn't paid enough attention to, the wetlands, grasslands, desert. Three families coming to an end was not enough. And what would it mean for him?

"The witch," he murmured. The woman in his arms pulled away, glancing around the room. "She is the heir to Sheer Rock."

"Would she want it?"

"I think she has grander ideas," he murmured. Although he didn't know what they were. She was only focused on giving back to the boy that which now belonged to Thom. "I want your brother gone," he said, and Dahli sighed. "I too want the boy gone. He may have travelled with the tribute, but it was not stolen."

"There was another, Belle."

"The girl your brother wanted for himself? He seems to want a lot. The kingdom received ten; that is all that matters."

She bowed her head. "I will talk with him."

"Only if you wish. If you are not comfortable, I'll send someone. There are only so many times I can explain the way of the world to him."

She smiled, looping her arm through his.

"Tell me of the boy," he said.

"I thought you said he was an imposter."

"I'm curious all the same."

"He behaved as a king might, demanding, yet…"

Thom waited, disappointed that she had paid Edwin so much attention. But the boy had grown, standing before them in this very room as a man. It could have been Barric twenty years ago.

"And?" he prompted.

"He was kind and thoughtful. He was interested in what the women wanted. He would have lined up with the soldiers to defend us on the road if required."

Very much like his father then, Thom thought. How disappointing. He had limited the boy as much as he could, inferior tutors, limited knowledge—other than the sword, which he had little influence over. The boy should have had no idea of how the kingdom worked or what his place would be in it. And yet he had become his father's son.

"What will you do if he appears?" Dahli asked, dragging him from his thoughts.

"The same as would happen to any other imposter," he murmured.

"You had best ensure the mage is close," she said with a small smile, and he stared at her. She knew who he was. Despite all that he had told her, she believed in the boy.

"Do you think he should be king?" Thom asked, closing his hand around her arm a little too tightly.

She shook her head. Thom wasn't sure if there was hesitation there or if he was looking for it.

"I thought you wanted to be here with me," he said, trying hard to keep the hurt from his voice.

"I do, my husband. I want nothing more. Only…" She leaned in close, despite the tight hold he still had on her arm, and ran a hand over his cheek. She smiled up at him, and he was lost in her deep brown eyes.

"Only…" he purred.

"To give you a son," she breathed in his ear.

"You are very good at offering just what I need," he said, but the doubt was there. Was she, like her brother, just out for what she could get?

"Yet no matter what I say, or what I do, you do not trust me," she said, stepping back from him as he let go of her. Deep finger-shaped bruises were already forming on her arm, but she didn't put her hand to it, and the niggling ache in Thom's arm reminded him that he could not trust anyone.

As he put his hand to his wrist, she stood taller. "I am not the witch. I don't know what else I can do to prove it."

He nodded slowly. She was right.

"What if I mark my skin, so that you are sure it is me? She wouldn't know."

He reached for her hand, shaking his head. It was a sound idea, but he couldn't bear to think of her perfect skin damaged.

She smiled brightly. "I could hold your hand a particular way when we are close." She stepped forward, lacing her fingers through his and running her thumb over his palm. A tingle raced through him as she traced out an unknown shape over and over.

"What is that?" he murmured, leaning forward to take in the smell of her hair.

"A tree," she whispered, pressing herself into him. "Perhaps there are other ways I could touch you that would assure you I am not the witch."

He burned hot at the image of her standing at the balcony in the sheer cloth, her slender frame too well revealed, and he remembered why he had wanted her for himself in the first place. He sucked in a breath at the realisation it had been the witch, not his wife, that evening. And as Dahli's hand travelled across his thigh, he grabbed her wrist. He glanced around at the guards by the door. "We need to take this discussion back to our rooms," he breathed heavily, wondering if he could make the distance.

He was somewhat disappointed that he could still be excited by the witch. His wife was beautiful and had shown far more interest in him as a man than any other woman had. Including Mariela.

16

Dray sat up, sucked in a deep breath and ran his fingers through his hair. He had dreamed of her again, although he was sure she hadn't been there this time. Ana hadn't been visiting him in his dreams lately, but he was seeing her in the shadows wherever he went. He hadn't seen her in the night since they had curled together in his room at the barracks, and he wondered where she slept.

As he squeezed his eyes closed, he saw her as she had been in his dream. Walking slowly towards him from the darkness. She had never appeared more confident, and he had never been more scared. Yet there was something of the girl in her, something of the maid he had seen fall from the Walk.

He shook his head and looked up at the king watching him across the room. Dray ran his fingers through his hair again and climbed to his feet. They might have been able to find soldiers to help protect Edwin, yet they were hidden away in this dusty space hardly suitable for a king.

"Perhaps we need to put you in plain sight," he whispered.

Someone had at least found a straw mattress for the king, and he was kind enough to share. Belle appeared somewhat more confident, as he had seen her before, but maybe now it was because she had found her place with the king.

As the king started to climb from the mattress, Belle murmured, reaching for him and then opening bleary eyes. "Is it morning?"

"Go back to sleep," the king whispered, running his fingers through her hair. She rolled away, pulling the blanket over herself.

The king tipped his head to the side, indicating they move to the door, and Dray climbed to his feet and followed. A single candle burned in the room. He looked back at the woman asleep and hoped that Ana's shadows watched over her as well as him. Although he hadn't needed to test them. If there was any danger, she would have the king removed, and possibly him too.

"What is it?" the king asked.

"Your Majesty?"

"Dray." He sighed, sitting on the edge of the step and indicating that Dray sit beside him. "We are friends, or at least I thought we were."

"Of course," Dray said, lowering himself to the step.

"Call me Ed, or Edwin at least. My father's friends called him by name."

Dray nodded once, but he wasn't sure he could bring himself to say it. The king sighed. "Edwin," Dray said slowly. "I have been trained a particular way my whole life. It is not easy for me to change."

"And yet you left your post to save a maid from falling."

Dray ran his fingers through his hair again and nodded.

"Does she trouble your sleep?"

Dray looked at the man beside him. "She has for some time, but this was different." The young man blushed, and Dray smiled. "Not in such a way. I wonder at times if I am a man like any other…" He looked up at the king looking at him seriously. "She visited me," he admitted. "When we were in the forest, she visited me while I slept. It was… confusing. But now I see something else. I don't know if she is trying to tell me something, or if it is just an idea of her."

"She worried for you," Edwin said, looking down into the darkness of the steps rather than at Dray. "She always worried for you."

"I don't know what we can do," Dray admitted.

"About Ana or my crown?"

"Both."

The king, Edwin, looked at him seriously. "We need to focus on one."

Dray nodded slowly. Ana was focused on making him king, it wasn't for Dray to worry about her. But then, someone had to, and he was sure no one did. Especially as she scared so many, including him. If she were to appear out of the shadows of the stairs, would he embrace her or jump in fear? He thought it most likely to be the second.

He looked at Edwin. The boy had become the man. Dray had seen it before, but it was more apparent now that they were in the capital. "The crown," he said. "Ana can look out for herself. And when it comes down to a decision, I know she will support you."

The young man nodded solemnly.

Dray looked back towards the doorway. How they were going to do that from a dusty attic, he didn't know. Barlow had insisted they were hiding him in plain sight and so far, neither the regent nor his men had come looking for him. Barlow thought the majority of the King's Men supported him, or at least believed the king to be who he said he was. They had seen his father in him standing in the throne room.

But would they go against the regent, with his mage and his creatures? Dray was sure that they were more Ana's creatures than the mage's, and that was because of what she had become. Or was it what she had always been?

"I worry that putting you before the people will put you in more danger." Dray took a deep breath. He really had no idea how to do this. In all the time, they had been moving closer to the capital. "Could Ende help? Could he stand behind you, burn the regent to a crisp?"

Edwin laughed easily. "I've had that dream myself. We need to discredit him. The people might believe in me, but there is too much fear of him. We need to show that we can keep them safe."

"That brings us back to Ana," Dray murmured.

Edwin nodded slowly. "If she can keep them in check."

"If she wants to," Dray said too quickly. As Edwin stared at him, he took another deep breath. It didn't seem to matter what he tried or whom he talked to—Dray couldn't calm his mind enough to form anything of use. "Belle," he said softly, and Edwin looked back towards the doorway, his face flushing a little.

"You were going to ask if it is proper," Edwin said.

Dray wasn't quite sure what he thought of the arrangement or what others might think. He was more worried the girl had annoyed Edwin to the point he had given in.

"I love her," he whispered, still looking towards the door.

"Oh," was all Dray could say. "You love her enough to risk the crown."

Edwin looked at him seriously, not quite hurt, but he appeared surprised that Dray would use such words.

Dray returned the look. "I worry at her reason for staying so close to you."

"She is what she always has been. She is strong and bright, and she cares for me. Not my crown," Edwin said clearly.

Dray nodded. "Then you have made the right decision. Does she have a plan?"

Edwin shook his head.

All Dray's years of leading men into all sorts of danger, and he was deferring the safety of the king to a farmer's daughter and a witch. He dropped his head into his hands. He was lost. More lost than he had been on the mountain, searching for a way to find help for Ana. And Ende had found them. But he had kept her safe and led her to where she was meant to be—beside the king.

Dray looked to the young man beside him now, who watched him far more closely than he would have liked. "I don't know," he said softly.

"Ana has the power to remove the regent..." Edwin said,

looking into the shadows rather than at him. As Dray opened his mouth to say something, he wasn't sure what, Edwin held up a hand. "She has the power to push him. Maybe we can use her to distract my uncle while we work on getting the people behind me. The distraction might also help the people see what he has done."

"I think the people have a very good idea of the kind of man your uncle is," Dray said. "What would you have Ana do?" And if she didn't agree, what might she do instead?

"Scare him," Edwin whispered.

"Like she does us?" Dray asked.

The king raised one shoulder in a half-hearted shrug.

"How do you propose to ask her? Call her? I'm not sure Ana is the kind of woman who would gladly do your bidding, just because you are king."

"I might do more than that, just to save him," Ana whispered as she appeared from the shadows before them.

Despite his heart racing, Dray stood slowly, although the king jumped enough for both of them.

"I know you don't mean to scare us," Edwin said quickly.

"Don't I?" Her voice was sweet, but there was something in her look that was even further from the girl Dray knew than the last time he had seen her. Something dark and distant. He realised he was staring at her, and she him. He sighed. Although she didn't say anything, he knew too well that she could read him even better than before.

If he had a bed, he might have hidden within the blankets and pretended she wasn't changed.

She raised her eyebrows at him, and he tried to keep the heat from his face. She looked past him then. Edwin moved to allow her by as she moved forward, although she ran a hand down Dray's arm as she stepped onto the step on which he stood.

As she disappeared into the room, Edwin raced in after her and Dray followed more slowly. He wanted Ana back, the girl, not this woman, and he didn't know how to make that happen. When he stepped into the room, she was looking at him.

"It will not happen," she whispered.

Edwin had put himself between Ana and the sleeping woman.

"You have seen this place before," Dray said.

She nodded once and stepped further into the room. She stopped by the blanket he usually rested on. A small cot formed beneath it, one like his own quarters. At the thought of the narrow bed, she turned to him, her eyes blinking as though confused for a moment. Then, with a small sweep of her hand, a larger bed with posts and thick curtains formed beneath Belle.

"Will the floor support that?" Dray asked without thinking.

The curtains closed in around the sleeping woman, and Dray wondered what Edwin would do with the increased privacy. He focused on Ana, who turned towards him, her eyebrow raised. "How does this help us?"

"You will be more rested."

"I'm never rested," he murmured.

"More dreams?" she asked, stepping closer, concerned like the Ana he knew might have been. "I no longer dream," she whispered, looking over his face as though she missed something. He wanted desperately to hold her then, comfort her, but he gulped the feeling down and looked to the boy standing in the middle of the room.

"I will do as you wish," she said, bowing her head to the king. "I will wear him down and raise you up."

Edwin smiled, the tension relaxing a little.

"But I will do it my way," she said, and Dray was sure he heard something else in her voice, something dark.

She flicked her eyes to him and then straight back to the king. Whatever he was thinking, she would know that too. And he nodded. Before Dray could ask what her way might be, she was gone. Perhaps there was more they could be doing while she worked on the regent. He walked towards the cot and then stopped. Edwin remained standing in the middle of the room, looking over the bed.

"What is it?" Dray asked, trying to keep his voice low.

"What does she expect of me?" Edwin asked.

Dray followed the king's gaze to the large bed. "Belle or Ana?"

Edwin took a deep breath and walked towards the bed, but as his hand closed around the edge of the thick curtain, he looked back to Dray. Dray gave him a nod and then turned to his own little bed. He wouldn't sleep, but he could try to rest and maybe come up with something to help Edwin reach his crown other than sending in a witch.

Ana stood in the smallest shadow of the room and watched the young woman from the trees struggle to fasten her dress. She should have had someone help her, and Ana was surprised there weren't multiple servants seeing to her every need. It appeared the regent trusted very few, and he wanted his young bride to himself.

Perhaps he thought she might be tempted by another. He was an old man, after all, and she was a beautiful young woman. As she struggled with a button, Ana stepped forward and closed her hand around it. The woman beneath her hold froze.

"I can help you," Ana whispered.

"I'm not sure I want the help you are offering," she returned, and Ana smiled at the confidence in the woman.

"You are a woman worthy of such a husband. A woman destined for great things."

"What do you want?" the woman asked, turning hard eyes on Ana. She didn't show the fear she had appeared to have when she was trying to placate her husband. Was she trying to show he was the strong one? Was that what men wanted?

"I can offer you the strength to keep your place by the man you love."

She laughed then, and Ana saw the woman she was inside,

someone very much like her brother. The young woman wanted power and a hold over others she would not have been afforded in the forest, for her brother would not have relinquished it.

"I can give you that," Ana whispered, leaning in closer. "I see what you want."

"I will not defy my husband," the woman said, her voice firm.

Ana looked her over. The want for power ebbed from her. "Family and children," Ana said, walking around her. "Yet a place before the people is a greater wish."

The woman remained unmoving, other than her head following Ana's path. Her heart beat fast in her chest as clear as her wanting and the fear of missing out.

"You can keep the old man; you can have his children. If that is your wish. You will stand beside him as long as you like. Whether that is before the kingdom or not is another matter."

"You want to remove him," she said.

"I want the king in his rightful place."

The woman chewed on her lip for a moment. "I would be happy with the younger man," she said, and Ana sensed she would stand beside anyone who gave her what she wanted. This girl had tried with Ed. She had tried to be more to him, but he only had eyes for Belle.

"Was it your suggestion that your brother take the blonde girl?" Ana asked. Although she knew the answer. This woman was just what she wanted, just who she needed.

"Perhaps," she said, her confidence growing.

Ana smiled.

"Will you give me what I want?" the woman asked.

Ana nodded once. "Draw the curtains and extinguish the flame."

The nervousness remained, but she did as she was bid. She drew the curtains and then looked over her shoulder at Ana before moving to the torches on the wall. She looked them over and then back to Ana.

With a click of her fingers, Ana extinguished the flames. In the darkness, the shadows moved from the walls. Several gathered close around her, and she let them inspect the woman who stood still and silent in the dark. Ana could taste the fear.

One called louder than the others, and Ana gave her permission with little thought. The other shadows disappeared as a soft moan left the woman's lips.

"Dahli," Ana said.

"Your Majesty," she whispered, almost hissed as she bowed down. The torches flickered back to life.

"Are you complete? Have I given you what you need?"

Both the girl and the shadow bowed in thanks. She appeared the same, yet different. She was the same creature the boy had become. Yet it was hidden so well within.

Ana wondered then at the magic the mage had used to give the maid to the first creature. How had he called it forth? He didn't have her skill, nor her hold over them, but he had something— something that had allowed such a transformation to occur. He had hidden far more from her than he had shown, and she was disappointed.

She wondered if the little girls were the same, if he had found some way to use them.

"What do you wish of me?" Dahli whispered, although it was the two of them now.

"Learn all you can from the regent and come to me when you have something to share."

"Do I behave as I did?"

"I thought you wanted to keep him," Ana said.

"My only thought is to serve you, Majesty."

Ana smiled. "Then that is what you shall do. He is yours to use as you see fit."

She, they, bowed, and Ana blinked from the room, thinking only of the mage and what she might learn from him.

17

The creature smiled at the mage as it stood over his desk. The mage glanced about the room automatically in case it smiled because the witch had returned. He was sure she appeared around him more often than he detected. He rarely found her in the shadows, and yet the creature knew she was there every time.

Sometimes it would tell him; other times it would not. He missed the maid. She had been keen to see the end of Ana, and he had thought she worked with the creature to make that happen, but now they protected her. The witch. How much of the maid remained, he wasn't sure. He might only be sure when they were separated, but he had never managed to succeed at that before.

Not that he had that much experience. Before Ana, he had only discovered two creatures. One Mariela had managed to bring, although she wasn't sure herself how she had done that. Ana, on the other hand, had very clear control. Perfect control. And she didn't doubt herself at all. In the beginning, she had been scared and unsure of what she was. She had fully embraced it now, only she was something very different from her mother.

Long ago, he had managed to capture the beast and hide it away in the book; and yet he had lost the girl. So far, the creature had given no indication of where she had gone, only that she was gone. And now that it had the maid, it wasn't willing to give her up. They still needed the anchor, no matter how many shadows had been seen.

And the regent wanted more answers that he did not yet have. Sarah appeared before the mage's desk, and he knew Ruth would not be far behind. There was something so different in the sister. She clearly did not have the same skill, yet he knew he needed to keep them together.

The creature, when it was present, watched them with hungry eyes. He wondered what could be done with them and how they could help him rid the world of the boy. The troublesome boy who was too much like his father and too hard to kill.

He sighed, and she stepped forward.

"I could search him out," she said.

"Who?" he asked, wondering just what she knew.

"Whoever it is you seek. I can sense the king. Would that be useful?"

"Sense him?"

"On the image of his mother," she said.

"In the ink," Ruth added, appearing beside her, and he wondered just what she could do. If a creature grew by absorbing someone, he wondered what one might do if it took on two.

The creature appeared beside him as though he had called to it, licking the air with its long black tongue. Sarah didn't even flinch. Ruth stared at it in wonder.

"Would you like to find out?" the creature hissed.

"I think it would benefit the witch far more than myself," he said, trying not to be too nervous that the creature knew what he wanted; what he thought.

"It might benefit you," it hissed.

"Not if it was a way to harm the king. She would not allow it, nor would you."

The creature growled and looked over the two before it. It stepped forward, reaching out a clawed hand. Ruth stepped back, and the other girl remained rigid. "I can't read you," it hissed, leaning over Sarah. She turned then and raised an eyebrow.

It looked to the other girl, still close but out of reach.

"I am not what you think," Sarah said.

"No," it hissed again, wrapping its long fingers around her arm and pulling her closer. She flinched as the long tongue touched her face. "You are something different." It glanced over its shoulder at the mage and then back. "You are stronger than when you arrived."

Ruth stepped forward then, looking at her sister closely. "You only wanted to borrow it," she whispered.

Sarah grinned, and the creature dragged her closer. "I could use you."

"What for?" Ruth asked, pushing forward. Before she could retreat, the creature reached out and took hold of her arm as well. She squealed, but Sarah didn't even look at her.

"You are worthless," the creature hissed, touching its tongue to her face as the child whimpered. "You may be worth a meal." The hiss was deeper, scarier as the sharp fine teeth were exposed in the too-wide mouth. The girl screamed. Her sister, still in the hold of the beast, didn't move. The knowing smile still on her lips.

"What did you take from her?" the mage asked, trying to keep the wonder from his voice. How could so many young girls be so talented?

"I took what we shared," Sarah said.

"You were only going to borrow it to find a way out," Ruth whined. The creature leaned in closer.

It touched her face again, tasting the air around her and the skin. The mage shivered. If it killed the girl here, would the sister do as they wanted?

"You have your own," it hissed, cocking its head to the side.

"We shared," Ruth whispered, the fear making the words catch in her throat.

"You shared something, but she has taken that. You have your own magic."

Now the smile slipped from Sarah's face as she looked from the creature to her sister. The creature gave her a little shove and pulled Ruth closer. She stifled a cry.

"Majesty will want you," it hissed, and they were gone.

The mage stepped forward into the space they had occupied and growled his frustration. The other girl looked around, but it appeared she was more worried she had missed out on something rather than for her sister.

"What did you do?" he asked.

"I took what I needed to be stronger. I can hear them calling." She held her chin higher and indicated around the room with a sweep of her arm.

"Then it would have wanted you. You may hold a similar power to the witch, and yet I hoped you would be something different," he said.

"There is nothing that Ruth has of any value," she said with the same confidence. "They will come to understand that."

"They might understand far more than you do."

Ana looked the girl over and nodded. Her light curls were dishevelled, her golden eyes sparkled with tears, and she hugged her body with her arms but it did little to slow her shaking. They were right—she was of use. There was something very strong within the girl, despite her overwhelming fear.

"I can make you stronger," Ana promised. She glanced at the creature at her side, still holding the girl by the arm. "I can make you more than your sister could ever be."

The girl wiped a hand over her cheek and sniffed. "Can you?"

Ana nodded slowly. "I will give you what you need, and you can help me in return."

"What do you want?" she asked, rubbing the back of the other hand under her nose as she sniffed again.

"The regent's wife is in need of a maid. You could learn from her. It would place you in the throne room and before other important people."

"I'm not sure I'm suitable enough for such a lady," the girl whispered, looking down. The creature beside her put a clawed finger beneath her chin and lifted it to bring her gaze back to Ana.

"You will be," Ana said kindly. "And you will come to understand what you need to do."

She waved the shadows forward. More and more were coming to her, understanding that she was helping them now to make her stronger. To help Ed, a small part of her whispered. They needed all the help they could muster to remove the regent.

The shadows moved around the girl, and although she tried to stand still, she flinched away as they drew closer. Then she stopped. Looking into the shadows, she stepped forward and reached out a hand as the creature released its hold. Ana watched the shadow move so quickly over and into her that the girl sucked in a deep breath. Ana waited for a scream, but it did not follow. She had selected well again.

The girl blew out a slow breath, looked at Ana with black eyes and bowed her head. "Majesty," she hissed.

"If you are to stay by Dahli, you must sound like the girl."

The girl cleared her throat and growled. The sound vibrated through the room. Ana waited. She cleared her throat again and then bowed, the same awkward bow her creatures gave.

"I will not let you down, Majesty," the girl purred. It wasn't the voice she'd had before, but it was what was needed. Dahli herself had a slight hiss Ana was unsure how to rid her of.

"See that you do not," Ana said. "Would the mage recognise you?"

She bowed her head awkwardly. When she looked up, her hair was dark and her complexion tanned, as though she had come from the trees with the tribute. She smiled and blinked her large golden eyes.

It would be enough. "Take her to meet her new mistress," Ana directed the creature. "Then return to me. We must find a way to get more people to see the regent for what he is."

The creature bowed its head, and they disappeared. Ana looked around the small hut and wondered why she had thought it would be the best place to hide, particularly as Phillip should have been present. At the sound of the latch, she sucked in a breath, and when she opened her eyes, she was in the room the creature had taken her to. The boy who would watch over her and allow her to rest. It appeared just as she had left it. For a moment, she wondered what the world around it would be like. But it wasn't her world. She would make the other world hers. She would find a way to rest and find nourishment within it.

That would start with removing the regent.

18

Ed looked around the room. It was still dusty and dark, and the new beds were an odd addition. He had struggled to explain how they'd managed to appear in the middle of the night. Initially, Belle had been quite enthusiastic about the more comfortable bed and the curtains, but the excitement disappeared once she discovered they had been gifted by Ana.

The soldiers filling the space had reacted in much the same way, and he wasn't getting anywhere with them either.

"There must be another option. You are hiding the captain and now me. The regent will become suspicious. I want to be able to talk to the people."

"I understand that, Your Majesty, only it may not be safe," Captain Barlow said, his calm voice clearly restrained.

"It isn't safe anywhere with those creatures," Kemp murmured. "I understand that she is on your side and sent them to watch over you before. But can we truly trust the witch?"

Ed could see the tension filling Dray's soldiers at the mention of Ana as a witch. It was something he struggled with, yet he had stayed away from her. He turned to Ed without responding to the remark.

"I want to go out," Ed repeated.

"I agree," Dray asserted. "Without the mage, the people might recognise him."

"We have some gold," Belle said quietly, and Ed nodded. He hoped the gwelka's money didn't turn anyone to stone. If he feared for anyone, he would just need to be sure that Belle handed it over.

"Take the lady shopping," Kemp murmured. "That should help the kingdom."

"It might," Dray said, stepping forward.

Ed looked at him seriously. "It was to help Ana…"

"Why in the…" Kemp stopped short when Dray turned his glare on him.

"Do you want to insist on questioning everything His Majesty does?" he asked, his voice flat, and Ed was more scared of Dray in that moment than he was of Ana when she appeared from the dark. "He is your king," he continued.

The man bowed his head, his fist across his chest. "Forgive me, Your Majesty. I just can't understand how it could help."

"It gets him amongst the people, talking, showing that he will support them."

The man nodded.

"Perhaps we could eat at a local tavern," Belle suggested, although the idea made Ed screw up his face. The last time he had looked at the food in a tavern, it was hardly edible. Despite his reservations, he nodded, and Belle grinned as she slipped her arm through his.

"And how would you introduce your lady?" Kemp asked.

"You won't be close enough to hear," Ed murmured. "I don't want the King's Men too close."

"You can't go out without us, Your Majesty," Barlow said. "It isn't safe, and we don't know who supports the regent."

"Either way, we are going. You can watch from a distance. I won't have your men in danger."

Barlow sighed and looked to Dray before he nodded. "Yes, Your Majesty," he said through gritted teeth.

"If I actually make it to the throne, I see I will have more than the general people's respect to earn."

The soldier pulled himself taller and bowed his head. Ed put his hand on Belle's and nodded to Dray. He might not be dressed as a soldier, but he was far more trustworthy than these men. They had claimed to be working for him, that they could all be trusted, yet Kemp seemed to do as he pleased. Ed wondered if he might not be more useful somewhere else in the kingdom.

Dray headed down the stairs and they followed, leaving the soldiers behind them. It was only once they were on the street that he paused to take in the world around him as Belle squeezed his arm.

"Can we trust them?" she asked. "They don't appear to treat you as well as they should."

"I'm still a boy to most," Ed murmured.

Dray waited patiently, standing like a soldier, rigid and tall and serious. Yet he was dressed like any other man, if all black.

"Are you well?" Ed asked Belle as she shivered.

"I am so excited," she whispered. "Who would ever imagine that I would be in the capital? I want you to show me everything."

"I fear it will be for Dray to show us both, for I know very little outside of my small part of the castle."

"How did you make it through the city?" Dray had stepped closer.

Ed shook his head. He wasn't really sure. No one seemed to notice him, and he had just kept walking north until he'd reached the outskirts and the road to the mountains.

"Can we see some shops?" Belle asked.

"I know just the place," Dray said, leading them into the small crowd that moved along the street. Although it wasn't as busy as he'd thought it might be, there were far more people than he had seen together in some time, and Ed felt more unsure of himself the further into the people they travelled.

"Ed," Dray said, dragging him back to the world from his overwhelming thoughts. "Forgive me," he muttered, "the market is this way."

Belle raised her eyebrows when he looked at her. "I did ask him to call me by name," he said.

They worked their way through crowd, turning into a wider road filled with even more people.

"You weren't answering to Edwin," Dray said when they stopped by a stall with silver bracelets.

Ed looked up at the man who appeared to be looking everywhere else. He didn't need the King's Men to look out for him; Dray would be enough. Although he also appeared to be looking for something.

"Do you want to look at something in particular?" Belle asked.

Dray shook his head and then looked back at her. "I saw a knife the other day." His attention was elsewhere.

"Has any particular piece caught your attention?" Ed asked her.

Belle shook her head too vigorously and looked about. He pulled her closer, wondering where her excitement had gone.

"There is too much to look at. I'm somewhat overwhelmed," she whispered. "Let us continue walking."

He nodded agreement and smiled at the old man standing behind the stall, who bowed his head and then turned to someone else approaching. Ed thought for a moment that it was Ana. He shook the idea away and followed Dray through the people towards the next stall. There were so many things to look at, and when Dray stopped at a stall and reached for a silver blade, Ed was sure again that he saw Ana amongst the crowd.

"That is quite a feminine blade for a man such as yourself," a quiet voice teased. Ed looked into the shadows beyond the stall at bright green eyes beneath a hood.

"It might be a gift," Dray said without looking up.

"Might it?" she asked, but she disappeared rather than step forward. Ed watched Dray run his fingers over it.

"Is it for her?" Belle asked, letting Ed go and stepping up to the soldier. "What do you think you can do to save her?"

"Does she need saving?" he asked, lifting his fingers from the blade and turning to her. "Does she?" he asked more firmly.

Belle didn't flinch, and Ed watched her with some level of awe. She was so much more than he had thought. Ana was helping him, or so she said, there was nothing they could do to change that. Did they want to change that? Did Dray want something different from Ana?

The large man huffed and turned from the stall, and Belle raised her eyebrows in a silent question before taking Ed's arm to continue on. They moved slowly through the stalls, looking over wares Ed had no idea one could buy. Belle stopped and made noises over some different items, including a gold chain, but any time he offered to buy her something she claimed she didn't need it. Despite their gold, she said it was all too much.

Ed was fascinated when they found a stall with carved pipes. They were made from a variety of materials, including different woods, bone and even stone. He turned one carefully over in his hand. The image on it could have portrayed a dragon, and it made him smile.

"Should we get one for your father?" he asked.

"It is some time since I have seen him smoke a pipe," Belle said, "but yes, it would be nice."

He motioned the stall seller over, indicating the pipe, and the man looked him over before offering him a price. Ed turned to Dray to see if it was reasonable or not. He had the gold, but he didn't want to encourage the people to steal from shoppers. Dray still looked into the crowd, but he nodded slowly.

He fished out a coin from his pouch and handed it to the man, fearing for a moment that he might turn to stone, but the man dropped it into his pocket and took the pipe from Ed's hands. He wrapped it carefully in a soft cloth, placed it into a box and handed it back. Ed in turn handed it to Belle, who smiled up at him. Then her face crumpled.

"Is it not right?" he asked.

"How can I give it to him? It might be so long before I see him again."

"We can ask Ana," Dray said quietly, his eyes still on the crowd around them.

"We never know when we might see her either." Belle pulled the box close to her chest, and Ed wanted to take her in his arms.

Dray nodded once. "Let's find a tavern," he said.

He headed into the crowd, and they had no option but to follow.

Ed looked more closely through the crowd as they walked, sure they were being watched and thankful Dray was always close. It wasn't that he was worried; he was just not quite comfortable surrounded by so many. And this had been his idea, after all. He had wanted to get out amongst the people. He wondered then if his father would have walked in the streets of the capital and introduced his son to the people, had he still been alive. Ed couldn't remember the man out of the castle, but then he hadn't really paid attention. He hadn't paid attention to nearly enough, and then it had been too late.

As he looked through the crowd now, sure that people were looking at him, Ed stopped. The crowd began to slow, people moving around him as though giving him space. He reached for Belle, but she was nowhere near. In the distance, as he searched the faces staring at him, was a hooded figure with bright green eyes.

Dray's hand landed heavily on his shoulder. "Ed," he said softly.

He nodded once. The crowd, now stationary, stared at him.

No one said a word. No one said anything that would indicate they knew who he was or what they wanted. He went to open his mouth, but the hand on his shoulder was heavy, and he could only focus on the green eyes amongst the shadows. Ed glanced at the man beside him, but he wasn't looking in the same direction, and when he looked back, she was gone.

Had she done this, or was this him? Would he always wonder if he deserved this or if he was placed here by Ana? Ana the witch.

He glanced around, sure that she was closer, sure that she knew what he was thinking and at any moment would take it all away.

A whisper started working its way through the crowd, and then Belle was beside him, her arm through his. The whispering increased. "This might have been a bad idea," she said.

"Your Majesty," someone said, an older man Ed recognised from one of the stalls they had stopped at. He had stepped from the crowd with confidence; it wasn't a question.

Ed bowed his head to the man. The whispering increased.

"You look so like your father," someone else said from the crowd.

"His mother," another voice corrected.

"Thank you," Ed said, bowing his head again.

"Why are you here?"

"We heard you were missing."

"I heard the regent had you killed." Voices talked over each other, questions and queries rolling over him.

"I heard you weren't the king at all." The murmuring stopped. Several turned to the man who had spoken and, in the silence, Ed could hear the King's Men growing closer with their armour and swords. As he looked, so did the crowd. Thankfully, it was Barlow, Kemp and a few of the other men he'd been assured he could trust.

"Your Majesty," they said as a unit and bowed, fists to chests.

The crowd around them suddenly dropped to their knees. Ed stepped forward to the man who had spoken first, took him by the arms and lifted him to his feet. "Please, sir. I might be King, but you need not kneel in the dust for me."

"King," whispered through the crowd. Despite his words, they remained where they were.

"Who is the girl?" someone called in the silence.

Belle stepped closer, her face red. "My friend," Ed said.

Other words were mentioned—beautiful, graceful, young. She seemed to burn brighter at every comment, and he wasn't sure how he could assist her without embarrassing her further.

"We should return," Dray offered quietly, although his voice carried through the crowd.

"We were to eat," Belle said.

A path opened in the crowd. With a quick glance at Dray, Ed walked between the sea of people, Belle still clinging to his arm, and wondered how the crowd had grown so quickly. They arrived at the doorway of a tavern. It swung open to reveal a short round man and a woman of similar size and stature behind him. They looked beyond him at the crowd and stepped out of the way.

Ed walked in to find it was both similar and different from the last tavern he had entered. It smelt very different for a start, hot bread and roast meat rather than wet animal and dung. He held a chair out for Belle and then sat beside her. Dray stood for a moment as people started to move into the tavern around them, and then he sat opposite.

Food and ale were set on the table before them without even asking, and Ed only paused for a moment before he started to eat. He had never had anything so tasty. He grinned at Dray, who picked at the food before him.

"What is it?" he asked, to have the room silence around them.

Dray shook his head, and Ed looked him over. He knew the problem, and he was starting to realise it had been a problem for a long time while he had ignored it. Ana. He glanced around the room and into the dark corners. She was nowhere to be seen. But that didn't mean she wasn't there.

Dray shook his head again and forced a mouthful of the roasted meat into his mouth. Then a sip of ale. As Ed looked around again, he realised that the King's Men had followed them in.

"Why is the king here?" someone asked.

"I wanted to see the world, as I've been locked away so long. I don't know anything of the capital or the people."

"The regent wouldn't listen to the likes of us."

"I'm not my uncle."

A murmur moved through the crowd, and then the older man

from the stall stepped forward. "If you would like to listen, Your Majesty, there is much we could share."

19

Salima was struggling to lift her arms, but she wasn't going to tell her father that. Either of them. Sitting on the windowsill, she looked at the two men sitting by the fire. At times she missed the mother she didn't know, feeling the hole in her life that she had left. Now she had two fathers. They had indulged her, she knew that.

Despite it being Papa's idea, she knew he had more doubts than certainty that she would be able to defend herself or Ed with a sword. She was grateful they had allowed her to find out who and what she was, but her only wish was that it would provide a way to help Ed.

She turned back to the window. She sensed Ed closer and wanted desperately for something to happen. But for now, it was quiet across the city, or at least what she could see of it.

Neither of the men beside her would allow her to look for him, despite her work with the sword. She was desperate to know how he was, if Ana had been able to form a plan to return him to the castle. She hadn't seemed very sure of herself the last time Salima had seen her, and the creatures that had caused so much fear looked after her as Dray would have done.

If Ana wasn't as strong as she had been, it was up to Salima to be the strong sister Ed needed her to be. She wouldn't be able to protect him as the dragon. The idea scared her more than she realised it could.

Salima might be a dragon, but she was human too, and that was something Ende didn't share with her. She wasn't pretending as he was; she had something of her mother, and Papa had strengthened that in the way he had raised her. She looked back to him by the fire.

"What else can I do?" she asked.

"Anything you put your mind to," Ende answered, and Papa looked at him as though he had said too much.

"Is that because I am a dragon?"

"Because you are Essa's daughter," he said, his smile sad. Salima tried not to sigh. She had so much to live up to, yet she didn't quite have a handle on what she was yet.

"Will that help Ed?" she asked.

He shrugged and looked back into the flames. "Ana will do all she can to help him."

"She can't protect him on her own."

"Perhaps she has a plan."

Salima looked back out the window. It was too quiet in the streets below. Usually there was a certain level of activity, but it seemed slower in some way. She was sure she saw more soldiers along the main thoroughfare from the castle.

"Something is happening in the city," she said, standing and pressing her nose to the glass.

Ende appeared beside her, much taller, and he stretched up even taller still. She wondered just how far he could see. "People seem to be gathering," he murmured.

"Why?" she asked.

He continued to peer out through the window in silence.

"Perhaps I could head out for a look," she suggested quietly.

"No," Ende said.

"We don't know what is going on. It could dissolve into something very dangerous," Papa said.

She turned and looked at him standing nervously before the fire and nodded once, although it pained her to do so.

"I'll go," Ende said. "I can hide a little more easily in the crowd."

"I can better sense where Ed is," she said.

"He may be safer if no one knows where he is," Papa returned, and she looked back to the window. He was right. She wanted to help, not bring more trouble or danger to his doorstep.

Ende rested his hand on her shoulder and then headed for the door with a nod to Papa. She wondered just how a tall man as distinctive as her father would disappear into a crowd. But then, Ed had thought he was an old man, and Ana hadn't recognised him immediately when he'd arrived at the castle. He might be able to shift between more than just dragon and man. She wondered if he would be able to teach her such a skill and what she might be able to do with it.

Dray woke from the same dream of Ana walking from the dark. Every time he dreamt it, it was clearer and clearer, although nothing else had happened yet. She had simply walked towards him from the darkness.

As unsettling as it was, the dream was of more comfort than when she had visited him in his sleep, and then when she hadn't. Sitting on the edge of the narrow cot, he looked into the dark room. Ana had given him the cot to feel comfortable in, he thought, but he could only think of her and it wasn't helping either of them, or Ed.

Ed, the boy king who was a man. Dray had far more respect for him from the conversations he'd had during the day. He was the king he was destined to be, and despite the regent's efforts he was his father's son. Edwin had proven that to the people at the market. He had listened, he had offered his ideas, and the people knew who he was.

Maybe the idea of just getting him to the capital had been the best one. He simply needed to be seen and heard by the people. But would the regent listen to them? Would he find a way to discredit them?

Dray looked up as the dim moonlight straining through the narrow window caught the edge of a blade. He stood slowly as the soldier stepped forward. The blade he held too tightly in his hand was the silver one Dray was so sure would suit Ana. The one from the market that he still had not bought for her. The green eyes in the shadows behind the soldier were almost a relief when he focused on them.

Kemp looked him up and down, his glare condescending. He didn't think he was worth the effort. Dray wondered if he felt the same for the king or if his feelings were reserved for Dray alone. As he looked beyond the blade to the woman in the shadows, Dray wondered if it was because of her that the man felt the way he did.

The shadows shifted. Dray was desperate to stand back, but he waited where he was. No matter what threat this man posed, he knew Ana was the greatest danger in the room; and she would not allow anything to happen to him, whether he wished her interference or not.

The shadows closed in around the soldier and the blade dropped to the floor, the sound echoing through the room. It was soon overshadowed by the sound of the man screaming.

And then he was gone.

Ana stepped out into the dim light. Dray wanted to cross the floor to meet her, but he couldn't move. A shadow creature appeared beside her as she bent and picked up the blade Kemp had dropped, and Dray was half aware of Ed's face appearing at the gap in the curtains of the bed he shared with Belle. Ana only looked at the blade, then held it out to him.

Dray sucked in a breath and stepped forward. "A bit girly for a real soldier," he muttered.

The beast beside her growled.

"You will appear as the man," she commanded, but her eyes never left Dray's face.

The creature beside her rearranged itself, and Dray watched in fascination as it turned into the soldier he had just seen disappear. It put its fist to its chest and bowed to Dray.

"He is your commander," she said, holding out the blade to indicate Dray.

"Yes, Majesty," the creature, Kemp, said. Dray looked at him, unsure what he was.

"Tell him," Ana directed, her voice clear and scary.

"Captain Drayton Sterling." He stood tall, Kemp and yet not. "How may I help you keep the king safe?" He didn't even look at the king or Ana. His entire focus was on Dray.

"You can check the perimeter of the building."

He bowed, fist to chest, and disappeared as though he had never really existed.

Dray looked at Ana after glancing briefly at the bed, knowing that both Ed and Belle were listening. She nodded once, and then she too disappeared.

He sighed, missing her.

He sat heavily on the edge of the bed and then slammed his fist into his thigh. Now she was expecting him to use the creatures, and he had no idea if they would help him keep the king safe or if they were working to another agenda.

After what felt like an age, he heard quiet whispering from inside the curtains, which became more insistent before the king's face appeared again in the dim light.

"Has it gone?"

"It will return. It appears that Ana has gifted it to us to help keep you safe."

"I don't feel safe,' Edwin murmured, climbing from the bed. Belle muttered something behind him but did not appear.

"Ana's only concern is you." Edwin looked him over but said

nothing. Eventually, Dray looked up at him. "Only you," he repeated.

"And yet she came for you."

Dray opened his mouth and then closed it. Perhaps she was just watching them and happened to be present when Kemp decided he was going to help the king a different way.

"She was here to save you," Ed said, something in his voice Dray couldn't place. Was it jealousy?

"She might have been watching Kemp. He appears to have been watching us."

"How do you know?"

"The blade," Dray said, but when he looked around it was gone. Ana had offered it to him, but he hadn't taken it. She had kept it after all. Had Kemp seen him looking at it? "Did he want to frame Ana?" he wondered aloud.

"What blade?" Edwin asked, raising his voice.

"The one from the market. The one I looked at for Ana. Kemp had it."

"He might have killed me and blamed you. Are we sure he was one of the King's Men that Barlow was so sure we could trust?"

"He was never far from Barlow, whom I do trust," Dray said, standing again to press his point, although he was starting to wonder if he should trust himself.

"Should we get Barlow here to ensure his men can be trusted?" Ed asked. "What if he is working for the regent after all and only wants to keep us hidden away?"

"That is not what he intends," a quiet voice hissed from the shadows beyond the doorway.

Ed took a step back, and Dray moved between him and the doorway, his sword drawn.

The shadows changed, morphing into the soldier he had not long ago sent out. The dark armour caught the moonlight and looked solid. He bowed his head to Dray, his eyes only on him.

"The area around the building?"

"Quiet, quieter now."

Dray nodded once.

"I was not seen," he whispered, his voice more of a hiss than the voice he'd had before. "I am the shadows."

"Where did the blade come from?" Dray asked.

"It does not matter what was done before. I am yours to direct. You are my master, and I will follow whatever you order me to do."

"Even over Ana?" Ed asked, stepping out from behind him.

"She is my queen. She is the reason I exist." He cocked his head a little to the side. "I will not harm her."

"We would never ask for such a thing," Ed said quickly.

"What do you ask?"

Dray wondered why Kemp didn't use the king's title, but then he had his queen. For the first time, Dray wondered what these creatures might do if Ed were to sit on the throne. It was his, after all, and Ana was working to get him there. She might be a queen in the shadows, but she wasn't Queen here. Despite what her creatures called her. "You will protect the king at all costs."

"That is what you have asked of me, and I will obey. He is safe. He is not to be touched. Nor are you, Master. For that is what my queen has instructed."

Dray tried not to sigh as Ed looked at him with raised eyebrows.

"You must call me Captain," he said.

The creature before him bowed his head, his fist to his chest. Although Dray knew the man he appeared to be was somewhere inside him, the movement was awkward.

"Will it be hard for you to protect us?"

"No. The man inside us is my anchor. His fears drive us, but my queen is stronger."

Dray nodded, swallowing down his uncertainty.

"The major," the king whispered, perhaps thinking something similar to Dray.

"He is of use to our queen."

"Doing what?" Ed asked.

"Whatever she wants of him."

"If your anchor was an enemy of hers, is there any question of your helping?"

He grinned then, the sight almost as frightening as when the large shadow creature had appeared before them in the forest. "She is strong. She will win them over, or she will destroy."

"Destroy the creature they have become?" Ed asked.

"Destroy," he said again. "Sleep now. I shall watch." It disappeared into the shadows and Dray tried not to shiver.

He looked at Ed, who shook his head slowly. "She is starting to really scare me now," he murmured, heading back for the bed and the woman waiting on the other side of the curtain.

"I am sure she does it all for you."

Ed stopped and turned back. "I think so too," he said. "But it doesn't make it any less frightening. What will she do with such power once I am King? Where will her focus be then?"

"Keeping you there," Dray whispered, or at least he hoped so.

20

"Who is the girl?" Thom asked, looking at the two of them in the flickering torchlight. The torches reduced the shadows, but the curtains had been drawn, and he felt a shiver.

"My love?" Dahli asked, looking up at him as though she had only just realised he was there. The girl continued to work at adjusting her dress.

He looked at the girl and then back, raising his eyes.

"I needed help," she said, then turned fully to look at him. "Should I not have help?" Her voice was soft. He opened his mouth and then closed it. Something was off, but he couldn't quite place it.

"Of course, you should have help," he said as she turned back to the mirror before her. Although that too didn't look as it had before. He walked from the room, back to his balcony and into the bright morning sunshine. He felt better when he was in the direct light. It gave the witch less chance to sneak up on him. Not that he had seen her for some time, but he wasn't taking any chances.

He jumped when Dahli appeared silently beside him, the young girl a pace behind. They both smiled at him, but again it felt unnatural, and he stepped back instead of towards her.

Her face fell, anger creasing her eyes. "What is it?" she demanded. She glanced over her shoulder to the girl, who still smiled. "Am I not to be considered as the wife of the greatest man of the kingdom? Am I not to have something to ensure I am the best I can be for that husband?"

"Of course not," he said quickly, stepping forward to placate her. Her brother was still around, after all, and he didn't know what she might say to him if she wasn't happy with what Thom offered. "You are to have everything you desire."

"Everything?" She stepped forward, leaning into him and pinning him against the balcony railing. Her breath on his skin made the hairs on his arms stand at attention, and he did his best not to shiver.

"Dahli?" he asked softly, looking over her shoulder at the still-grinning girl.

"I want a child," she breathed. He felt his face flush as he glanced down at her bosom pressed into his chest.

"As do I," he murmured, running his hands around her waist and pulling her tighter against him, his excitement building.

She grinned up at him, but the look in her eyes gave him pause. Was she only there for the power of his position? Should he complain if she was? He had only selected her for her beauty and what he could gain from such a match. She was more beautiful than the witch, after all. If she was willing to share that body with him, he was content. He looked back at the girl behind her, her smile too contrived.

"Will she accompany you to the court today?"

"She will go where I go," Dahli said, pushing away from him. He stood away from the railing. "She will be my shadow."

Thom looked at the dark-haired girl. In some ways she appeared similar to Dahli, and very different at the same time. "Does she know the witch?" he muttered.

"She is my servant," Dahli growled, and Thom took a step back. "Why must you connect everything to that woman?" The anger was apparent despite the soft tone she used. "Do you long for her?"

He shook his head. Dahli turned sad eyes towards the girl, then motioned for her to follow as she headed out of their rooms at speed. He wondered where they were going, but he didn't ask. Maybe she was after her brother. He watched the doorway for some time after they had disappeared. She felt the same pressed against him, as she had in the night. But he shivered. The feel of her skin on his had been different, although he couldn't say how.

He would need to be in the throne room soon enough, listening to the whining of the people. They rarely brought him anything he could use or work with. They just wanted answers to their petty problems, and he had enough of his own.

Despite the number of people still coming in and out of the castle, no one seemed to be aware of the boy or where he might be. As Thom moved down the steps, he wondered where Ende could be. He had seen him with the sword master. He had been in the capital when the boy had returned, and he had known Barric well.

Thom stopped, leaning into the wall to catch his breath as he considered who might know the boy. Did Ende know, or had he guessed that the boy was the king? What might he do with such information? Although Thom wanted to be confident that he had convinced the people the boy was not who he had appeared to be, he knew they doubted him. He veered along another corridor and out into the courtyard. The sun was warm on his skin, yet he searched the shadows that hugged the walls.

Would he ever stop wondering where she was and what she might do? He headed across to the mage's workshop. The mage had been distracted as well of late with his girls and creatures, and he should be focused on ensuring the boy was gone for good. The sooner they could prove him gone, the sooner Thom could step up to take the throne and all that went with it. Once his bride produced a child, a boy of his own, he could be assured that the line would continue.

He shook his head, thinking of his young wife. She had been eager enough, and it didn't matter if she only wanted him for the power and position he gave her. That was what he was interested in, after all, and it would mean she would do all she could to maintain her position. But as he thought of his wife, the strange girl behind her came to mind. He shivered.

Thom entered the mage's workshop to an odd silence. He stopped as the mage and the creature he had tamed stared down at the young woman before them. She seemed small, yet something strong and familiar pulled at him.

"I thought there were two," Thom murmured.

"We lost one," the mage muttered.

"Where?"

The mage turned his glare on the regent, who might have stepped back at any other time, but he scowled instead.

"I am not here to worry about your maid." The creature growled, and he tried not to look at it directly. "I need to know what we can do about the king."

"He is gone," the mage said, turning his glare back to the girl, who smiled at them both.

"Are you sure?"

"Are you certain he will return?"

"Yes!" the regent bellowed, and all three turned to him. "He wants my crown," he insisted, trying not to sound like a petulant child. "He wants to be King. You saw him. No matter what might have happened to him, I think he has found his purpose and will return to claim it. I also think Ende might be involved in keeping him safe."

"Ende?" the mage asked, putting a finger to his pointed beard and dragging it through the grey curled hair. "Why do you think that?"

"He is friends with Forest. He was friends with my brother. I think he has recognised the boy, and I worry what he might do."

"No one will believe it is him."

"Because of your little adjustments? That may not be enough."

The mage stared at him and then turned to the creature beside him. "Where is the king?" he asked. Instead of answering, the face split into a wide, sharp-toothed grin, and its black tongue licked at the air around them. The regent tried not to shiver.

"It works for her," he snapped. "It will not tell us."

"My queen has determined that the king is not to be touched, by anyone. We keep him safe."

"We?" the regent asked, stepping closer. It bowed its head, and he was reminded at just how unnatural this creature was. "Did you take the other girl?" he asked suddenly.

The mage glared at him. "It is not important where Ruth has gone," he muttered.

"She didn't have any real power," the girl said, and Thom turned from the beast to look at her. She could have been any other girl, but he knew that if the mage had her, it was for a good reason. "She wasn't as strong as me."

"Did she need to be for the witch to take her?" the regent growled. "So far, she has taken a boy and a soldier. Although I must admit that the major was a loss."

"Those are just the ones you know of," the girl said sweetly, and he stared.

"What do you know?" he asked.

"Not enough," she admitted. "But given time, I can find out."

"Can you?" he asked. "And how will you do that?"

"I am stronger than I look." She squared her shoulders and held her head high.

"You were stronger together," the mage muttered.

"I have all I need." But her confidence had slipped somewhat.

"Have you unlocked all that you are?" the mage asked, stepping forward, his wiry fingers closing around her shoulders. For the first time, the child appeared frightened.

She glanced over his shoulder at the creature behind him, and Thom wondered if Ana allowed the creature time with the mage to report on what they were doing. It turned dark eyes on him, and he shivered.

"She does not need us," it hissed. "Not like you think she does. The child is right; she has many others to do her bidding."

"Many?" he asked, his mouth going dry at the idea of more creatures such as this one. She had used her shadows to take, but had she created? He wondered if that was what she was doing, but he hadn't allowed himself to believe it. "At least they would be easy to see," he murmured.

The creature before him grinned and disappeared into the shadows. Thom gulped down the rising fear and turned back to the mage.

"We don't know what she is doing, we don't know where the king is and we don't know how to get to him. I would like to suggest we use the soldier against him, but I doubt Sterling could be so easily turned."

"If you can find him. If you were to visit the cells, I think you would find him gone. He too has more allies within the castle than either of us would like to admit."

"A man who abandoned his post for a girl!" the regent roared.

"A soldier who stood by his king," the girl responded, her confidence returned. "That is what the men saw."

Thom growled and swung from the room. He would not be told by a child. He stopped by the door and turned back. "Did she run, or was she taken?"

The girl just grinned at him. She knew far more than she would tell, and he wondered at the mage finding these children to help him when they only came to help themselves.

Ende watched the regent emerge from the mage's rooms and stomp across the courtyard, wondering what the mage had told him that had put him in such a mood. As he had moved through the castle, he had heard the servants talking about the king listening to the people. Salima would have a better idea of where Ed was, but at least he agreed with Forest that it wasn't safe for her to go out looking. And he had found no sign of the activities the day before.

As Salima came to mind, he saw her sneaking towards the practice halls. Not that she needed to sneak, for so far the three of them had been the only ones to visit the halls since the death of the boy. There was too much that didn't make sense. Had the creature that had killed the boy so many years ago returned? Was that the same creature the mage attempted to keep as a pet? Ende thought it far more likely that it answered to Ana.

He wondered where she was, and what she was doing. Dray was so sure she was trying to help the king, but was she? She could be hiding with him in the capital somewhere.

He rested his hand on Salima's shoulder as she put her hand to the door, and she jumped. "You should sense me," he murmured. "What are you doing?"

"Practicing," she said, smiling up at him.

"Then why sneak? Your father has told you that one of us must be with you at all times."

"I'm not sneaking, and you are my father."

He stood back and crossed his arms. He knew the child found it somewhat confusing, but she cared for them both. He felt that from her when Forest was in the room. He might be her father, but Forest had raised her, and she had bonded with the man. Ende also knew he would do anything to keep her safe, no matter who her true father was.

"I think I can look after myself," she murmured, opening the door.

"What if the creature or one of them wants you? We thought it sought out power. You might be strong, but so are they," he said, following her into the space and looking at where the boy had been ripped apart. He wondered then if the mess had simply been because he had been interrupted. What if he had chosen to go with the shadows? What if the boy had thought it was an option to make him stronger? Perhaps the interruption somehow disrupted the joining. If that was how it happened, it was no wonder the major had screamed as he had.

Ende stood slowly after examining the floor where the boy had been. The major had screamed. The boy had screamed. Had Ana done this? Had she allowed the shadows to take the child? And what exactly did that create? The creature he had seen stand beside her in the throne room… Could that be the boy, or the major?

"She's making an army," he whispered. Fear covered his body and his wings longed to be free. Others might have dragged the shadows closer, but she was using them. Ana was creating more creatures from the shadows. But was it to help Ed become King, or was it something else?

"Ende?" Salima was staring at him, her eyes wide, and he blinked to refocus on her.

"What is it?" he asked.

"You look different," she whispered.

He looked himself over. He had grown, perhaps, but there was something in the way she stared at him. He put his hand to his face and ran his fingers through his short, neat beard. His hand brushed over rough skin. One side of his face was not the man he thought he portrayed.

He pulled the sword from his belt, and with the bright light streaming into the room, he stared at his reflection. Half of his face was burnt, the scales marked and damaged. Was this caused by Ana's shadows? He looked to the child who stepped towards him. Or was this something else?

He realised then that the windows were clear, and the light in the room was from the sunshine rather than the torches that seemed to have filled the castle. He looked back to the blade, and his face was as it had been.

"You saw that?" he asked, allowing the sword to drop as his hand returned to his face.

She nodded slowly. "What happened?"

He shook his head. Could it have been a vision, or had he done this by focusing on Ana? She was much stronger than he had thought. His fears returned. She was something other than the girl trying to help the king. "Does she need them to become what I saw her to be?" he asked himself.

"Ana?" Salima asked, her hand on his now, her eyes searching his face for the marks that had disappeared. "Did she do this?"

"She might be yet to do it," he murmured, then looked up at the narrow windows. "Who cleaned them?"

"I didn't like the shadows," she whispered. "I don't think Ana would harm Ed."

"I'm not so sure," he said, looking back to her face.

Salima opened her mouth to say something else and then stopped, taking a small step back. He looked at her closely, his hand to his cheek again. And then he turned and looked behind him.

Ana stood in the sunshine, her hood back, her green eyes bright. She looked like the girl he had met in the mountains. Young, innocent and haunted by something in her dreams she couldn't understand.

"I understand now," she whispered, stepping forward. Ende reached out and pulled Salima closer as she stepped back from Ana. He didn't want her disappearing into the shadows.

"What do you understand?"

"What I am," she said without hesitation. "And why I am the only one to help Ed."

Salima made to step forward then, but he held her close. He could feel the power pushing at her skin, but no matter what form she took, Ana would win any fight.

She smiled at him then.

"I won't let you take her," he growled, the walls vibrating with his anger.

"I don't take," she said, stepping forward. "I offer opportunity."

"Opportunity?" He allowed his disbelief to be heard.

"They become stronger. They become a way to remove the regent."

Ende took a deep breath, trying to calm the beast as it tried to rip through him and the woman before him. "This isn't about Ed," he said.

"Of course it is. He is the rightful king, and the regent has worked all these years to prevent him being what he is."

"Are you going to restore his crown?" Ende asked carefully.

She bowed her head, her smile wide, but there was something different about her, something off. He wondered what they could do to stop her.

The shadows around her shifted, even in the bright light, and a creature became solid beside her. Salima stiffened against him. Again, he was sure he could feel her trying to become the dragon. He blew out a soft breath that warmed the room around him, and Ana smiled. Another creature appeared behind her. How many of the creatures did she have? he wondered as a third appeared, blocking the doorway.

What might Ana intend by making such a show? Was she reading him still? A fourth creature appeared, and he sucked the warmth back, holding it still in case he needed to use a flame he hadn't for far too long.

Ana waved one hand to the side, and the creatures were gone. He had the feeling this little show was only part of the power she had.

"Just what will the little dragon do?" Ana asked, her voice dark. He was reminded of the shadows that no longer stood behind her.

Ende looked down at the child pressed against his body, warm and getting warmer. He didn't think she would be a threat to Ana; of all of them, Salima was the most trusting that Ana wasn't the witch she was thought to be. And yet Ana was showing him something very different.

"How will this help Ed?" he asked.

"Everything I do brings that boy closer to his crown," she almost hissed, and something dark covered her face.

Was she losing herself to the shadows? She blinked at him as he thought it, her features clearing somewhat although her eyes were more brilliant than he had ever seen them.

"You are nothing like your mother," he whispered.

She was there in a blink, from the other side of the practice hall, now standing right before him, and he pushed the child behind him. The fear he had felt in the mountains returned, and the room warmed instantly in response. She grinned at him, looking deep into his eyes as though she saw his every thought. Then she nodded once.

"I am what I am," she breathed. The hiss was gone, but something dark still lingered. "I am as I have always been."

He shook his head. This was not the girl he knew.

"Of course I am," she said. "I am Anaise Merrin, daughter of a soldier and a mage. I am strong and magical." She stepped back. Her green eyes sparkled in the sunlight. She looked up then, as though his thinking of it reminded her of the change in the windows. "I am doing what I need to do for our king," she said, looking back to him.

"I don't believe that," Ende said too quickly.

"Believe as you will. But don't get in the way of my army."

"Your army?" Salima asked, her hand still tight in Ende's although she stood behind him.

"The King's Men cannot be trusted," she said. "They belong to the regent."

"How many do you have in your army?" Ende asked slowly.

"Not enough." The hiss was more evident in her voice before she disappeared again.

"That was scary," Salima admitted, moving slowly out and around him into the patch of sunshine in the middle of the floor. "What did she think I might do?"

"Become the dragon," he said, unsure if that was what she thought.

"That won't help Ed," she said.

"And using a sword will?"

"Maybe. Do you think she is right? Are the King's Men not to be trusted?"

"Some, perhaps. I know at least one man who won't leave the king."

"But then what is he to Ana?"

"Or what is Ana to him?" Ende murmured. He was so sure he'd had that worked out. She couldn't be parted from them initially. But she didn't need either of them now to work her magic or find her strength. Ende had felt the increase in her power when they'd been drawn to her. But she was something else now. Maybe she only needed them to realise what she was. And now that it was realised, she was something strong enough to destroy them all.

21

Ana stood in the dark as the cool shadows wrapped around her. She shivered and pulled her cloak tighter, but it was a comfortable feeling. The sun had been too bright, too hot, and she had not wanted to show them just how much it hurt her. She preferred the shadows, but she didn't need them. She had even managed to move to where she wanted with the bright light, and she wondered for a moment how the windows had been cleared. The little dragon peeking around her father's back might have been responsible, but she would never know.

The girl was annoying, far more annoying than Ana wanted to admit. She was also sure the girl would work out soon enough that Ed was back in the capital and go searching for him. She didn't think that would help either of them. But it appeared Ed was finding ways to help himself.

Ana had watched him at the market and listened to his discussions with the people. Dray and the blade, she thought, pulling it out of the folds of her cloak. It shimmered, even in the dim light of the world she preferred to her own. The dark room disappeared to nothing around her, only the table and bed sitting in any clarity.

Blowing out a soft breath, she reached to put the dagger on the table, but she couldn't seem to let it go. It wasn't even as though he had given it to her. He had intended such a gift, although she wondered at it. It had been the soldier who had bought it, wanting to suggest Dray was responsible for something, yet she wasn't quite sure if he would have killed the king and blamed it on Dray, or if Dray had been his intended victim all along.

She sighed and pushed it back into her belt. It was cool against her side, and the feel of it pressing against her provided some comfort.

She was gathering her forces, although she wasn't quite sure what she could do with them. The regent's wife would be of use. She would start to unsettle him, although Ana had managed to do that quite well on her own. He wasn't reaching for the wrist, but he was watching every corner and had insisted on torches all over the castle. The new maid would be of use too, and for more than helping the wife into her clothing. She was very special. Her sister might have stolen more than she had been willing to give, but she had something very special of her own. Ana just had to work out how to use it.

And to keep it from others. It appeared that even her sister didn't know what she had, and therefore the mage wouldn't either. At the thought of the girl, she appeared in her changed form so that the mage wouldn't recognise her. Or the regent, for Ana feared he visited the mage far more often than he should. Although what the old man thought he could do now was anyone's guess.

"Ruth," Ana said softly. "Welcome."

Ruth bowed her head, still more creature than girl. "Thank you, Majesty. What would you wish of me?"

"What would you wish to give?"

She studied Ana as a girl might, trying to determine what she wanted from her. Like her sister had wanted from her and taken from her. Trust had been broken.

The creature shifted, turning into the one she knew that looked like all the others, only Ana could see the child inside and identify everyone. The major came to mind then, although she didn't call him. She would have work for him, although not with the regent.

"She is strong," the girl said in the creature's voice.

"Your sister?"

They bowed their head. "She wants more."

"You are far stronger than she could ever be. That is why you were chosen. That is what we saw in you."

They bowed their head again, their unnatural grin broad.

"What do you think the mage intends?" Ana asked carefully.

"He wants the regent to be King. He wants the boy dead."

Ana waited. She had given the instruction that Ed was not to be harmed, nor Dray, and although the creature that had once been the maid upheld that wish, she knew the mage tried to work around it. "How would he use you?"

"He hoped we would be like you. He waits for us to hear the beyond, to see it in the workshop bottles."

"Do you? Did you?"

The creature sighed. "No, Majesty. Not until you granted us this peace. Now I feel the beyond. Now I know the beyond, but as a girl I did not."

"Your sister?" she asked.

The creature looked down, and Ana could feel the disappointment ebbing from it.

"You are stronger," Ana repeated. Not that she had to reassure such a creature to have it do as she desired. Just pulling them together, giving them the chance to move between worlds, was enough. She too now visited the beyond. Initially led here by another, she could come and go as she wished. She was stronger than she had ever imagined she could be, and therefore she could remove the regent. It wouldn't be hard. But destroying him, as she wanted, wouldn't help Ed. The people would turn against him when she needed them with him.

Ana looked over the creature before her and rested her hand on the dagger at her hip. She needed the people behind Ed.

Why is that? the familiar voice asked in her mind. *Why do you need them?*

Ana shook her head, though not to dispel the thought, for it was one she had wondered on herself. One that kept repeating. She needed the people.

"Perhaps I should spend more time with him," she wondered aloud. "Be seen with him."

Would that help him and the people?

Ana growled her frustration. They didn't trust her—that was why she needed them to trust in Ed.

"How may I help you, Majesty?" the creature before her hissed. They were worried for her; she could feel it. She reached out her hand to take that of the girl and noticed her own dark nails. She lifted them closer. Perhaps it was the light, the strange world of the beyond. She waved the hand, and a mirror appeared before her. Studying herself, Ana wondered when these changes had started. Was it when her magic found her again, or before that? Or was it simply how she appeared to be in this world?

"Am I you?" Ana asked her reflection. It grinned at her. The lips smiled too wide, the tongue that licked over them too dark. Ana put her hand to her face and thought she appeared too pale, almost grey, but as she looked around the room, so did everything else. It was this world. She might have changed, but not that much.

She remembered Dray flinching when she had appeared in the dark. He had tried to keep calm, particularly in the face of the king, who had jumped like a child. But she had seen it, the fear and uncertainty deep within him. It caused a sharp pain to move through her chest. She doubled over with the pain, calling out, and the creature was there, wrapped around her. She looked up as she slipped to her knees, putting her hand to their cool and scaly face.

"Majesty?" they hissed, a soft and comforting sound.

She shook her head, unsure what she needed, unsure what she wanted to happen. "I need Dray," was all she could manage.

They moved as one, appearing in the light of a tavern. Ed sat surrounded by people, Belle at his side, Dray standing behind him. They loved their king. She could feel some uncertainty, but there was more trust from the people in the room. Dray lifted his dark eyes to focus on her in the shadows, she gulped down her fear at the confusion on his face, the sadness she saw reflected in his dark eyes.

"No," she breathed, and the creature dragged her away again, but not to the shadows, to a small room.

Ana stepped away from them as she focused on the world around her. This was not a room she had visited before. A narrow bed, a small table, a fireplace with a kettle hanging over long-dead coals. Yet there was something here, something familiar.

She turned back to the creature, who bowed its head.

"Why here?" she asked, her voice shaky. She tried desperately to clear it, but a lump had formed.

The creature bowed low. "Your mother," they hissed and then disappeared.

Ana sat heavily on the edge of the bed. Dust rose into the air, making her cough. She looked about. There was a narrow window, and she stepped forward to look out over the marshes. She was somewhere in the castle. She turned then and realised there was no door. It was a room only she could enter. She ran her hand over the table, leaving thick lines in the dust.

She waved her hand as she had in the beyond, and a mirror appeared leaning against the rough stone wall. Ana looked as she always had, or so she thought, although she dressed quite differently. The cloak was always around her shoulders, her straight hair long and curling a little towards the ends. She leaned forward, and her green eyes sparkled in the light.

"What do you think I can do?" she asked herself.

A chuckle filled the room.

She leaned back. "Tell me."

More than your mother ever could. You are the queen. You shall find a way to prove to the people what and who you are.

"I don't want to be Queen here," she said quickly.

Don't you?

Ana stared at herself, unsure what she could say.

You belong to both worlds. You will join them.

22

Ed looked up at Dray standing behind him as he mumbled something. Then he blinked slowly and looked at Ed as though he didn't know what he was looking at.

"Did you say something?" Ed asked.

Dray shook his head.

"You sure?" Ed asked. The room had grown quiet around them. Dray nodded, but his gaze moved to the shadows, and Ed wondered if Ana had been to visit.

"What can we do?" a man asked from across the room, and the crowd turned to him.

"I'm sorry," Ed murmured.

"The regent," the man said. "We know you are the king; we trust in you. As your uncle and regent, he was to protect you until you came of age, and that was some time ago. We must make him give up the crown."

Ed released a long breath. "I had hoped it would be that easy, but he will not give it up. He will not admit that I am the king. He'll have the mage change me again to create doubt, or have me killed."

"What of the witch?" a woman asked. She stood off to the side, and Ed thought there was something familiar about her.

"She is not a witch," Dray said, his deep voice carrying through the space. The gentle conversation hushed completely. "She is our friend."

The murmuring started again. "Could she help you?" the woman asked.

"She has tried," Ed said. "I think she continues to try. She has some gifts that allow her to reverse what the mage has done, although my uncle would tell you that she created me from someone else."

The murmuring continued.

"My brother is a soldier," the woman said. "He saw you in the forest and said you are the king. If he says it, then I believe you are."

Ed bowed his head. "The King's Men have helped protect me. What is your brother's name?" he asked.

"Kemp," she said, bowing her head to him.

Ed opened his mouth and then closed it. He tried not to gulp too loudly thinking of what had happened to the woman's brother. Did she know he was gone? Or changed? He could still appear as Kemp when they needed him to. And although Ed knew he was close now, he hadn't seen Kemp for a time. He wondered what would happen if this woman saw him, for he didn't look himself, even when he did.

A strange thought occurred to him in that moment—Ana might not be Ana. She hadn't been acting as herself for some time, and he knew that the creatures of shadow, or whatever they were, called her their queen. What if she too was half shadow creature, only looking like Ana to make it appear that she was helping them? He looked up at Dray, suddenly more afraid than he had been for some time.

"The regent," someone said, drawing his attention back, and he wondered if his uncle had appeared in the room.

Belle gave him a gentle nudge. Ed shook his head. He didn't know what he was doing.

"We need to make him step down. We have to find a way to convince him that stepping down and giving the crown back to me is a good idea, and one he supports."

"And then what will you do with him?"

"He is still my uncle," Ed said, looking for whoever it was who had asked the question. Although he was sure whatever the future held for his uncle, it would involve a small cell.

The room moved into general conversation, leaving Ed to his thoughts. He tried to listen to what they were saying, but he couldn't focus. The ideas of how to remove his uncle were leaning towards mobs and swords, and he didn't think that was the best option. He would need to make the decision for himself. It was the only way.

But how he could do that, he had no idea. Now that he thought he had a better understanding of Ana and what she was, he wasn't sure she should be the one to help. Although he certainly didn't want to be the one to tell her that. The idea of her turning into one of those creatures before him, her face becoming the wide-eyed, sharp-toothed, black-tongued monstrosity, made him shiver.

"What is it?" Dray asked, leaning over his shoulder.

"Ana," he whispered, and the tall soldier looked about the room. "She isn't here," he added.

"She was," Dray said, leaning down again so that those around them couldn't hear.

Ed gulped down the fear rising in his chest. Was she really there to help him, or was she there to help herself? He blew out a slow breath, worried he was shaking as much on the outside as he was on the inside and these people would grow to doubt him even more.

"She wasn't herself," Dray whispered.

Ed pushed himself to his feet, and the soldier stepped back as the room dropped into silence. He could feel every set of eyes on his back, even though he looked at the soldier. Belle's hand had reached for his, but he had pulled from her reach.

"What is it?" Dray asked, his voice low.

"What do you think she is?" Ed asked just as quietly, although he worried that everyone was listening for what had upset the king.

"What she always was," Dray said, his chin held high, but Ed knew it was a lie. He wanted to believe in her, wanted to trust that she was the same as she had always been, but Dray too had seen something different. As Ed continued to stare him down, Dray lowered his eyes and sighed. "She looked as though she was injured," he said. "Or unwell. She was struggling to stand, and one of her creatures held her up."

"Did her eyes glow?"

Dray nodded once.

"Then she is as strong as she has been every time we have seen her. She doesn't need us," Ed said, the realisation stinging more than he thought it would.

"She never needed us," Dray said.

"She will always need you," something hissed from the shadows behind them, and they turned together to find there was nothing there.

"She is one of them," Ed whispered hoarsely. "She is a creature of the shadows, pretending to be Ana."

Dray shook his head, although he continued to stare into the shadows.

"That wasn't..." Ed started, looking through the crowd for Kemp's sister.

Dray shook his head again, his jaw clenched, and Ed wished he could read the big man as well as Ana seemed to be able to read him. She knew too much. She knew it all. Whatever they planned, whatever he thought. Any doubt he had in her.

"I need her," he said, disappointed at the realisation. "I might think I can do this, but any plan that will work must involve Ana and her skills."

Dray continued to stare into the shadows.

"There are others who would like to talk with you, Your

Majesty," the innkeeper said, and Ed turned to nod slowly at the man. They had been there two days running. If his uncle found out, what might he do? Ed was sure that word would have already reached him, but maybe Ana's shadows kept him safe after all.

He sat slowly back at the table. "I need to learn all I can of the kingdom," he said to the room as Belle rested her hand on his arm. He gave her a brief nod. He needed her here after all, he was certain of that. "Please, share what you can, and when I am restored I will do all I can to help you."

By the end of the day, Ed's head was spinning. He had been offered too many ideas about how to remove his uncle, most of which involved killing him. And as tempted as he was, he knew it wasn't the way forward for him. His father would have been able to consider something else. What advice would he have offered if he were alive?

Dray had remained at his back, his comments few, although Ed was sure he watched the shadows for Ana rather than the crowd for a threat. But then, he also knew that Kemp was watching from the shadows to keep them safe.

Barlow hadn't questioned his man missing, but he would have assumed he was helping protect the king, or at least that was what Ed would have thought if he were in Barlow's position. Although, if there was a threat and Kemp stepped forward from the shadows to protect him, what would the people think? Ed looked then for the sister who had disappeared. Some of the crowd had moved on during the day while others had come. Word was out that the king had returned and was willing to listen. The idea only confirmed for Ed that his uncle must know he was in the capital and not hiding. But he couldn't very well have Ed killed before all these people.

Or could he? They wouldn't know it was him. He hoped between Dray and the shadows that couldn't happen. He glanced at Belle as she wiped a hand across her eye and tried to stifle a yawn. It had been a long day, and although she hadn't said very much, it was of great comfort that she sat beside him.

Someone had asked who she was at one point, and she had introduced herself as from the Grasslands. She hadn't given away their relationship, but Ed wasn't always sure he knew what that was. He cared for her very much; he had admitted as much to Dray. But he had made no real commitment to Belle, and although they shared a bed, it wasn't as he hoped it would be. Or could be. He burned at the idea of what it could be. She looked up at him and smiled.

"Did you eat?" Dray asked, stepping between them.

She shook her head, putting her hand over her mouth as she yawned again. Ed's face burned hotter. He wasn't even looking after her as he should.

"I have a private room," the innkeeper offered, appearing before him. "I have laid out a meal. I appreciate you have somewhere safer to stay, but please." He indicated the way with his outstretched arm and Ed nodded, taking Belle by the hand and following. The man stopped by the door but did not go in. Dray pushed ahead and opened the door, and Ed gaped at Kemp standing beside a table laden with food. He bowed his awkward bow as Ed followed Dray into the room, the door closing behind them.

Ed let out a sigh at the privacy. Would he ever get used to so many people? Dray pulled out a chair for Belle. Part of him wanted to note that he was the king and should be seated first, but they were all friends and she was tired. And he should have considered that before Dray. Particularly when Dray wasn't as focused as he should be.

"What did you mean about Ana?" Dray asked as Ed took a seat.

Ed looked at Kemp standing in the corner, the shadows closing in around him. Ed shook his head. He wanted to share what he thought with Dray, who seemed to know her best and would have a better idea. But he didn't want to voice those concerns around one of her soldiers—creatures—who might report it back to her.

Dray looked at the creature, took a step forward and nodded, and it disappeared from view.

"Where did it go?" Ed asked.

"Patrol. He knows his place."

"Are you sure?" Ed insisted, hoping his fear couldn't be heard in his voice.

"What is it?" Belle asked, and he knew he had failed.

He took a deep breath, looking around the room, then looked to Dray first. "She is one of them."

"Who is one of what?" Belle asked, yawning again as she reached for the plate of meat.

Ed stood, leaning over the table, and dragged it closer to her, then waited as she piled it onto her plate. He dragged some of the bowls of vegetables closer and wondered at the spread. Not something you would usually find at an inn, at least not in his limited experience. "Did we pay for this?" he asked.

"What do you think Ana is, exactly?" Dray demanded. He put the bowl down and then sat back in the hard chair.

"She is one of those shadow creatures."

"How do you know?" Belle asked through a mouthful of food. She moaned with contentment, juices dripping down her chin as she looked up at him.

"She is their queen. So she has something like them inside her, only she is showing as Ana, as the Ana we know so that we are comfortable with it, like Kemp."

Belle dropped her fork, and Dray stood slowly. "Why?" he asked, his voice just as deep and scary as it had been before.

Ed shook his head.

The large soldier stood over him. "Why don't you trust her?"

"I trust Ana," Ed said, climbing to his feet. "But she might not be Ana."

"She is," Dray snapped.

"How can you be sure? You are just as uncertain of what she has become. You are distracted, fearful almost. Can you truly say she is the girl you saved from a fall and led through the mountains?"

"You aren't the boy I met there either. Much has happened, Ed, over the time since we have met that has changed us all." He motioned to his own body, and Ed noted the lack of armour. He wasn't the soldier he had been either. He was still dedicated, he was still strong, but he was different.

"What is she to you?" Ed asked.

"What is she to you?" Dray shot back.

"My friend," Ed said quickly, with no hesitation, although he wasn't sure it was true. He didn't know her anymore, not like he had. And since he had watched Kemp so often during the day, he seemed to understand something very different about her. "What if she doesn't support me like she said? What if she works for another cause?"

"Then she wouldn't be trying to make you King," Dray snapped, his whole body stiff, and Ed knew he was on a knife's edge by challenging the large man.

"Is she?"

"Of course," Belle said, blinking up at him. Then she pushed another large piece of meat into her mouth.

"You are sure?" he said.

She crinkled her eyes and swallowed the too-large mouthful, coughing a little and reaching for a pitcher of ale.

"Why do you doubt her?" Dray asked. "I'm not sure of anything anymore. The world is not what I thought it was, but I have to believe in Ana."

"And if you are wrong?" Ed asked.

The large man put a hand to his cheek in a move Ed had not seen in some days, although it wasn't very long ago that his fingers had searched his cheek all the time.

"She wasn't right about that," Ed said as Dray allowed his hand to drop.

"Not yet, but that doesn't mean it isn't to come."

Ed sighed. "What if she isn't strong enough to stand up to

them? What if she dragged them here and they are using her?"

Dray shook his head. "I don't know," he whispered, falling into a chair, and Ed sat slowly.

"The three of you have worked together from the beginning," Belle said, her voice soft and reassuring. "Even Ende saw that."

Ed looked from Belle to Dray and stood. "Where is Ende?" he said. "What does he know that he hasn't told us?"

"It is never that simple with Ende," Dray said. "He has his own agenda."

"Salima," Ed whispered, anger building suddenly in his chest. He had thought Ende a friend to his mother, yet he had abandoned her when she needed him. Assumed them lost. Could he have saved her if he had truly wanted to? Although when Ed thought of him standing in the cottage, his arm around Salima, he understood just how much the dragon had loved their mother.

"Why is he interested in Salima?" Dray asked.

Ed opened his mouth and then closed it. Ana had known. The moment she had seen her, she had understood the link between them. And that was only because of the link she herself shared with Ed.

"Why won't you tell me?" Dray asked, something sad and almost lost in his voice. Was the strongest man he knew crumbling before him?

"He is her father," Ed whispered, looking around the room, fearing who else might hear their story. The more who knew it, the more danger it put her in. No matter what she was deep inside, she was still his little sister.

Dray stared at him and then nodded slowly. "He isn't as he appears to be," he said. "None of this is how it appears to be."

Belle took another gulp from her ale and sat it loudly on the table. "Really?" she said, her words a little slurred. Ed wondered how much ale she had managed to drink.

"You are just as you were," Dray said to her, lifting another cup himself.

"What good is that when everyone else had changed?"

Ed opened his mouth and stopped as Kemp reappeared in the room. He bowed awkwardly and turned to Dray. "Soldiers come," he hissed.

"King's Men?" Ed said, standing slowly.

"They talk of the imposter," Kemp hissed.

Dray growled something under his breath, and the soldier stepped forward.

"Master," it said, reaching for him, but he stepped back.

"Take the king and his guest first."

Belle hiccupped and grabbed at Ed as the soldier turned into the creature. Before Ed had a chance to say anything, the darkness closed around them and they were back in the little room hidden away from the world. As the creature disappeared, Belle said, "I was still hungry."

"I'm sorry," he muttered. He wasn't doing a very good job of looking after her. She had sat beside him all day, and he hadn't even thought to ensure she ate. She leaned into him and pressed greasy lips against his. And then stepped back, grinned, hiccupped and jumped into the bed.

Ed smiled at her as Dray appeared beside him. "Ensure we weren't followed," he instructed, and the creature was gone again.

"I'm not sure whether it is more unnerving when it is the creature or when it is Kemp," Ed said. Dray nodded agreement and sat down on his narrow cot. Ed looked back at the bed to see Belle had fallen asleep, her hair loose and her shoes still on. He sighed and sat next to Dray. "If Ana is not what she was, what do we do?"

Dray stared at the floor. "I don't know."

23

Thom seethed as the soldier stood at attention before him. There was too much going wrong. He had never expected the boy to find his own way to the people, nor the people to rally around him. Threats had been made, but the people were still gathering.

"We were too late, Your Highness," the soldier said.

Thom was sure that they hadn't tried very hard. Were these men on the boy's side after all? "Explain it to me," he growled, trying not to glance at the woman beside him. Dahli appeared interested in the conversation, but not as concerned by his tone as he would have expected.

"There was word that there was a gathering at the same inn. It was claimed the king…" The man had the decency to colour a little. "They claimed it was the king, but we know it was the imposter," the soldier went on. Thom didn't even have an idea of his rank or name. He would need to replace Field at some point, but he hadn't yet found anyone he knew he could trust in the same way. He wasn't even sure which men were his.

"Imposter," he said, waving his hand for the man to continue.

"We sent men to investigate, but there was no crowd and no sign of the imposter."

"None?" Thom asked.

He shook his head.

Thom thumped the armrest of the throne. Dahli ran her hand

over his wrist, but the movement burned and he pulled away from her. The soldier looked at her and then back. He hadn't been the same since Ana had appeared as Dahli in his room. The feelings he had for her had been even more unsettling—so much so that he was struggling to look at his wife as he should. Despite her best efforts.

He cleared his throat and refocused on the man before him. "They have met there before?"

The soldier bowed his head.

"Then can I suggest you have soldiers there when the inn opens tomorrow in case they decide to meet again?"

The man bowed, his fist to his chest, and then he was gone.

He turned to Dahli, who smiled at him, although he could tell her heart was not in it. He held his hand out again, and she placed hers slowly in his. "You don't trust me," she whispered.

"It is not you that I don't trust, although you did manage to heal me before. It seems the pain has returned."

"Should I fetch the mage for you?" the young maid asked, a step behind his wife's chair. She was always close, even in their bedroom last evening when he had tried to focus on Dahli and not think of the witch.

"He is preoccupied," he said.

"With what?" Dahli asked, her voice a little different. He turned back to study her. He expected an apology, but she simply raised her eyebrows. "He is to serve you. What is more important? Or a cleric?" She turned to the maid and waved her hand towards the door.

"I don't think either would assist me," Thom said, and the girl halted. He should have let her go; she smiled too much, and it unnerved him. "Has your brother gone yet?"

Dahli opened her mouth and then closed it, drawing her eyebrows together. "I don't know," she said. "He would hardly tell me his plans." She waved the maid towards the door again. "Child, go to his rooms. Tell him to come."

"I don't want to see him," Thom groaned. "The man is a thorn in my side."

"Then tell him to go." Dahli straightened her skirts and squared her shoulders. She was always a picture of grace, but as he watched her settle in anticipation of her brother, he thought he saw a black tongue lick at her lips. He leaned forward.

"Now is not the time," she whispered, grinning at him. She leaned forward to meet his gaze, her hand on his knee, and as it ran slowly along his thigh, black eyes blinked back at him.

He sat back and shook his head. He was searching for the witch wherever he looked, and it had to stop. "When your brother is gone," he breathed, leaning in close again, despite his fears, "we will have some time alone."

Her brown eyes smiled back at him, and he breathed out slowly as the guard at the door announced the Lord of Near Forest. Thom wondered what he would do if he no longer had to worry about the lords.

"What do you want?" the lord huffed as he stood before them, and the guard who had shown him in put his hand to his sword. "Don't you think you have taken enough?" he asked, looking pointedly at his sister.

The woman stood and stepped forward. Her body moved fluidly, and Thom's eye was drawn to the sway of her hips. He was tempted to lick his lips, for he was keen to get her alone now. It had been too long. He had allowed Ana to influence him, and that would stop.

"What do you think you want, brother?" she asked, her voice husky as she walked slowly around the lord, her hand trailing across his skin. He shivered.

"What is rightfully mine," the lord said, but the strength had gone from his voice.

"And what is that?" Thom asked. "Do you want your sister returned?"

"The blonde," he breathed, distracted by the woman beside him in a way no man should be by his sister.

"Is she so much more beautiful than I?"

He licked his lips and shook his head.

"Ruth, child," Dahli hissed, "show the man."

Thom's heart beat too fast for his chest as the little maid stepped out and changed before his very eyes. She became the beautiful blonde woman who had travelled with Edwin.

"Is this what you want?" she asked, her voice almost a hiss as she breathed in his ear.

"The witch," Thom breathed.

"Is that what you want, husband?" Dahli asked, turning her attention to him. She had never looked more beautiful, and he had never been more afraid. He waited, but she didn't turn into the woman he still longed for.

"I am needed," the maid said—no, the blonde woman said.

Thom pressed his hands to his temple as the girl disappeared. He gulped down his fears. Was she the missing sister? He hadn't really paid her much attention, but he was sure she looked very like the overconfident girl who had remained with the mage. He remembered her sister grinning in the workshop. She had taken something from the girl, and he wondered then if that had allowed her to be taken by the dark. But then she had appeared normal enough, until she had changed into someone else and disappeared. His focus moved back to the woman walking slowly towards him; she stopped and tilted her head to the side.

"What do you want?" he asked.

"Power. A place before the people. Very little."

"You are just a woman," the brother growled, remembering himself, no longer quite so entranced.

"A woman has more power than you realise. How do you propose to raise future lords and kings without us?"

The man gaped. She turned back to him, her back to Thom, and the man paled and staggered back. When she turned back to Thom, smiling, he wondered what could have frightened him so.

"Go home," she snapped, and the lord turned and ran from the room. "Are you happy, husband?"

Thom nodded, but he wasn't sure he was. His wife was not as he thought, and he was sure she wasn't who she had been when she had first arrived at the capital.

She moved quickly, pinning him against the throne. She had more strength than he had given her credit for. She sat in his lap and pressed her lips to his in the quiet room. He wrapped his arms around her and kissed her.

She pulled away, grinning, then kissed along his jaw line. Something warm stirred in his chest. How had he doubted this woman?

"Husband," she hissed in his ear, and a shiver covered his skin. He clung tightly to her as something cool and dry flicked over his cheek and into his ear. "You are mine," she hissed.

He tried to answer, but his mouth wouldn't work, and the room grew dark around him.

The creature, the boy, appeared and bowed low before Ana as she sat at the table and picked at the dark fruit. She could sense the trepidation, the uncertainty, and knew she would be disappointed as she followed the shadows back to the royal suite in the castle.

She looked over the room, allowing her anger to flare, and the woman cowered at her feet. She sighed, and the woman flinched. "This is not what I asked of you," she said, allowing the darkness of her voice to fill the room.

"I wanted him."

"And you may keep him. But we need to find a way for him to give the crown to Ed, not die before he can give it up. The people will blame me, and I won't have it." Ana tried to keep her voice level, but it was hard.

"You promised me," Dahli hissed.

Ana turned from the prone man on the bed to the woman at her feet. "Do not question me or my gifts." She leaned forward. "Or I shall take them away."

She looked up then with hard eyes.

"I can anchor you with another."

"I like this anchor."

Ana sighed again. "You are to do as you are told. Or I will take him away."

The woman looked back to the floor.

The child standing in the corner smiled and stepped forward. "You can use me, Majesty. I can be anyone you choose." She bowed her head and then became Belle, then Dahli, and before Ana could wonder at how to use this child, she turned into Dray.

"Enough!" she bellowed, and the remaining candle went out.

"Dahli?" the regent whispered from the bed. He sounded like a child. In some ways, Ana was happy with such an outcome, but she needed him to hand it over. Or for Ed to take it. Maybe she could find another way.

"Husband," Dahli purred, standing slowly and running her hand along his arm. He sighed, and Ana put her hand on the other woman's hand to stop the movement. The regent cried out, and Ana glared at the other woman as a torch sparked to life. Dahli flinched beneath her hold as shadows moved around the bed. "I will do as you wish," she whispered.

The uncertainty of the creature anchored to this world with Dahli overwhelmed Ana for a moment. She wanted to allow it to do as it saw fit, as long as it ended with the crown being handed to Ed. "If you go against me again, I will end this arrangement."

They bowed before her, awkward and conflicted. Ana nodded once and walked from the room, dragging the child with her. They waited. She could feel their eagerness to please, the excitement of what they might do.

"Majesty," they hissed, bending forward. "Tell me what you want of me."

She thought of Belle, but Ed needed her. "Do not do that again," she whispered.

The creature before her bowed low. "Majesty, let me help you."

"You do help. Watch over them." She indicated the room where she had left Dahli with the regent. "Has he seen what you are?"

She bowed her head.

"And Dahli?"

She shook her head slowly from side to side. "But he knows something."

"She is to be careful. You are to be careful, but not too careful. I want him nervous and watching."

She bowed her head again and headed to the room.

"Ruth," Ana called after her. "I may call you again."

"Majesty," she said with a slight tip of her head. A black tongue flicked out through her lips before she was gone.

From the regent's balcony, Ana looked over a city she didn't know and rarely got to see. She had visited much of it, yet she hadn't seen it. Little corners, deep shadows. So briefly she had seen Dray, and he had looked worried. Did he not know she would look out for him as she did for Ed?

If this creature was not doing as they were told, she suddenly wondered if the others weren't as well. She appeared in the small attic room beside the sleeping soldier. The curtains were drawn on the larger bed, although she could only hear sleeping noises from within. The dagger pressed into her side. Kemp was nowhere to be seen, and she wondered if she had made a mistake. If they weren't helping her as she thought they were. Should she send them back? Could she, if she wanted to?

Kemp appeared before her, they appeared, as the creature who had looked after her so well before. She stepped forward from the shadows, her hands outstretched, and the creature took them, turning them to look them over. Then the creature held her hands tight.

"Majesty," they breathed, the devotion and loyalty filling the room and her heart. She breathed out. Why did she have such doubts? She knew what and who she was. She knew what she was to do. She knew what she could do.

Ana raised a clawed hand to her cheek and felt the power of the darkness, the link to the beyond. She longed for the little room, and yet she needed the shadows.

"I will take you, Majesty."

She nodded once, and as the shadows closed around them and they blinked from the room, she was sure Dray had watched her.

Ana sighed with the relief of being in the darkness. She thought of the little room and wondered if she could hide Dray away there. Had her mother hidden her father at any stage? Had he known what she really was? She had been like Ana, and yet so different.

The mirror before her caught her eye. Despite not being bright, the reflection seemed even duller than it had been before. She blinked and then raised a hand to her image. She turned the hand slowly before her. Her nails were black, her skin grey. But the image was something else entirely.

"Are you me or am I you?" she asked the creature before her. It was taller, darker, broader than the creatures she had called. Those she had created by anchoring them to her world and allowing them to travel between the two.

"Both are true," the creature hissed from beyond the mirror. "I become stronger as you become stronger."

"Then I am just as those I create?"

"Oh, my little queen, you are so much more," the voice purred from the glass, and Ana stepped forward. The creature who had travelled with her, Kemp, was gone, but she didn't miss him.

She reached clawed fingers towards her reflection, but instead of glass they touched cold, leathery skin. She locked fingers. Hers appeared longer as they moved between the black, narrow, long-clawed fingers that reached out to meet her. The cold skin met her palm, and she looked up into the grinning face, the eyes far blacker than anything she had seen in Ende or Salima. In her heart, Ana saw what she was. She stared harder, understanding so much more than she had before. As though she could see so much further. She stretched her neck from side to side, the weary feeling she had been carrying lifting from her shoulders as she looked herself in the eye. Nose to nose, hands still clasped.

Ana shivered as a hand reached forward and took the dagger from her belt. She felt a loss as it was taken, noticed the lack of it pressing against her skin.

"He did not give it," she hissed, her tongue strangely dry as it brushed over Ana's skin. "He did not take it." Her voice was lower, dangerous.

"No," Ana said. "He fears me."

"As it should be, for you are his queen."

Ana wondered if she was right, if the world would come to the end as she had dreamt. Dray amidst a battlefield, his face bloody. For a moment she felt like the girl who had seen him in the lord's office, a stranger with a scarred face. But he wasn't. He would never be a stranger. She had always known Dray—she would always need him.

"Like the boy?" her reflection asked, now free of the mirror. "He can only be King if you allow it to be so."

"All of this was for Ed," Ana whispered, finding the long tongue difficult to speak with, her voice more like a hiss. "Ed must be king!" she growled, allowing herself to let go.

The creature before her squeezed her hand tighter. The long claws cut into her skin. Ana could feel the blood flowing between them, dripping onto the floor. She reached for the dagger, but it was gone.

"He is mine," she hissed.

"He is ours," the reflection purred. "It is all ours."

"Ours," Ana repeated.

"Ours."

Ana blinked in the dim light of the room. The image before her had gone, and she ran her own tongue over her dry lips. She turned back to the table and reached for a goblet to find her hand bloody, dark red dripping from deep puncture wounds. She took the goblet with the other hand and gulped down the wine. It barely wet her lips, and yet it was satisfying. She appeared to be herself again, although her skin was still pale and her nails dark.

Looking into the mirror, she took a step forward. She placed her bloody hand against the icy glass. Dray came into focus, sleeping peacefully, although she was sure she could see the red and angry scar across his face.

"Ours," she whispered as the image faded and a long black tongue licked over her dry lips.

24

Forest looked at the girl sitting with the dragon and tried to curb his jealousy. They were spending just as much time with him, and it was all focused on trying to find Ed, but she looked at him differently. It hurt him more than he had realised it could. He had known one day she would discover who she was, and in many ways it would be fitting that she didn't look at him the same when she learned she was the princess. But she wasn't, although she was. She wasn't the king's daughter; she was the dragon's daughter. She was his daughter.

"What is it, Papa?" she asked.

He tried to smile, but he had heard news and wasn't sure how to tell her. Partly because he knew she would leave and it wasn't safe, no matter what skill she had. With a sword or with wings.

"Ed," he murmured.

She leapt to her feet, and he tried to keep himself together when he just wanted to wrap his arms around her and run. They had lived in a small village far to the south, where he had grown up before becoming a soldier. They could return there and no one need know. He looked up at Ende's knowing look and tried not to sigh.

"He has been meeting with the people."

"What?" she demanded. "Where?"

"In the city."

"Here?"

"You knew he was close," he said, wondering at all the questions and how long he would have before she bolted for the door. But instead she looked to Ende.

"I had heard the same news," Ende admitted, and she glared at him, the room warming with her anger. "Is it time to bring him back to the castle?"

"Will he be safe?" Salima blurted.

"Is it enough?" Forest asked. He might have been meeting with the people, and from what Forest had picked up amongst the soldiers, they believed he was the king. But would they back him if required? Would it be enough, or would the regent have a way to discredit him? In all the talk of the imposter, it had been forgotten that the king was missing, and no one seemed to be doing anything to try and find him. No one. Not the soldiers, not the regent, not even the mage. The focus of the crown was to disprove that this man was the king he claimed to be.

More and more of the people queried whether he was still the boy they had been led to believe he was. There was more open talk in the castle of the regent and what he might be hiding, why he hadn't supported his brother's son.

"The regent will have to step down," Forest said.

Ende nodded once.

"Is that what Ana plans?"

"Why do you ask that?" Salima asked. "She is helping Ed."

"But how is she helping? What is she doing other than scaring people with her shadows? Does she plan to kill the regent?" Forest asked.

"If she did, he would already be dead," Ende said matter-of-factly. "And the people would blame the witch for his demise, and that might not help Ed either."

"He seems distracted by his new wife," Forest said, "and yet…"

"What is it?" Ende stood, and Forest was reminded just how big a man he was.

"There was talk amongst the soldiers that he might not be as trusting of the new bride as first thought. He shies away from her when she tries to touch him. She has taken on a maid, an unknown."

"Did she come from the forest?" Salima asked, but he shook his head.

"She just appeared."

"Do you think Ana had something to do with that?" she asked.

"Now you think she is busy giving maids to the regent's new wife. How clever is this woman?" Forest looked around, a little nervous that she might appear from the shadows again, then disappointed when she wasn't there. He turned back to Ende's raised eyebrows. "What do you think?" he asked the tall man.

Blowing out a long breath that warmed the room further, Ende sat back down.

"Can we ask her?" Salima asked quietly.

"Do you want to bring her here?" Forest asked, wondering what his daughter, Ende's daughter, really thought of the woman. They had seemed close, and yet Salima was scared of her. "Did you see her dreams?" he asked, thinking of the time Salima had slept with her when she was recovering from the ice. Before the darkness and her magic had seemed to take hold.

The girl nodded, but looked to Ende.

"The Walk," the dragon murmured.

"And more. Some of it I didn't understand; some of it hadn't happened."

"What hadn't happened?" Forest asked gently, stepping forward.

The girl lifted a hand to her cheek. "The soldier," she whispered.

"Dray?" Ende asked. "You saw him injured or scarred?"

"It was a battle, a big fight in the mist. Ana was lost and scared, and then Dray was standing in the middle of it all, his face cut here." She indicated the slice across his face. "Blood dripped down his face, and she screamed."

"That was when she woke. I thought she had seen something truly terrifying."

"It was," Salima breathed. He could see her heart racing as she reached for Ende's hand. "She thought he was lost."

"Maybe we need to make sure the soldier is on board," Forest said.

"He wouldn't leave the king unprotected," Ende insisted.

"You're sure?"

The dragon nodded. "But there is a link, and one we may be able to use if we need to."

"Ana won't like that," Salima said.

"Ana might not have the choice," Forest said. "Get your sword. We are going to find the king."

Salima grinned at him, but she remained by the dragon, holding his hand tight.

"Did she really think him lost?" he asked as she tied the sword to her belt. His hand wrapped tight around the handle of his own, just to reassure himself it was there.

"I think it would kill her if he was lost," she whispered, looking up at the dragon rather than at Forest, and he nodded. Now they just had to make it out of the castle unseen, to find a king hiding amongst the people before the regent worked out where he was.

It was Kemp who had guided them to a different shop this time, although the people gathering in the street were a good indication that something was going on. They worked their way through the people, Dray more nervous than he should have been at the crowd, worried they might not be as trusting of the king as they appeared.

The soldier standing by the door surprised him. It wasn't someone he immediately recognised, but Kemp nodded to the man and they continued inside. When they entered the space, there were only more soldiers inside. Dray turned a hard look on Kemp, who stared back and bowed his head. No matter what he thought of what Ana had done to the man, he was Dray's man, if only because she had declared it to be so.

"There is something going on with the regent," one man said, stepping forward.

"What kind of something?" Dray asked.

"He isn't quite himself, nor those around him."

Dray waited. He could do with Barlow at this moment, and he wondered where the man might be. They were to be looking after the king together, helping him find a voice amongst the people. Despite being in a room full of soldiers, Dray wasn't sure he could trust any of them.

"The wife," the soldier said.

"Dahli," Ed answered.

The soldier nodded. "She has sent her brother back to the trees."

"That is not so unusual," Belle said. "She hardly liked the man, and he didn't treat her very well."

"He was still claiming he had been tricked."

"I am sure my uncle set him straight on that matter."

The men looked amongst themselves, and Ed stood taller. "You don't believe I am the king?"

Dray scanned the room again, subtly bowing his head when he made eye contact with Kemp. The creature disguised as a man moved as though to the door, but put himself between Ed and the group, his hand on his arm.

"We believe," the soldier stuttered, and several of the others nodded. "But proving it without it looking like the witch has tricked the whole kingdom is another matter."

"What is different about the regent?" Dray asked, hoping the soldier didn't disappear with the king before the others and break the small amount of trust they seemed to be building.

"He's nervous," one suggested from across the room.

"Ana," Ed breathed. Kemp nodded.

"Will she convince him to hand the crown back?" Belle asked.

"We can only hope, but we have more of the people behind us," Ed said, looking the men over. They nodded.

"But the regent knows you are here, and he wants you stopped."

"Because he knows who I am and what it would mean for him."

"Either way," the soldier continued, "he wants you removed and the people dispersed."

"And what will you do?" Dray asked. Kemp stepped forward. Dray put up a hand, and Kemp bowed his head.

"Most of the kingdom support you, Your Majesty," the soldier said, his fist to his chest as he bowed. Ed let out an audible sigh. "We have the people behind you. We now just need to get you back inside the castle and convince the regent he is no longer needed."

"What men does he have behind him?" Dray asked.

"Not many, although it is hard to be sure," the man admitted. "Field was clearly his, but since his disappearance, no one will willingly go against or support the man in fear of what the witch might do."

Dray took a step forward, but it was Kemp's hand on his arm holding him back, and he gave a small shake of his head. He wondered at the movement, as though the man were still a man, when Dray knew very well he was not.

There was a murmuring of increased noise coming from outside the building, and Dray nodded to Kemp to check it out. Ana could defend herself well enough against these men. He needed to find the king allies first, not more enemies.

Then Ende, Forest and Salima entered the room. The girl even carried a sword, and Dray wondered what she truly was as she threw herself at Ed. He smiled as he squeezed her in return. She released him sooner than Dray expected, bowed her head and then stepped back to stand between the two men.

"We are here to help, Your Majesty," she said.

Ende nodded slowly, and Forest moved forward to put his hand on Ed's shoulder. "I am so pleased to see you safe."

"Thank you," Ed said.

"How did you find us?" Dray asked.

"Half the kingdom knows where you are, including your uncle," Forest replied.

"What is the plan?" Dray asked.

"We put him before the regent, with the people behind him."

"It can't be that easy," the soldier murmured. "Or we could have done so before. I would suggest we assess what has happened to the regent and see if we can use that to our advantage."

"Why don't we ask the people?" Ed said, indicating the people outside filling the streets. "Could we take a representative?"

"And have the regent kill them on the spot?"

"Ana would know," Salima whispered, and Dray looked her over.

Something moved in the shadows, as though called by the thought. Dray looked to Kemp, but he moved to shield the king with his body. Ana wouldn't allow anything to harm him. "Can you give us some time to discuss this?" he asked the soldier. Although he seemed reluctant, he called the other soldiers from the room.

Forest and Ende remained with them, and despite the soldiers leaving, the room still felt crowded as Ana stepped from the shadows. But she didn't look at him. She looked at Ed, and Kemp growled.

They waited in silence until Kemp stepped forward. "You are not my queen," he hissed, and Dray noticed Salima move closer to Ende.

"She has sent me," Ana whispered. Her voice was soft, yet it contained the same hiss of the soldier, another of her creatures. "I thought you would find me more comfortable this way," she continued, pulling the cloak closer around her, and Dray felt an uncertainty he hadn't in some time. He'd had doubts about Ana, many at times, but this was something else.

"Child," the soldier hissed. "Tell us what my queen desires."

"For the king to be safe. We have the uncle," she said with a grin that scared Dray far more than he would like to admit. The girl's dark tongue licked her lips, and she changed before his eyes. The cloak slipped away as the hair changed to something curly and fair; she was just a girl. But as a long tongue like the shadow monsters' licked at her face, Dray barely controlled his shiver.

"Where is she?" he asked, and she turned her gaze to him for the first time. "Ana."

"You would question my queen," she hissed, growing somewhat, her skin becoming darker. Then Kemp was standing before him.

"He is protected. She has directed me."

The creature before them nodded. "She has gone to where she is safe. She has left the regent to us."

"What have you done?" Ed asked, stepping forward. "She wouldn't allow him hurt; it would destroy any chance I have."

The creature blinked at him, taking him in as though she was weighing whether to answer. "She trusts us."

Dray could feel the room getting warmer, and he wasn't sure if it was the dragon or the fear of what Ana had started. She had dragged these creatures here to help Ed, but were they helping or acting for their own benefit? She had gone somewhere, but had they put her there instead of her choosing to go?

"Take me to her," he demanded.

Kemp blinked slowly and then nodded once, putting his hand to Dray's arm. The room darkened around him as he saw Ed reach for him.

"Will he be safe?" he asked, too late, as he left them far behind.

"She will not hurt him," Ana's voice echoed through the darkness. He had wanted so desperately to see her, and now he was lost, although he could feel the tight hold and the sharp claws of the creature at his arm. "You should not have brought him here."

"The connection is strong. My master's wish is mine," the creature hissed, and then Dray focused on the grey world around him. Although it was difficult to focus, it was as though he stood in a thick fog.

"Where are we?" he asked Ana's outline before him.

"Somewhere I can be myself," she whispered. He heard the difference in her voice, the soft hiss, the deep dark shadows that surrounded them echoing in her voice. "Dray," she breathed, her hands in his. They weren't the hands he remembered. Her fingers were longer, her nails sharp. Her hand was wet, and as he turned it, trying hard to see what it was, she flinched and pulled away from him.

"Ana," he said softly, reaching for her in the dark. "Tell me what you are doing."

"Helping the king," she said.

"How is this helping?" he asked, allowing his frustration to be heard. "The king is still hiding away, the regent not himself."

"Dahli," she growled, and he stepped back. "She is mine, and she will do as she is told."

"Ana?" Dray asked into the darkness.

"Majesty is strong," the creature beside him hissed. "She will save your king."

Dray sighed. "Why does she come here?" He was still unable to make out anything through the darkness.

"She is happy here. She is stronger here."

"What if I stayed?" he said, unsure what he was asking.

"You will die," the creature hissed softly, "and my queen will not allow it."

When the fog cleared, he was standing in the room with the king and the others. The girl still stood before them, wearily looking at the creature beside him.

"You are to do what your queen demands," it hissed.

She smiled up at him and stepped back into the shadows. "I only do as my queen demands," she hissed and was gone.

"Where did you go?" Ed asked.

Dray shook his head and ran his hand through his hair. He was losing himself. He had no idea what he was doing, whom he was supporting.

"What has she become?" Ende asked. Dray turned slowly as the creature dropped his arm and stepped away, becoming the soldier again. The girl sucked in a breath.

"He is here to protect us," Ed said, indicating the man.

"She sent him," Ende said. "She is directing everything. How can you be sure that she protects you?"

The soldier stepped forward and Dray held out a hand, halting his movement. "Master," he hissed, bowing his head. Dray looked at him. "Captain," he corrected himself, sounding more like the man he had been before.

"She has given you your own pet?" Ende growled. "You trust her too much. She is not what she was."

"No," Dray admitted, "she is not. But she works to save the king."

"Are you certain?"

Dray wanted to be, but as he looked over the strange dark liquid on his hand, he wasn't sure in that moment that she had as much control over her own creatures as she claimed.

25

Ana stood on the balcony in the cool afternoon breeze, allowing it to pull at her hair. For a moment, she was reminded of the sheer drops she had grown up with, surprised that she no longer felt the same sense of fear about anything in her life. Except, perhaps, for Dray. She couldn't understand why that remained when all other fear had left her.

He had looked so worried when he had appeared in the shadows. His focus should have been on the king. Did he fear she wasn't doing as she had promised?

Why would her creature bring him to such a place? Or at least try, for he was still a man and couldn't reach her. In many ways, she was relieved. She didn't want him to see her as she was now, and yet her own creature had felt the connection between them. It had been enough to bring them so close.

The girl should have been enough to keep them placated. Ruth appeared beside her then as called. The other was taking too long to respond to her call, and she was unsure how to punish such a defiance. She needed the woman. She needed to be close to the regent.

The girl beside her continued to smile.

"Be Dahli," Ana commanded, and the face turned to one of concentration before it became more tanned, the freckles fading. The girl's shape shifted to one of a woman, and she smiled again from her new face.

She bowed awkwardly, the shadows moving around her. Ana breathed out slowly, trying to calm the beating of her heart.

The shadows formed into a creature, and she looked the maid over. They bowed before her. "Majesty," they hissed.

"I did not call you," she said. "Where is the one I want?"

"With the regent, on the throne."

Ana growled, and the creature remained too still. "What has happened?" she asked.

"It appears the little girl has found her magic," they hissed.

Ana sighed.

"It is not as yours, Majesty. She is not as strong as you."

"But she will use it against us, against the king." The anger was building inside her, and she wanted to release it on someone.

The creature bowed her head. Ana was very tempted to stomp her foot. Why was no one doing as they should?

"Return to the mage. I shall be there directly."

The creature disappeared.

She turned back to the new Dahli. "You will hold this shape until I tell you otherwise," she commanded. The woman blinked dark eyes at her, black eyes.

Ana moved in a breath to the throne room, where too many people stood around the regent. They were quiet, unnervingly so. As she took a step forward, he looked up slowly, his eyes vacant. The woman whose hand he held stood with him. She grinned, and Ana glared at her.

"You have no hold over him," the creature hissed, and Ana wondered at the strength of the woman within.

The regent remained silent. Ana heard movement behind her and turned on the crowd. "Go," she hissed, and they turned and ran.

"He is mine," the creature hissed, holding tighter to the regent's hand as the man winced.

"What have you done?" Ana growled.

"You wanted him compliant."

"I wanted him scared," Ana hissed, feeling the darkness grow inside her. Her link to the beyond grew stronger. "He must hand the crown to the boy."

"Must he? We could rule through him."

Ana reached out a hand, clenched it into a fist and dragged it back towards her chest. The creature stumbled forward, pulling the regent to the floor. He barely moved to right himself.

The creature before her shifted, trying to free itself from her hold even though Ana hadn't laid a finger on her.

"What did you do?" Ana demanded.

"I told him what I was. I planted a fear so deep inside him that he will never act against me."

Ana tightened her hold.

"Us—you, Majesty."

"You useless beast. Who are you to go against me?"

"I would be Queen of this world," she hissed, then whimpered. The regent looked up, his eyes unfocused.

"Now," Ana breathed. The girl, the new Dahli, raced into the room.

"My love," she cried, taking the regent in her arms and pressing his face to her bosom.

"Remove it," Ana hissed.

The creature in her hold started to laugh, the odd hissing sound filling the room. She looked to the girl, who nodded once and extended her long forked tongue, which she pushed into the regent's ear. He looked up at her as though seeing her for the first time.

"Dahli," he whispered. "What has happened?"

"You have been unwell," she returned, her voice every bit Dahli's, and the creature in Ana's hold growled again. "It tried to trick you," the girl said, holding him tighter. "Help us!" she cried.

Soldiers ran into the room, then halted as Ana squeezed her hold tighter and the creature fell to her knees. She tried to change, a flash of Dahli appearing on her face before it was gone. The regent stood shakily, pushing the woman behind him.

"You tricked me," he spat. "The witch is behind this," he growled, and Ana heard swords being drawn.

"Wait," the new Dahli said, clinging to his arm. "She appears to be helping."

"This creature is not mine," Ana hissed, her claws starting to dig into the creature's skin as she squeezed her hand tighter and tighter. The creature groaned and then cried out.

"Kill it," the girl said.

"No, Majesty. I shall do as you bid," it pleaded.

Ana released her hold, and as her blood dripped onto the floor, the creature rose slowly to her feet. She bowed her head, but Ana could taste the deception in the air, the greed for what should be Ana's. She sliced her hand through the air, and a dark wound opened across the creature's chest. It screamed as Ana sliced again and again, cutting it to pieces. Until there was nothing left but shadows. Then Ana growled out her anger, and the shadows dissipated.

The regent stared at her, the overwhelming fear in the room evident on his face. The woman clung to his side. Ana nodded once, then took a shaky step forward as the soldiers closed in around her.

The maid's creature appeared, wrapping long dark arms around her, and they were gone.

She breathed out her relief as she fell to the floor of her dark world. Breathing in the dark shadows, she could feel herself calming and growing stronger.

"Can you trust the little one?" the maid asked.

"I wondered if I could ever trust you," Ana replied.

"Majesty," she bowed. "I am yours."

"You have seen what will happen if you are not," Ana returned, climbing to her feet and brushing down her skirt. She ran her fingers through her hair before noticing the blood on her hand. The creature poured wine into a goblet from an ornate bottle without the request being spoken and held it out to her with her head bowed.

"They are gone," it whispered.

"In this world and theirs," Ana said, taking the offered cup with her bloody hand. "The child will be a better companion for the man for now. She might help convince him to give it up."

"Is that truly all you want, Majesty?"

"I need the crown to go to the king. I need the people behind him."

"They appear to be."

"Tell me of the girl's sister," Ana prompted. "What power does she have?"

"Something very different, which does not share the beyond."

"As does the girl. But the sister has stolen it, and she may not be able to keep it. Ensure the mage does not use it to harm Ed. The end is near, and I will not have it jeopardised."

"Majesty," they hissed, bowing low, the movement fluid and natural in this world. Ana smiled.

"You may go."

In a blink, the creature who had wanted her harmed not so long ago was gone and knew to do her bidding. She opened her fingers to reveal a small shadow, all that remained of the woman and creature who had worked against her. She closed her hand around it as it screamed, and an odd silence filled the world. She was the queen, after all. If they would not follow her, they would not follow anyone.

26

The regent stood in the throne room looking over the men who surrounded him. The woman beside him dropped to the floor with a sigh, as though the weight of the world pushed down on her. He knelt and put his arm around her shoulders, helping her back to her feet. She nodded her thanks and clung to his arm across her.

"She was pretending to be me," she whispered, her voice shaking as she looked up at him with wet eyes. He pulled her close and breathed in her subtle citrus scent. Something very odd had been happening.

"Did she just save me?" he asked the men in the room. They turned to look at him and then back to where the witch had been.

"I think so," one man murmured. "What was that thing?"

The woman in his arms whimpered.

"Have you not seen them before? She brought them to the throne room often enough. Field," he added in a hushed tone, wondering if the woman he had been kissing was in fact the major. He shivered, and the woman in his arms looked up at him.

"Would you like to return to the room?" he asked her.

She shook her head vigorously as she stepped back from him. "I don't want to go anywhere on my own. What if another one of those creatures appears?"

He nodded and pulled her close again, then led her to the seat beside his. "Fetch the woman some wine," he directed one of the soldiers. "I could do with some myself." He felt dry, as though he hadn't eaten or drunk anything for days. "What happened?" he asked.

"She…" Dahli stammered. "It tricked you into believing it was me."

"Where is the maid?" he asked.

"What maid?" she returned, looking around the room.

"You had a maid," he said, looking at her seriously. "How can I be sure it is you?" he asked, and she burst into fresh tears.

"How do I know you are the regent?" she sobbed. "Or that any of these men are not soldiers but more creatures?"

He shook his head then, reaching for her hand, but she pulled away from him. "I don't know who to trust," she murmured as the tears continued to stream down her cheeks. "And you don't trust me."

"Your Highness," a soldier interrupted, handing her a cup. She sipped at it slowly as Thom took the one offered him and gulped it down. The world was not as it was, not even a little, and he couldn't quite understand what he could do to put it back.

"Send the mage," he said, waving the man away.

"Would he know how to stop her?" another asked, stepping forward. When he raised his gaze, the man lowered his. "I am sorry, Your Highness, but things are not as they were."

"No," he muttered, putting the now-empty goblet back to his lips. He looked at it with disappointment and waved the man forward. "Find some more," he said, handing him the cup. The man looked at it as though this was not what he was for, but he left the room, cup in hand.

"There were people here," Thom continued, standing again, and the movement made his wife flinch. "Where did they go?"

"You were not behaving as yourself," a soldier muttered, looking from him to his wife and back. "Neither of you."

"I would think that creature had some spell over me."

"Can we be sure that it no longer has a hold?" the man asked.

Thom took several steps forward, hoping to intimidate the man, but he held his ground.

"What news of the imposter?" he snapped, too close to the man.

"He meets with people in the city. We went to where he met before, but they had moved. We have managed to stop him talking with them so far."

"Today, but what of all the other talks?"

"I am sure they understand he is not the king. He does not appear to have made any promises to them. Just listened."

"Listened!" Thom bellowed. "Too much like his father."

He turned back to the man, but he stood as he had, not indicating that he had any real idea as to what Thom had just given away.

"What does he want?" Dahli asked, clinging to her goblet still.

"Who?" he asked.

"The boy pretending to be King. What does he hope to gain?"

"The throne, my lady," the soldier said, but his eyes were on Thom.

"Do you think he could get it?"

The man tilted his head a little to the side as though thinking it over. "It may depend on how many he can convince. The people won't support a bloody uprising," he added.

"Are you sure?" Dahli asked, stepping forward. "If they believe the imposter is the king, would they not try to remove the uncle who will not step aside for him?"

Thom blinked at her for a moment, but she came up beside him and slipped her arm through his, the feeling warm and comforting. He sighed with the relief of it, as though he hadn't seen this woman in so long. He wondered then how the creature had managed to get so close.

"Where were you?" he asked.

"My love?"

"While that creature tried to ruin me, where were you?"

"Never close enough." She sighed, her hands slipping from their hold. He put his hand on hers, and she smiled up at him.

"What do we do?" he asked the soldier as the mage appeared in the doorway, his little girl beside him. The woman at his arm clung a little tighter. "He won't hurt you," he whispered.

"Are you sure? He seems to work just as much with the shadows as the witch does."

Thom looked to the man standing at the edge of the room. the girl with him even more confident than the last time he had seen her. Where had the other one gone? "Do you think the people will rise up?" he asked, returning his attention to the soldier.

"It is hard to say."

"Then find out," he growled. The man slammed his fist to his chest, bowed his head and headed for the door, many of the soldiers going with him. "Leave men on every door," he called after him, and the man waved at two men who moved back to the door.

"What has happened?" the mage asked, and Dahli pulled in tighter against Thom.

"The witch was here, only she was saving me from one of your creatures."

The girl looked at his wife, and he glared at her. "Why are you here?" he asked.

"She is important in this," the mage answered for her, but her eyes never left Dahli. "What did Ana do?" he asked, too calm in his tone, as though he was bored by the events.

"One of your creatures was pretending to be my wife," Thom snapped. "The witch destroyed it."

"Destroyed it?" the mage asked slowly, turning to the girl. "How?"

He waved his arms around, trying to repeat what she had done. "I don't know," he muttered. "She just tore it to shreds until there was nothing left. Not even a shadow."

"She is stronger than I thought possible," the mage murmured. "Why would she save you? She wants the crown for the boy."

"Maybe she doesn't want to start a war."

"Maybe she already has," the mage returned, and the woman beside Thom let out a squeak. He looked down at her, worried she had entered far more than she'd expected, when he noticed the girl had stepped up close and was looking her over.

"What are you doing?" he growled.

"I can feel her," the girl whispered, reaching out a hand, but the regent moved Dahli out of the girl's reach.

"You will do no such thing."

"I know her as I know myself."

"We have never met," Dahli squeaked.

Thom put himself between them but held Dahli out by the shoulders to look her over properly. She blinked her deep brown eyes at him, and he had the sudden image of black eyes and a long black tongue. He grabbed at her face, and she squealed. "Show me your tongue," he growled.

She opened her mouth without question as large tears tracked down her cheeks. He released her face, and she shook from his hold. "You don't trust me," she stammered. "I would be better with the witch if this is how you treat me." She sucked in a sob and wiped her hand over her nose. Her chest rose with obvious fear. "My brother even treated me better than this. He can take me back to the forest."

"He's gone," Thom said, unsure how he knew such a thing.

"What?" She blinked back more tears. "When?"

A soldier shuffled by the door, drawing her attention, and she raced towards him. "Help me," she begged. "Tell my brother what has happened."

"He has gone, my lady."

"When?" she pleaded, desperation making her voice break. Thom wondered why he didn't trust her. He had dragged her into this, made her his wife, put her at the mercy of the witch.

"Dahli," he said softly, stepping towards her, but she flinched away, standing closer to the soldier. "I'm sorry, it has been a difficult time."

She burst into sobs again, and the soldier looked uncomfortably between them. Thom took her in his arms then and pulled her back to his chest. She was so vulnerable, so young, and he wondered why he had thought marrying her would be a good idea. It had all been lust, and now he didn't want her in danger. He looked back at the mage and the girl, who continued to stare at Dahli.

"Find the boy," he declared. "I don't care how you do it. Find him. End him and this nightmare."

The mage bowed his head and shuffled towards the door. The girl waited too long before she followed, and Dahli shivered in his arms.

"What is she?" Dahli asked. "Could she be another witch? I thought the mage supported you, yet he keeps bringing these women in who could harm you."

"That isn't what he does," Thom whispered, pulling her closer. But he wondered if she was right. First Ana and then this girl, and there was something very odd about her. At least the shadow creature wasn't with the mage. But Thom had seen it with Ana when she had destroyed the creature; it had taken her away. Maybe she was working more closely with the mage than he realised. The idea made him very nervous.

"What did you get a sense of?" the mage asked the girl as they entered the workshop. He breathed in the scent of it, frustrated that he had been called away. He wasn't getting a clear idea of what Ana hoped to achieve. She was trying to help the boy, yet she had saved the regent from the shadows.

None of it made any sense. He watched the girl as she walked away from him rather than answer his questions, and he wondered if she had been another mistake. Already she was too sure of herself. He had sensed a magic, yet she was very different from

Ana. She entered the bedroom she had shared with her sister, the one Ana had occupied not so long ago, and yet it felt like an age.

He followed her into the room as she sat on a bed, closed her eyes and dragged in a deep breath.

"Well?' he demanded, a little pleased that she jumped at the sound of his voice.

"Ruth," she whispered.

"You felt Ruth?"

She sighed and opened her eyes. "There was something of her in the room, in the woman, and yet it wasn't her."

"Are you certain?"

She shook her head. "What if the witch turned her into a creature and then killed her? It would be her acting against us, not helping the regent."

"Do we know if Ana can create such creatures?" he asked, reminded of the soldier being devoured by the shadows. Yet the soldier had not reappeared. The mage only knew of two; one he had created while the other had formed a bond on its own. It was almost as though they needed permission, and he doubted Ana would give permission to something that would destroy the boy.

"Call your creature," the girl demanded, her bright eyes staring him down. They glowed golden like sunshine, and he was reminded of Ana and her green eyes that seemed to glow brighter every time he saw her.

"I doubt it comes…" He stopped as it appeared before her, bowing its head awkwardly.

"Mistress," it hissed.

"Where is my sister?" she demanded, standing up from the bed, and the mage stepped forward as the creature's grin widened. He wondered just what he would do for this girl.

"She is better than you. She is stronger than you. She is needed and you are not."

Her mouth dropped open as the creature taunted her. "I am strong," she murmured, then clenched her jaw closed again.

"Majesty has seen something great in her."

"Then she didn't destroy her?" the mage asked. The creature turned black shiny eyes on him, and he missed his little maid. The eyes blinked as though reading his thoughts, but did not answer his request. She was lost.

"She will not be defied."

"Then something did upset her, went against her?"

"If she can't control the shadows, they will not exist," the creature returned. "She has control. She is stronger."

"The shadows?" the mage asked, his mouth drying. "How many does she control?"

"All of them," it hissed, and then turned back to the girl. "I will not answer to you." It leaned forward, flicking a black tongue over her face, and she shivered as it touched her skin. "You are nothing."

The mage felt the spark before he saw it, a bright light that made the creature shy away, but it lasted only seconds. The creature screamed; an ear-piercing sound that made the girl put her hands over her ears before it disappeared.

"It will not come again," he snapped.

"We don't need it," the girl said, but her strength and confidence appeared to have disappeared with the creature. He wondered if she was as strong as he had thought she was.

27

Barlow pushed his way into the room. "The crowd is growing. If the regent hasn't worked out where you are, it is only a matter of time."

"If he does know, what will he do?" Ed asked, looking around the small group. He could hear the crowd in the street beyond.

"Something has occurred in the throne room," Barlow said.

"Ana," Dray said, and Barlow turned to him, nodding. Ed wondered how the man always knew when she was involved, but then she nearly always was.

"She appeared to help the regent."

"Help him how?" Ed asked, stepping forward. While it might have appeared as though she helped him, he doubted she had. But then, he wasn't really sure what she was.

"The wife was one of her creatures."

"Dahli?" Dray asked, looking at Ed.

"So, it seems. She was challenged, and she took on the witch, who…" Barlow shook his head slowly, and Ed wondered if she had been hurt.

"What happened?" he blurted after too long a silence.

"She destroyed the creature with a move of her hand."

"What?" Belle asked, stepping forward.

The soldier moved his hand in front of him, a wave really.

"Did you see it?" Dray asked.

"There are men I trust all over the castle, and the regent said something that indicated he knows you are the king. Word has spread quickly."

"But is it enough?" Ed asked. "Ana helping, the regent's admission, the soldiers backing me. Will it be enough to get my crown back?"

Ana appeared in the middle of the room, and they all took a step back, Dray included. Although Ed expected sad eyes, she only had dark eyes focused on him. It took a moment, and he wondered if it was the pretender again, for her eyes had always been green, even when he doubted her, when everything else had changed. As he thought it, they changed before him, glowing even brighter than before. Then a creature appeared beside her, falling to its knees.

Belle stepped forward then. Ed reached out a hand to stop her, but she was out of reach. The creature raised black eyes to her and leaned back. Was it afraid?

Ana leaned over it, her hand cupping its oversized face, sharp teeth apparent as its tongue licked the air. "Child," she whispered.

"She is too strong," it hissed.

Ana looked up at Belle, her face unreadable, but Belle stopped dead.

"She shines too bright," the creature continued.

"Rest. I shall deal with the girl."

"Majesty," the beast hissed, leaning forward, clinging to Ana, "you cannot."

"Go," Ana said more firmly, and as the creature disappeared from sight, she stood slowly. "I will not be dictated to," she growled. Belle took a small step back. The movement caught Ana's attention and she turned, then tilted her head a little to the side. "You shine brighter," she whispered, and Ed was sure there was a hiss to her voice like that of the creature.

"Are you helping the regent?" Belle asked.

Ana blinked slowly, and Ed could see a similarity between her and the creatures she called. She turned a hard glare on Ed as he tried to remain calm. She was just what he feared. With a small motion from her hand, Belle stumbled to the side and Ana marched forward. From the corner of his eye, Ed saw Dray put his hand to his blade, but his creature—the soldier who followed Ana—put a hand on his and stopped him.

"I am doing all that I can for you to be King," Ana said. Despite the fear that filled the room, her voice was calm and sweet, the girl from the mountains who had healed his shoulder.

"There is talk," Ed continued, trying to sound like the king he wanted to be.

"Is there?" she hummed. "If the shadows will not follow me, they cannot be trusted to keep you safe. The woman wanted more than I could give, more than I was willing to give, and so she was going to take it for herself."

"Dahli?" Dray asked softly.

"She is not what she was," Ana said, something softening as she looked at him. But the hardness returned as she returned her glare to Ed.

"Why did you help the regent?"

"I helped you by allowing him to think he is safe. You wanted to use me," she said, stepping forward, her voice soft, and his heart beat too fast. "You want me to get your crown."

Ed wanted to nod, but he wasn't sure her words meant what he thought they should. Was she getting it for him, or from him?

Standing far too close, Ana turned her head a little to the side, and he knew she was reading his every thought. She smiled then, a smile that scared him as much as the shadow creatures, which made her smile all the more. She knew what she did, and she knew what she did to him. He didn't know if he could trust her.

"The regent must give you the crown," she breathed, too close. He wanted desperately to step back, but he feared what she would do if he did. "The people trust you. They know you, and they will follow you. If the regent dies before he can hand you the crown, they will blame me and you will lose that trust. I must keep him alive to give you what is yours."

The silence in the room was almost as overwhelming as the woman pressed against him. Ed gulped down the growing fear and nodded once.

She smiled as she stepped back, then looked to the soldier, and Barlow's brow creased. "Watch them, protect them and do as your master orders."

"Majesty," he said with a bow of his head, and she disappeared.

Barlow turned slowly from Ed to Dray, and to the soldier he had placed to watch over them. His gaze stopped on the soldier, who bowed his head, but did not salute the captain as he should. Although he stepped closer, it was Dray who prevented the creature from doing anything.

"What do you think you are doing?" he asked the creature. It blinked at him, appearing like the man he had been and yet something very different.

"He couldn't be trusted as he was," Dray said quietly.

"You did this?" Barlow asked.

"He tried to kill me. Ana did this," he said, looking to the space where she had stood not so long ago.

"Despite all you hear, you trust her. What would it take to break that?" Barlow asked.

"Ana is something we should focus on later," Ed said. "My uncle has shown himself; we need to find a way to push him further. Ana will have a way to weaken him."

"She will have another creature close," Barlow said.

"Are you sure?"

"She just told you that the girl was untrustworthy and went against her. Yet the regent was holding his sobbing wife when we left him watched over by the guards of his choice."

"How could he believe such a thing?" Belle asked.

"The maid was blamed, but I think the maid is also one of her creatures."

Dray looked to the soldier at his side, who wasn't giving

anything away.

"You wouldn't tell us what she was doing, even if your master demanded it," Ed said, resenting the creature who had kept him safe so far.

It turned black eyes on him, but made no indication of agreement or not. He wanted to ask so much more, yet he knew where its loyalties lay, no matter whom it looked to or whom it looked like.

He looked around the room then. Ana had appeared with several of them previously, a show of power perhaps, and her words rang in his ear. She wanted more than for him to be King, and helping him was only helping herself.

"Don't doubt her," the soldier hissed. Ed looked up at the wide-eyed man and the growing anger on Dray's face. He doubted her more and more, although Ed knew it hurt him to do so. Yet he would never admit it.

He turned back to Belle as the noise outside the room started to increase. "What did you do?" he asked, but she took a step back from him. "Why did it react as it did to you?"

"I couldn't hurt such a creature," Belle whispered. She shook her head. "What do you think I could do?"

"You shine bright," the soldier said, and Dray stepped closer, grabbing it around the wrist. "Do you see it?"

"In the carriage from the forest, Ana said that she shone bright," Dray said.

The soldier nodded, and another man came through the door. "They are getting restless, Captain. Forgive me, Your Majesty," he said, bowing his head towards Ed. "They want to see you."

"I don't know," Ed said.

"Yes," Belle said. "They need to see you. They need to know you."

Ed looked around the already crowded room. "How much longer will we do this?"

"As long as it takes," Barlow said.

Kemp had not taken his eyes from Belle.

"Do I scare you?" she asked the creature. It turned its head in a similar fashion to what Ana had done not so long ago, as though taking her measure.

"One day you will, but not today." He bowed his head to her as though in respect, but he grinned, and Ed shivered. Did he see a future where they were on opposing sides? Was that future very far away?

Ende studied those in the room and wondered how it had come to this. He should have stayed in the mountains, for he wouldn't be able to help Essa's son. The best he could do was take his daughter for himself. But he knew that she would not leave the brother she loved more than anyone else. He would have to allow her to be what she wanted to be before he could take her far away.

He tried to get Dray's attention. If anyone could see a way through this, it would be him, but he was not what he had been. Ende would have to draw him back from wherever his doubts had led him, and he wasn't sure how to do that. He was feeling the pressure of the room, the anger and anguish and uncertainty, and it was pulling at his wings.

Dray looked at him as though he could feel the heat rising in the room, and Ed was also looking towards him. "She is going to be what I feared," Ende said.

"No," they said at the same moment. Ende could feel the certainty in the room, yet he knew it was hope and not what they thought might actually happen.

"She is doing this for Ed," Dray said. Ende wondered at his using the King's name. "She has always done all of this for Ed."

"It may have started out that way, but I don't think it is going to end the way you want it to."

"I have to trust her," Dray murmured, and the man beside him nodded slowly. Ende could feel the strange cold magic around him.

"You keep her pet too close," he growled.

"This isn't helping," Dray said, stepping forward, his voice as deep and frightening as Ende's. "The king must be seen by the people. He must be known."

"I agree," Ende said quickly. "Do you want to let them in or go out to them?"

"How many are there?" Ed asked.

"Too many," Forest muttered, and Ende wondered what he thought of the situation.

"What will I say?" Ed looked more like the boy from the mountains than the king Ende was sure he saw in him. Despite his fears and worries, this was where he was meant to be. This was who this man was. Ende wanted to think of Essa in that moment, but it was Barric who came to mind. Barric's boy, for Ed could have been him. And if Ende could see it, so would the kingdom.

"Forest is right," Ende said, stepping forward and taking the king by the arm. "You must go out and stand before them."

"What if he finds out?"

"Let him try to deny who you are. The people will see it. The men will stand with you."

Dray nodded once, and the creature hidden as a man beside him did the same.

"I'll lead the way," another soldier said, making his way through the group and to the door. The noise increased as the door opened, then fell away to a murmur as the soldier stepped out.

"Who is that man?" Ende asked Dray. "Can he be trusted?"

"Barlow," Dray mumbled, standing close to the king as he nervously looked towards the door. "I would trust him with the king more than I would trust myself."

"That is saying something," Ende said.

"I'm not ready," Ed whispered.

"Of course, you are," Belle said, giving him a gentle prod from behind.

"Will you come?"

She shook her head. Dray indicated the door, and he and the creature moved forward as one. Ende did not trust the creature, yet it appeared to do as directed for now.

As they passed him and headed outside, he took Belle aside. "The creature," he breathed.

"Follows Dray," she whispered, looking towards the door, and he wasn't sure if it might return at the mention of it or what was occurring outside. "Calls him master," she breathed.

"A gift from Ana?"

"Kemp, the soldier he was, tried to kill Dray in his sleep. She saved him and made the creature swear to protect them."

"Them?"

"Dray and Ed."

"Still the three of them."

"I worry," she whispered, looking towards the door rather than at him. "But so far she has done nothing but ensure they are safe."

Ende put his finger to his lips, and she looked around at the edges of the room as though Ana might be there, listening to every word. He wondered how lost to the shadows Ana was.

The silence outside was unnerving. He left Belle and headed outside to see for himself.

Someone had placed a box on the street, and Ed had stepped up onto it. He looked more nervous than the time he had to remove his shirt for Ana. Ende stepped around to stand beside him. He nodded once to the boy, who dragged in a deep breath as he turned back to the crowd.

"Not many of you will have seen me since I was a small boy," he started, clearing his throat. "My father always wanted me to learn what it was to be a king, but with his death I was denied the lessons. My uncle was to care for me, but instead he ensured I was kept from the world, hidden away and poorly schooled. He wanted the kingdom to think that I was still a boy.

"I stand before you now as my father's son, hoping that you will see in me what you saw in him. I hope you will enable me to learn all I can of Ilia and be the king she so desperately deserves. What my uncle has denied you all."

He took a deep breath, and the hush of the crowd continued.

"He is the king," someone whispered loudly.

"How can we be sure?" someone else asked.

"He looks like his father," another voice called, and Ed smiled. It could have been Barric, and Ende was both glad and disappointed to be looking at the man who had taken so much from him in the end.

"What will you do?" another voice called.

"I only want what is mine," he said. "I want my father's crown. I want the chance to make my father proud. And once my uncle is proved to have kept me from the people, he will hand it back."

"Are you so sure?" a deep voice called, and Ende looked through the people for its source. Was it someone he knew? For it raised something old and familiar in him.

But he couldn't make out who it might be. The crowd then raised their collective voices, arguing over whether they believed he was the rightful heir. The majority supported him, it seemed, but it didn't take long before a fight broke out amongst some of those gathered. The soldiers moved forward.

"Wait," Ed called as the sound of metal rang out through the street.

Silence descended.

"The people are welcome to their opinion. I am only here to state my case, not make more trouble. Ensure no one is hurt," he commanded. Ende could hear it, the sound of a king in the boy standing before the people of Ilia.

28

Ana stood in the shadows, lost to them. She didn't even need to pull her cloak around her now to hide. She didn't need it, yet she still clung to it. She watched across the sea of people between her and the boy standing a head above them, telling them who he was.

It was a risk, but she felt the certainty in those who had gathered in the street, and more were coming, drawn by the sound. Ende watched the people, and she wondered if he did this for Ed or himself. For the woman he had lost. Ana looked through the crowd for the child; neither she nor Belle could be seen, and they must have remained inside.

Did he not want to explain the women in his life, or was he keeping them safe? They trusted him, no matter what he did, and these people saw him for who he truly was. Those that scuffled and questioned did so out of fear of what the regent might do.

He had waited too long, insisted too loudly that the boy was not who he claimed to be. And yet the world knew it to be so. If a boy was lost, a true king missing, his uncle would have done all he could to find him. That was not the case.

Ana wondered if she was truly needed in all of this. The regent was doing well enough in turning the people against himself. For he had done very little in his time on the throne to win them over. He had not been the leader they needed, and he would never see that. But would he bend to their will and hand the crown to the boy who was?

They all feared her—Ed, Dray, the people of the world she wanted. She hoped that Dray would forgive her, would allow her to be who she truly was and remain her friend. She wasn't sure why she needed that, but a small part of her did. She reached for the dagger that had been taken and tried not to sigh.

The shadows beside her shifted, and she wondered at the major. He was one of her strongest and most committed soldiers. She would need to ensure she chose more carefully. The thought of the forest girl still irritated her. But this anchor would do as he was told. Soldiers always did what they were told.

Her gaze rested on the tall, dark man across the street. She missed his armour, almost as much as she knew he did. And yet he was more a man to her without it. He had always done as he had been told, but then he hadn't. It had been Ana's voice in his head, even then, demanding he save her.

The creature growled softly.

"You will not touch him."

"I feel your need, Majesty."

She blew out a soft breath. Dray was not something she wanted any longer. He was not one she could bring into her army. He would fight her every step, and she would have no option but to destroy him as she had the forest girl. The memory of her loss still weighed heavily. The girl had shown her worth.

"What do you sense?" Ana asked the creature, looking over the crowd before her. She raised a finger, feeling the pull of the darkness beside her and the uncertainty in the young man standing back from the edge of the crowd only a few feet from them. "Take him," she breathed. He was gone in an instant, barely a squeak leaving his lips, and no one seemed to notice. The man standing in front of him turned but didn't appear to notice him gone.

There was something else, someone else in the crowd. Ana could taste the strength in them, although taking someone from within the crowd would only weaken Ed's connection to them.

Their trust in him. She had to hold their trust. She tasted the air around her again.

"Mark him," she breathed.

"Majesty," the major hissed. Ana saw the shadows hazy around him, and then they were gone. She looked back at Ende to ensure he hadn't seen her, for he would be the one to ruin her plans. He was the one who still insisted she could not be trusted.

His eyes were focused on another part of the crowd, and the shadows would follow the man until she gave her permission to take him. She needed more, so many more, yet she knew she would get what she wanted with only a few.

Ed had understood what she was saying in the little room filled with too many people. She had told him what he wanted to hear, yet he had heard her true intention. He hadn't quite believed her, as he wanted so much to trust her. To trust the girl he knew, the girl whose skirts he had held as she had healed his wounded shoulder.

She could still feel his firm, warm skin beneath her fingers and the wonder at what she had done when the nasty, infected wound had disappeared beneath them. She had never repeated such a moment, and yet she had achieved so much more. She looked down at her fingers, her hands that had once only been good for carrying tea. She hadn't been very good at that either.

The deep puncture marks in her palm were still present, still tender. She ran her fingertips over them. The sharp pain made her bite her tongue rather than cry out. She could heal them, but she wouldn't. She needed that pain.

"Majesty," the creature beside her hissed, drawing her attention back to the crowd.

People were clapping and cheering. Ed was being assisted down from the box and led back inside. As people were starting to move away, Ana could feel the others the creature thought would be of use.

"You may follow them. Take them after I have what I want."

The creature bowed its head and disappeared.

Something dark pulled at Salima, and she tried to shake it off. As Ed entered the room, she tried not to throw herself around him.

"What is it?" Papa asked, but she could only shake her head again.

"Salima?" Ende asked, his deep voice drawing the attention of the room.

Ed stepped forward and smiled, reaching out a hand to take hers. She breathed out the relief in being able to hold him. But her eyes moved to the soldier who moved behind him into the space.

"She was there," Salima whispered, unsure how she knew. Dray nodded once. "You feel her too."

Dray looked up, his face flushing, his beard and shaggy hair disguising the soldier she knew he was inside. He would always be a soldier, and it would only cause him pain. She looked to Ende, who nodded slowly. She didn't want to be able to feel so much or understand as much as she did.

Ed squeezed her hands and drew her attention back to him. "Who?" he asked.

"Ana," she said, then chewed on her lip. "She seeks more." Salima looked at the man who wasn't, standing beside the soldier who no longer looked like one. "Nothing is what it seems," she whispered, looking up into Ed's worried face.

"What did Ana seek?" he asked, but she shook her head and threw her arms around him instead. He was going to need her far more in the time ahead, but she couldn't tell him that.

She squeezed her eyes closed, fearful of the new feelings in her chest. But it wasn't darkness she saw; it was bright white light. She released her hold and stepped back. Ende looked at her closely but said nothing. She couldn't see what she thought she could, yet she was very certain.

"Salima?" Belle asked, stepping forward. Salima thought she could see a faint glow around the woman, as though the sun shone behind her, lighting her up. Ana had mentioned the light. Perhaps she was starting to think she saw things that weren't there.

"Breathe," Ende said, his hand on her shoulder. "Let them come. You may not understand what you see, and you are better to keep it to yourself until you are sure it is right to share."

Salima looked up into his comforting face. The warmth moving between them helped calm her racing heart. "Can you see what I see?" she asked.

He shook his head. She looked around the room again. She could see the girl glowing faintly, the soldier creature dark and shadowy. She sucked in a breath as she looked at Dray. The broad man stood at attention, still looking every bit the soldier, and across his face a deep, red, angry scar made her step back. His eyes locked on hers, and he put his fingers to his face, but the mark disappeared as she blinked.

"I'm sorry," she breathed.

"Maybe we need to get you home," Papa said, taking her hand. A strange feeling washed over her, but before she could grasp what it was, Ende lifted his hand from her shoulder and the world before her returned to what it had been.

"I think we need to get Ed to the castle," she said.

"You think we should act now?" Ed asked.

Salima nodded as everyone in the room focused on her. The soldier creature narrowed its wide eyes. And she nodded again, wondering just what it might do.

"She is just a girl," another soldier said—Barlow, she remembered as he stepped forward. "I mean no offence, Sword Master, but why is the girl directing when we move?"

"Because she knows," Ed said, something sad catching in his throat, and Salima nodded once. He looked from her to Ende. "She does know," he repeated.

She turned at the silence of the dragon. Ed knew what they were. He knew what Ende could do and so might understand that what she thought she saw might be true. The idea scared her more than what Ana might do.

"Ana," she breathed.

"What of Ana?" Dray asked. "Did you see her in the crowd?"

"I felt her," Salima continued, unsure how, but she had. "I couldn't see her, but I knew she was there, and she wasn't there for Ed. She was there for something else."

"What?" Ed asked.

Salima shook her head; it was too hard to explain. "All I know is that you must return to the castle."

"Will it end how we want it to?" Belle asked, running her hand around Ed's arm and pulling herself close to him.

"I don't know," Salima said honestly. "But I think we are far from the end."

29

"What do you mean they are coming?" the regent bellowed, pushing up from the throne. Dahli remained in her seat. She had finally stopped crying, but she clung to the goblet as though it kept her safe from any creatures that might appear.

"I heard he spoke to the people," the soldier said.

"How many?" Thom interrupted, despite needing to know what he talked of.

"All of them," the man continued, and Thom sat back in the throne. "They are on their way here to claim the crown. What would you have me do?"

"I would have you protect me from this imposter," Thom snapped, looking to the doorway. "Assemble the King's Men."

"I'm afraid that many of the King's Men are with the king," the soldier said, looking a little uncertain for the first time.

Thom stood slowly from the throne and stepped forward. "What?" he demanded. "This is treason! Arrest them!"

"Who, and with whom?" the soldier asked. Thom was sure the man smirked.

"How dare you," he growled, stomping towards the soldier, but the man held his ground. "I am the King's Regent of the Kingdom of Ilia."

"It appears the king has come of age, and there is no need for his regent to continue."

Thom was lost for words. Half expecting Edwin to come marching into the room, he turned to the door to find the soldiers who had been there disappeared. He opened his mouth to scream an order as though they were just outside, and the mage wandered into the room. "I sent for you hours ago!" he directed at the old man instead, although it was not long since he had left. The soldier bowed without raising his fist to his chest and walked from the room.

"What is it?" the mage asked. The girl trailing behind him made Thom turn back to his wife, but she wasn't looking; she was focused on the goblet in her hands. "I have work to do," he grumbled.

"The king is on his way, with half the kingdom behind him."

The old man looked at Thom seriously. "Is this Ana's doing?"

"I think he has somehow managed this on his own. How do we stop him?"

"The witch has her shadows everywhere," the girl said, looking at Dahli. "I can hunt them out. I can stop the witch."

"Can you?" Thom asked, hoping he didn't sound as desperate as he felt. Despite thinking that Ed had managed to rally the people, he knew Ana was the problem. Ana had always been the problem. If he could find a way to remove her once and for all, then he could maintain his hold on the throne.

The girl nodded, and as he glared at her, she gave a small half-hearted curtsy. She was just another girl out for what she could get. He looked her over seriously. She was a child. "You want what she has," he said simply. "Why do you insist on bringing in these girls to help? They only help themselves. They come with little, and you give them the power to take it all away from me," he said to the mage.

"I am doing this to help you. I told you Ana was dangerous," the mage returned curtly.

"And yet you insisted we bring her here, that she would prevent the boy from taking the throne."

"I saw the power of them together. When they were apart, I thought she would understand what we wanted."

"Oh, she understands it," Thom snapped, "and she embraced it for her own purposes. To bring that boy to the capital and give him the crown he thinks should be his. It is mine, and it will remain mine!" He was shouting, but he didn't care. This man used his magic to help, or at least he was supposed to, and he had only ever helped Ana to become what could destroy Thom.

"I can stop her," the child repeated. Thom looked her over again. She was young and small, and she grinned too confidently for him to take her seriously.

"They are on their way. The king, his soldiers and most likely his witch. You will have your chance."

The smile slipped from her face then, and she glanced back to Dahli, who was still staring into her cup.

Dray wondered if it could truly be as easy as it appeared. They moved through the streets of the capital, the king surrounded by the King's Men and the people of the kingdom following behind. Could they march into the throne room and demand the regent step down? What might they face when they got there?

He stopped as he noticed Ende and the girl pause at the side of the road. Ende was talking urgently to her, but she simply shook her head. Dray had recognised it within the shop when she had looked around the room, beyond Dray and yet at him. She had seen something, something like Ende might have seen. She was his daughter, after all; she might share the same skills, or perhaps even more. Ende had held Ana's hand and seen a future that scared him. The girl had looked around the room and seen something similar.

"Are you coming with us?" Dray asked Ende, whose hand was holding tight to the girl's arm. He turned his glare on Dray.

"I cannot," Salima said.

"I thought you would want to be with Ed," Ende said.

"Now is not the time. He will need me later. I cannot help him here."

"What have you seen?" Dray asked, but she simply shook her head.

Ende released his hold and stood taller.

"Come with me," she said, her voice soft. Ende looked at her for too long, and Dray was aware of the people moving forward without him. He had left Kemp beside the king, but a nervousness pulled at him to return.

"This is not going to be as easy as we hope," he said.

"No," the girl agreed. "Come with me," she said again to Ende, who nodded, blowing out a slow breath that warmed Dray.

He surprised Dray by holding out a hand. Dray took his forearm, wondering if he would ever see the dragon again. An odd thought formed that they might not be on the same side, if they were to meet.

"You will always do what is right, Drayton Sterling," the girl said, her eyes focused somewhere far away rather than on him. "That is what you are and why you are here."

He bowed his head to her, his fist to his chest, and she smiled. "Princess," he whispered.

"Go with Ed, keep him safe."

Dray bowed his head again, then turned and pushed his way through the crowd he hadn't realised was so large. The soldiers marched rhythmically ahead of him, and he worked his way to the front to stand beside the king.

"Is there a problem?" Ed asked.

Dray shook his head and looked at the soldier on the other side of the king. What had the girl seen that made her hold back now? What was to come? She had said this wasn't the end, or that they were far from the end. Ed would have some challenges once he was on the throne, but Dray was certain that by the end of the day, the king would be sitting just where he was meant to be.

The soldier turned dark eyes on him then, and Dray turned to look along the street to the gates of the castle. They were wide open for them, welcoming. As the crowd followed, filling the courtyard, Ed held up a hand and silence fell.

"I appreciate your support, far more than I can fully express," Ed said quietly, his voice carrying around the courtyard. "But I must face my uncle alone."

Barlow opened his mouth and then closed it. Ed nodded in his direction.

"I will take a small group of soldiers to protect me," he said, looking to Dray. And then he reached out for Belle's hand. Dray thought there was a little shake before Ed held her tight, but he might have been mistaken, for the king looked more confident than he had ever seen him.

Dray wondered if there would be any resistance to their entering. At the idea, he turned to the entrance that led to the throne room, sure that Ana hid in the shadows just beyond the sunlight. Salima had been right. He felt her, knew her, and she had come to support them as she had promised.

They headed inside the castle, and Ana bowed her head to the king as they met outside the throne room, although Dray thought that she winced. Did the movement cause her pain? He looked at her hands, but they were hidden beneath her cloak. He was so sure she had been injured when he had found her in the shadows; he wondered what else had happened.

Now they were together, the three of them in one place, he was sure it would be all they needed to help Ed to the throne. Despite Ed's murmurings of talking with his uncle, Dray drew his sword and entered the throne room.

He was surprised that there were no soldiers present, only the regent, Dahli and the mage. A girl who grinned too broadly stood in the middle of the room, her arms outstretched. As the small group entered, a shadow creature appeared, and Dray tried not to flinch as dark shadows crossed Ana's face.

30

Ana looked at the girl glowing in the middle of the throne room and growled, the sound reverberating from every surface. *I will not have this,* she thought.

"She is too strong," the maid hissed, shying away, the shadows of the room lost to the brilliant light.

"Ruth," Ana cried. The creature moved from the throne to her side in an instant as Dahli and then in a blink changed to the girl she had been, her arm raised to shield herself from her sister's brightness.

She looked at Ana with wide eyes, the creature lost to the fear of the child. Ana stepped forward and put her hands on her shoulders. "You are stronger than any of them," she breathed. "You need only take back what is yours."

She blinked at Ana for a moment as though taking in what she was saying. "Take it back?"

"You did only lend it to her, didn't you?" Ana asked, looking towards the too-bright girl and knowing she was stronger than just the light she used. Ed looked not at the girl but at the woman beside him. Ana let out a slow breath, trying not to show her anger. She would wait. Belle was necessary now, and she was too close to Ed.

"She is working against the king," Ana said loudly, as though all she did was for the boy.

Ruth stepped forward, her hand still raised to shield herself somewhat. Ana hoped the girl was strong enough to do what she needed her to do.

"Sister," Ruth hissed, and there was an intake of breath from her sister, doubt forming in her mind that the mage and the witch might work together. Ruth took another step forward.

"This is all you, witch," the regent shouted.

The girl who had not so long ago appeared as his wife turned dark eyes on him and hissed. He stepped back, sitting heavily on the throne, closing his fingers around the armrest as though that would be enough to keep him in it.

"Sister," Ruth hissed again, and the girl turned her light on Ruth. Ruth closed her eyes against the light and held out her arms in a stance similar to her sister's when they had entered the room. She took a deep breath, and the girl only grew angrier, glowing even brighter. Ana felt the sting of the light for a moment, and then it dimmed.

"You are not worthy," the girl snapped. "I was always stronger. You were stupid to give me what you had."

"But I had so much more," Ruth hissed as the light dimmed and the other girl looked over her hands. "I have always had more."

"No," she sobbed as the light went out completely.

Ruth blew out a contented sigh and turned a smiling face to Ana, bowing her head low. "Thank you, Majesty," she hummed and licked her lips. The maid growled softly as the mage stepped forward and put his arm around the child, pulling her back.

"She is yours, as I promised," Ana said.

The maid looked to Ruth first, and at the smallest nod from her, the maid stepped forward. The mage held up a hand.

"You never had control," the creature hissed, leaning over him, and he cringed away from it. "You did as you were designed to do. That child is mine. Move," they growled. As the child dropped to her knees, tears running down her cheeks, the mage faltered for only a moment before he stepped out of the way.

"Please," she begged, looking to her sister, but Ruth said nothing, only morphing back into the wife long lost to the regent and reappearing beside him. He yelped and shied away from her, and she put her hand to her chest. "My love, what is it?" she asked in the sweetest voice as Ana laughed at the silliness of it all.

She continued to laugh, feeling the release of trying to be so much to so many for so long. The maid lifted the girl from the ground, and she kicked and screamed as the long, clawed fingers bit into her arms. Then they were gone. Ana wasn't sure what the maid wanted with the girl, but she could do as she wished. She might eat her or try to join with her. Either way, she knew the little maid who had wanted her dead so long ago was one of her truest soldiers.

Ed took a shaky step forward. Although Dray reached for him, he was too far ahead.

"What do you want?" he asked.

"For you to be king," Ana said, feeling the freedom she hadn't in so long. She smiled, and although she wanted to laugh at him, she didn't. The hurt on the man's face behind him dampened her joy somewhat.

"I..." the regent stammered.

"The people don't want your involvement here," Dray said, stepping forward. "They believe in their king. They want him seated where he should be."

"Of course, they do," Ana hummed. "And I have done as he has asked to help put him there."

Ed gulped down something. Was it regret?

"Didn't you?" she said, stepping forward. She was pleased to see he was man enough not to flinch away from her. "This is just what you wanted, when you worked out what that was. You wanted the power, the crown, the throne." She indicated the man cowering in it now, the wife leaning over him. "You wanted me to make this easy for you."

Ed shook his head then, but he chewed a lip rather than answer.

Belle stepped forward, but Ana held up a hand, holding her in place. She could have used one of the many shadows, but she didn't. Her own magic was enough. She wondered why she hadn't used it as often as she could have.

"Edwin," she said, turning her focus back on the boy. "Didn't you ask me to do this?"

He nodded slowly. She could feel the regret and pain and fear bubbling from him, and she stepped forward as she drank it in. She could have done this so long ago.

"This is not what he wanted," Dray asserted, and she was disappointed. "He needed help."

"I gave him help," she said, her voice soft and sweet. "What did you want, Captain?"

He glared at her.

At a cry behind her, the room's attention shifted. She turned as Ruth, still disguised as Dahli, assisted the regent from the throne.

Ana waved her hand, and he stepped forward reluctantly. "Give him what is his," Ana growled, feeling the power. She wondered if Ende could have rumbled the world in the same way.

"Never," he returned through gritted teeth.

Ana snapped her fingers, and the crown appeared in his hands. The world focused on it. For it was not something they had seen for so long. Ed took a step forward. The regent might not have worn it openly, but he had kept it from the boy. He had taken it from his brother after all. Ana could feel it in his desperation to hold it.

"What exactly did you do to get that?" she asked, allowing the darkness to be heard in her low voice.

The boy took another step forward.

The regent, his lips pressed together, tried to drop the crown, but it was tight in his hand. Ana grinned. "Tell us," she breathed, looking to the girl who stood taller and then changed to the creature Ana knew her to be.

The regent's eyes grew wide as her grip tightened on his arm.

"What did you do?" Ana asked again.

"I took what should have been mine," he snarled, brandishing the crown like a weapon in her direction.

"How?" she asked, a singsong quality to her voice, and the creature beside him became the brother lost so long ago.

"Father?" Ed stopped mid-step, his gaze focused only on the creature.

The regent squealed and pulled from the creature's hold, standing alone in the middle of the room, the crown still tight in his hand. The brother he had taken it from was suddenly alive beside him, the boy before him. He looked between the two of them.

"Tell me," Ana hissed, appearing beside him, her arm through his, her long tongue flicking over his skin.

"I killed him," he blurted. "I took what was mine and I killed him."

"And what about me?" the boy asked.

Ana moved to the raised platform behind him, running her hand over the tall back of the throne.

"You didn't deserve it. I am King. I just needed the title." A sudden confidence came to the regent as he stood alone, looking at the crown in his hand. "And so, I took it the only way I could."

"You *never* deserved it," Ed said, stepping up to him, and the older man stepped back. He feared the boy, feared what he said was true. And then Ed was standing over him, taller, one hand on the crown, the other on the blade he had pushed into his side. The regent looked down, releasing the crown, and Ed stepped back, staring at the blood on his hand.

Ana clapped slowly as she sat down, as though this show had all been for her. She had provided the blade, after all. Ed looked more like the boy as his lip quivered, and she smiled. "You have what you wanted."

"I wanted him to give it to me," Ed stammered.

"He did," she said as the regent dropped to his knees and dragged in a ragged breath. His hand pressed to his side, too much blood pushing through his fingers.

Ana leaned on the arm of the throne and put her chin in her hand. Did she want this man? Could she use him? She looked at the creature who appeared as the previous king, and it stepped forward. As it leaned over him, the fear widening his eyes, the regent tried to push himself across the floor away from it but fell on his back instead. The creature of shadows returned.

"Do you want him?" Ana asked.

"No thank you, Majesty." The creature bowed and then disappeared.

"Now then, Your Majesty," Ana said to the king as he stared at his dying uncle, the crown in hand. "What is the plan?"

He stared at her and then lifted the crown. She could feel his frustration, the sudden anger and hatred for what she had made him do, as he looked over the silver crown in his hand. The anger pushed through him as he hurled it towards her before he wiped at the blood, only to have it stain his other hand.

"No!" Dray cried as he raced forward, but he was too slow.

Ana held the crown firmly in her hand. She turned it slowly, wondering at the tarnished metal and the dim reflection of her green eyes. She was finally free.

The boy reached for her then, taking a step forward, but the soldier placed a hand across his chest to hold him back. Kemp stepped forward then and bowed low before her, becoming the creature she knew him to be.

The crown slowly turned to hard, black stone in her hand. Ana lifted it and placed it on her head, the stone cool. She smiled at the weight of it. She breathed as though for the first time and sat back into the throne. Tightening her hold around the armrest, she felt the cool stone form under her fingers.

The men before her took a step back. She wondered briefly where the dragon had gone. Odd that the little dragon hadn't stayed close to her brother when she had always sought him out. She shook her head. It no longer mattered. The crown was hers, and she was Queen.

We are Queen of both worlds.

She nodded slowly, looking over the leaking regent in the middle of her throne room. "Does anyone want this?" she asked, pointing at the man. A shadow formed easily in the middle of the room, and as the regent screamed, they disappeared.

Dray made a strange noise, and she stood, stepping forward from her throne, pleased he waited for her to meet him.

"Would you like a similar gift?" she asked, raising her fingers to his cheek. He flinched away from her, his hand covering where her fingers had touched the skin. "I shall leave you alone," she said, turning away. "It ended well enough, did it not?" she asked, allowing her cloak to disappear as she moved back to her throne.

She stood before it alone, the crown firmly on her head.

"You didn't even end up scarred," she said to Dray as she sat down.

"You can't..." the boy stammered.

"I already have, thank you," she said, sitting back and running her long, dark nails over the cool stone. "You may go." She waved her hand towards the door, then sighed as they remained standing in the room. "Show them out." She allowed the dark to fill her voice as a creature appeared beside her, and then another behind the king. She nodded once, and it leaned forward and tapped his shoulder. He jumped but didn't move.

Ana pushed herself up and huffed. She did not want her rule to start this way. "Go now, or you will remain as one of my soldiers," she growled as more of her creatures filled the room. The major was amongst them, and it appeared he had selected well.

Belle murmured something, and Ana realised she had not released her. But as she raised her hand, the woman started to glow a little brighter. "If you want him to survive the night, I suggest you stop that," Ana hissed, taking a step forward, her focus solely on the blue-eyed woman who stared back.

Ana looked between them, and they slowly glanced at each other before heading for the door. Dray was the last to go, and she wondered at the hatred in his eyes. But it no longer mattered. None of them mattered now.

31

Forest tried not to snap as the large soldier turned on his heel and paced back the other way before the fire. He understood the loss and frustration the man felt, and there was nothing he could do to calm him. Nothing he could say to reassure him. He felt the same loss, the same frustrations. Not only at Ana, that she had become whatever she was or that she had betrayed them, but that Salima had gone, and Ende with her.

"I thought she might have said something," he murmured.

Dray stopped and looked at him as though just realising he was in the room. "She had good reason," he said.

"I'm not sure the two of you are in the same conversation," Ed said, looking up from the sleeping woman whose head rested in his lap.

Returning to the quarters he had shared with his daughter might have been a bad idea, but so far, they had been left alone. Neither Ana nor any of her soldiers had been to visit them, but he doubted they were safe.

"Do you think she will send her creatures after us?" Forest asked, and the large soldier shook his head and sighed as he finally sat in the chair beside him.

"I think she will protect us in her way," Dray murmured.

"Her way?" Ed asked, his voice too high. The sleeping woman murmured something and shivered. Ed rested his hand on her shoulder and took a deep breath.

"She could have turned us into her creatures without any effort," Dray said, something sad in his voice. "She could have removed any threat you might be to her crown."

"Her crown," Ed repeated.

Dray looked around to him and nodded. "It was always hers."

"Ende saw that," Ed said, running his fingers through the girl's hair absentmindedly. "None of us believed him, not even Ana. And now she is whatever she is, sitting with my crown on her head."

"It isn't quite yours," Forest started but then stopped himself, thinking of how she had changed the metal of the crown and the wood of the throne, and how Ed had given it to her. "Did you know she was that powerful?" Dray shook his head slowly. "To change them as she did, and to hold Belle in place. Would it have been different if Ende had been there?"

"But he wasn't," Ed said sadly. "All that way to find a man who was a dragon, and he didn't want to help me in the end."

"He will," Dray said, certainty in his voice despite his distant gaze.

"When?" Ed demanded, rousing the girl. "It is all too late."

"Are you going to sleep?" Belle asked him, but he shook his head and looked back to Dray.

"I saw them," Dray said, "Salima and Ende, before we entered the castle. She saw something, something like Ende saw in the mountains, but she didn't need to touch us to see it. She might be stronger than him," he added, looking at Forest. "Whatever it was, she knew she had to go and that she would return to help later. That you would need her later."

"I need her now," Ed whined. "Is she really that strong?"

"Ana or Salima?" Dray asked.

"Salima," Ed said. "She is just a girl."

"She could read more of that room than I thought possible," Dray returned. "When I spoke to her, she was confident in what would be needed of her. She asked Ende to go with her, and although he was torn, he will always put her first."

"As he should," Ed sighed.

"Why would he put her first?" Belle asked.

Ed opened his mouth and then closed it.

Dray turned to Forest and raised an eyebrow in question. "Is there a threat to her still?"

"There is a threat to all of us with Ana on the throne, with Ana as Queen," Forest added softly, unsure just what that meant for any of them. He had no idea what her creatures were truly capable of and what that might mean for the rest of the kingdom. "There was some form of friendship between them, but Ana isn't the woman she was when she first arrived here."

"No," Dray said with a sigh, and he looked back to the flames.

"What are you not telling me?" Belle asked, sitting up and rubbing a hand across her eye as she yawned. "You all know something of Ende you haven't shared."

Ed looked back to Forest. He wasn't sure why it was his place to explain, but Salima was his daughter—although she wasn't. He sighed and turned to face the woman.

"Ende is not a man," he said, "and Salima is his daughter."

"I thought she was your sister," she said, turning to Ed.

He nodded once. "I did tell you she was his daughter at the inn, but I think you had too much ale."

The young woman's cheeks glowed and she looked back to Forest.

"They share a mother," Forest continued, "but I thought the child I had taken to raise in safety belonged to King Barric. It turns out that she is as much dragon as Ende."

"Dragon?" Belle asked, her voice somewhere between disbelief and fear.

"Ende is a dragon," Dray said. "When Ana and I first met him, he was a dragon. Then he appeared as an old man. Now a younger man. You didn't think there might be something different about him?"

"That was why he could hold the gwelka as he did," Belle whispered.

Dray nodded.

"Does no one else know what she is?"

Ed shook his head this time. "And they don't know who she is. If it were discovered that she was the princess, she might have been in more danger."

"What if Ana learns the truth?" Belle asked, standing suddenly.

"She already knows," Forest said. "She knew before any of us. Before I knew her true parentage. Before the king knew his mother had been more than the dragon's friend."

"Did he love her?" she asked.

Forest wanted to laugh. Of all of this, that was what the girl focused on. It seemed that no matter how much of a girl she still was, Salima had grown far more than he could have supported her. He might always love her as a father, but she needed Ende close to teach her what she truly was, and that was far more than he could ever understand.

"Ana," Ed said softly when the conversation stalled. "What do we do?"

"Dray?" Forest prompted as the soldier remained silent, looking into the flames. "There is a bond with you; there is something she feels for you."

He shook his head.

"She does," Ed added. "She looks at you differently. It was almost like the old Ana was there when she looked at you."

"Ana is lost," Dray said. His deep voice left a sad mark on Forest.

He had hoped for something else of the girl himself. Although what that was, he wasn't sure. Either way, the soldier was right. She was gone. The girl from the cell who had shivered in his arms when Salima had hidden her in the storeroom; the girl who had cried out in her sleep for a soldier lost. Forest studied the man beside him. Ende had said that he would be the way to save her, and he wondered if that really was an option. For now, they only needed a way to stay safe.

They couldn't stand against her soldiers, no matter what relationship or loyalty Dray shared with his soldier earlier. They belonged to Ana. They had always been loyal to Ana, and for the moment she had complete control of the capital, and likely the whole of Ilia.

ACKNOWLEDGMENTS

The team at Deranged Doctor Designs (DDD) for absolutely brilliant cover design work and all the marketing extras. Thank you for your support and clear emails around what is needed from me to make the magic happen.

TWG members and Melissa for listening and support in all things writing related. Special thanks to Yasmin for taking the time to read my draft and providing ideas to make the story stronger.

Allison E Wright for wonderful editing work to make my sentences smoother and my intentions clearer.

My parents, Francine and Ken Smith. Amazing, supportive people who I don't thank often enough. Thanks for keeping me grounded and being the best grandparents ever.

As always, Temwa for being my biggest supporter.

ABOUT THE AUTHOR

Georgina Makalani survives life as a servant of the public by hiding in her office at lunch time with dragons, witches, a laptop and a little bit of magic.

For more about Georgina and her books visit her website: www.theflowofink.com